Fill Your Cup, Valentine

Rachel Anne JONES

FILL YOUR CUP, VALENTINE
Copyright © 2023 by Rachel Anne Jones

ISBN: 979-8-88653-111-4

Published by Satin Romance
An Imprint of Melange Books, LLC
White Bear Lake, MN 55110
www.satinromance.com

Published in the United States of America.

Cover Design by Caroline Andrus

For Mark and Shelli—because sometimes, no matter how little or how long you know each other, you just know.

one

Maggie Post FaceTime's her daughter, Ali, nervously. There was a time when these calls would bring joy and longing to Ali's face, but these days she barely covers her annoyance. Ali's not answering, and Maggie almost hangs up, but then she sees one of her beautiful green eyes hiding behind layers of heavy eye-shadow and magnetic eyelashes. "Ali?"

"Oh, hey, Mom."

Maggie frowns at the darkest shade of lipstick she's ever seen on her daughter as her lips appear on the screen. She laughs nervously. "Am I interrupting something?"

Ali seems distracted. "What? No."

Maggie can't help but notice the low-cut blingy top, or her fly-away hair looking all shiny and crimped. "I think I am. Is this a bad time?" Ali blinks back a tear, and Maggie's heart drops. Ali's never been an easy crier. "Honey, is everything alright?"

She nods, swallowing hard. "It's going to be Mom, it's going to be."

Maggie studies her daughter, searching for the right words. "I called because I need a favor."

Her eyes light up. "You need me?" Is there hope in her voice? Maggie's heart lifts a little.

"I really do. I, ah, I lost a friend unexpectedly, and she wanted me to come and see her, but I never got there, and now she's gone." Maggie fights back her own tears.

Her daughter's eyes focus on the screen. "Oh, no, Mom. I'm really sorry. Was this your vlogger friend from college you loved to follow?"

Maggie smiles through her sadness, happy that her daughter was paying attention. "Yes. Her brother's trying to go through all of her things, so I'm going back there to help him."

Ali giggles. "Isn't her brother the one you had such a thing for?"

She hopes she's not blushing as she rolls her eyes. "That was years ago. We're adults. I'm sure he's married by now."

Ali winks at her mom. "You never know." She swallows hard. "One of us needs a happy ending." She mutters under her breath and wipes away another stray tear.

Maggie's ears perk up. "Honey, what is going on? Where is Jason? Don't you two have big plans for Valentine's Day, what with your wedding coming up so soon after?"

Her daughter looks off to the side, taking a deep breath. "There's no wedding, Mom. Jason called it off."

Maggie gasps. "What? How long have you known?"

Ali sighs into the phone, looking caught. "Oh, since two days ago. He called from Europe and said he wasn't ready and that he was sorry. And then he hung up." Maggie bites her tongue, trying to find the right words. Ali stares at her, speaking softly. "I was going to call, but I've just been processing it. It's going to be okay, Mom. I know he wasn't your favorite. I could tell."

Maggie frowns in silence, deciding now isn't the best time to argue with Ali's opinion, which is spot on. She chooses instead to focus on the positive. "Are you sure you're up for coming home? It looks like you're going on a trip."

"I was, Mom, o-kayyy. But it was just a girl's weekend to Vegas."

Her eyebrows raise. "With whom? I mean, most of your friends are scattered. Are they all flying in? You don't want to let them down."

Her daughter looks embarrassed. "No. Most of these girls are Jason's friends, but they were all so inviting, especially since we broke up."

Maggie's eyebrows shoot up again. "So you're going to Vegas with your ex-fiancée's girlfriends?" Ali makes a face at her mom. "I'm not judging, I'm just trying to understand." There's more silence. "Okay, maybe I'm a little judgy, but do you really want to spend a whole weekend in Vegas with *his* friends? I mean, that's not really your thing."

She shrugs. "I don't know, Mom. I just wanted to get away from it all, you know? And I'm tired of people saying I never try anything new."

Maggie giggles. "Well. I've definitely got something new for you. Here's the rest of the favor."

Ali plops down on an airport chair beside her solitary suitcase. "Okay, Mom. Lay it on me."

"Well, you know I run a café." She clears her throat nervously. "I can't afford to lose business for a few weeks, so I need you to run it when I'm gone."

Her daughter blinks a few times. "What? I thought you just needed me to house-sit or something."

She laughs. "Nonsense. If that's all I needed, Alex could do that."

Ali's immediately suspicious of the warmth she hears in

her mom's voice at the mention of Alex's name. "Alex? Who's that?" She looks all alarmed.

Maggie sighs. "He is my renter and my friend. He's also a writer. How cool is that?"

Ali listens with impatience. "How does *Alex* fit into the café equation?"

"He can help you with whatever you need. I left all my lists with him. I even made you a spreadsheet. He has everybody's numbers if you need them, and a daily schedule, and the café menus."

"If he's so wonderful, why can't he run the café?" Ali answers in a pouting voice. "Why did you need me?" Her voice is much quieter, and it worries Maggie. Ali has never seemed so insecure.

Maggie wants to ask more, but she doesn't want to push Ali away. "Don't be silly, Ali. I'll always need you." She exhales slowly. "Could you please do this for me? Otherwise, I don't know if I can get away."

Her daughter wipes a tear away, takes a deep breath, and waves her hand. "Chillax, Mom. I'm sure I can figure it all out. Now, go get ready to see your old crush, and don't do anything I wouldn't do."

Maggie giggles a little at Ali's teasing. "Nice to see Jason didn't squash your sense of humor." They exchange a mutual look of I-can't-believe-you-just-said-what-you-just-said through the phone.

Ali rolls her eyes, reliving her teenage years. I love you, Mom."

"I love you too, honey. Thanks so much for doing this for me."

Ali winks at her mother and her mother's furrowed brow of love. "As Grandma Irene always said, 'Where you're needed most is where you're meant to be.'" Ali ends her facetime call, muttering, "I swear. My mom's forty-five, and she gets more man-action than me."

An elderly woman sitting two seats down turns and makes a face at her. Ali throws up her hands. "I didn't mean that kind of action, just attention, oh just never mind." She pops up out of her seat, tugging at the hems of her short red tank dress, pulling her matching sparkling red suitcase behind her.

two

"M aggie, are you sure you're going to do this?"

"What do you mean, Alex, am I sure? I'll be fine. My daughter Ali's coming to take over for me at the shop while I'm gone. She's plenty capable. Besides, you'll be here to help if she needs help."

"I don't know. From all I've heard from you, she may not want any help from me."

Maggie smiles, gathers up her laptop, phone, and keys, and heads out the door of the café. "Just the same, I'll feel better knowing you're here. And remember where I told you all the lists are—my daily schedule, the inventory, the meal plans, and the list of support for the Valentine's Dance." She pauses in the doorway. "I don't know. The big dance is just a week away. That's a lot to put on her."

Alex gets up, crosses the room, and gives his landlord a gentle shove out the door. "I was kidding, Maggie. We'll be fine. It's only seven days. Get out while you can. Go catch that plane. Have a drink or two and relax. You haven't taken a vacation since this place opened two years ago."

She turns, giving him a big hug. "Thanks. I really do need

a break, and Natalie's brother sounded so distraught in his last message. He hasn't got anyone else to help him sort through everything." She turns away, wiping the tears from her eyes before turning back to Alex for half a second. "Oh, and be kind to Ali. She may seem strong, but her fiancée just dumped her. They were practically on the way to the altar." She claps a hand over her mouth in embarrassment. "I shouldn't have said anything. Please don't mention it to her."

Alex gives her a playful shove. "Mum's the word. Now go, or you're going to miss your flight."

Maggie races down the sidewalk to her ride parked on the corner, opening the door. "Hey, Cathy. Thanks again for giving me a lift."

"Oh, that's no problem. I've got some things to pick up in the city. There's a new cake supply store I've been wanting to check out. I just love crowded city sidewalks in winter with everyone bustling about window shopping on a snowy day like today when big, fat snowflakes fall just right on my tongue." She sticks out her tongue.

Maggie laughs out loud. "You've been watching Christmas Hallmark movies again, haven't you?"

Her friend starts up the car, pulling away from the curb. "Guilty as charged. I know we're coming up on Valentine's Day, but I keep those Hallmark movies on standby—they always get me in the mood for making pretty cakes and cookies."

"Did you get a lot of orders this year for romantic goodies?"

"I'm working on it. I like to add a new twist or design every year. I haven't quite gotten there this year, but the image is brewing." She taps her graying temple. "So, how are your kids?"

"Well, Ali's coming down to run my shop while I'm gone. She's in an in-between spot with her job and her love life."

"What? I thought she was engaged to that fella she's been seeing. Hasn't it been a year?"

Maggie sighs, fiddling with her earring. "More like a year and a half, but I guess it wasn't meant to be."

Cathy harrumphs. "Well, things are tougher these days for young people. Why, in my day, a person knew after 3-6 months of dating if they were walking down the aisle, and then as they say, the rest is history."

She squirms in the car seat. "Yeah, I know. But who's to say? I mean, I thought I signed up for forever, and things were going great, but then he traded me in for a faster, younger model."

Her friend frowns. "Maggie, you're not a car, but if you were, I'd tell you, you still got plenty of good miles left; what with that killer engine under the hood, you're definitely a classic."

She laughs out loud. "Boy, Cathy. I can tell you and Paul have been to your share of old car shows."

Cathy smiles. "Yep. That's what marriage is, give and take. I learned to like old car shows, and he learned to leave my Hallmark movie channel alone."

The two women pass the rest of the car ride, chatting back and forth and listening to the radio. Cathy pulls her SUV up to the sidewalk. "Here's your gate number. Have a nice flight. See you in a week."

"Thanks! Good luck at the cake store."

three

Ali pulls into her mother's house late Sunday night, parking her maroon Legacy in the carport. She piles out of the car, stretches her long legs, and enjoys the cool night air on her skin as she tugs her tank dress back down to mid-thigh. She raises an eyebrow at the black motorcycle hugging the side of the house in the shadows, muttering, "Did Mom get a bike and not tell me?"

A tall man steps out of the dark. He heads down the sidewalk along the side of the house, startling her as he clears his throat. "That's *my* bike, and I'm Alex."

She releases her mace, letting it hang off her keyring to shake his hand, noting his lean, muscular build as they stand beneath the porch light. "I'm Ali."

He studies her at his leisure before answering. "I figured as much. You're much taller and blonder than your mother."

She stands up straight and tall, feeling slightly insulted. "Thanks, I think. I take after my dad in looks."

He steps closer and lays a hand on her suitcase. "Do you need a hand with anything?"

She shakes her head and dismisses him, thoroughly

annoyed by the fact that his feathered hair whisking here and there with a mind of its own would normally irritate her, but on him, it's utterly charming. "Nope. I've got it."

He gives her an ingratiating smile, and it rankles. "If you're sure. I'm just trying to be a gentleman."

She turns back to him and speaks more sternly. "I said I've got it."

He chuckles to himself, sticks his hands in his pockets, and rocks back on his heels. "What time should we meet at the café in the morning?"

"I was thinking like ten?"

His sky-blue bedroom eyes open wide. "I'd say more like six."

She groans. "6:00 a.m.?" She whines as she tears her eyes from his full lips and deliciously stubborn jaw covered by a 5 o'clock shadow; shaking her head to clear it. She's never been *over the moon* for a man, and she's not about to start now. "Why so early? Isn't it *Mom's* café? Can't she set her own hours?"

His patience runs thin. "Yes, she can, and she has. The people here depend on her."

She hears his explanation, but she's not done protesting. "Yeah, *retired* people I imagine. All they come in for is coffee and gossip. So what if their social calendar gets delayed a few hours? Just *thinking* about 6:00 a.m. gives me a headache."

"They come in for other things besides gossip. You can't just reset your mom's café hours to fit *your* schedule. The café is her place of business. It's run a certain way," he grumbles as he stares her down. He can hardly believe what he's hearing.

She crosses her arms, glaring. "*Fine*, but it's 1:00 a.m. and I drove all night. I'm beat. I'll see you tomorrow."

He smiles at her frowning face. "I'll be up with the rooster's crow at dawn."

A startled look crosses her face. "Are you for real?"

He chuckles again. "Relax, big city girl. It's an expression. I was kidding, since this is a small town and all. We're country folk 'round here." She gives him a funny look, not answering. "Forget it. Just never mind. I'll see you tomorrow."

She drags her sparkly red suitcase past a quizzical Alex up the front porch stairs and lets herself in. She stumbles up the stairs to her old bedroom and crashes on the bed.

He follows her in, shuts and locks the front door quietly behind him, and shakes his head. "So that's Ali." He exits out the back of the house and locks that door as well before entering the separate, attached apartment.

Ali wakes to the sound of banging on the front door. She jumps up and sleepwalks down the stairs to answer it. "Yes?"

"Open up, it's Alex. It's 6:30, and we were supposed to meet at 6:00."

She flips the deadbolt, throws the door open, and snatches the dangling keys from the hook by the door, holding them out. "Here, I'll be down there at 7."

He frowns at her, steps inside, and leaves the keys dangling in her hand. "Nope. Go brush your teeth and your hair and take a quick shower." He leans into her space, sniffs her shoulder, and makes her jump. "You smell like a 14-hour car ride."

"Gee, thanks. Are you this charming all the time?" His hand reaches for her face, and she jerks back. "What're you doing?"

He doesn't stop. "Hold still. You've got something." His fingers brush just below her eye. Unexpected heat, along

15

with a new awareness, rush through her, making her eyes widen.

He holds out his hand, palm open, almost whispering. "You had eyelashes?"

She snatches it from his hand, all annoyed. "They're magnetic. Thanks." She spins around and marches toward the bathroom as he calls after her.

"Get a move on it! We need to get to the café before Bernie does. He'll be hot under the collar if you don't have his oatmeal and Chai tea ready by 7."

She ignores him and continues on her slow and steady pace to the bathroom. Soon, One Direction blares from the bathroom. He chuckles at the off-key voice accompanying it. Minutes later, she steps out in a towel that barely covers all her parts, making him just about swallow his tongue. Her face turns a cherry red. "I thought you left."

He recovers quickly, smirking at her from his utterly masculine slouching posture on her mom's pink velvet accent chair, the most feminine piece of furniture in the room. His jet-black hair is a stark contrast to the pale pink chair. "You didn't tell me to, so..."

She makes a beeline up the stairs to her bedroom and slams the door. She throws open her suitcase, and grabs the first thing she finds, another slinky, sparkly gold tank dress. It slides into place with a tug here and there. She makes quick work of slapping on some lotion and deodorant, grabs a pair of booty shorts and yanks them up before stepping into her favorite pair of heels that match the dress. She runs a brush through her shoulder-length straight blonde hair, pulling it back in a tight bun before leaning over in the mirror to put on a touch of mascara and lip gloss, muttering, "Café life here we come."

She strides into the living room with her eye on her watch and the front door behind it. He chokes again at the transformation. "You sure you want to wear *that* to the café? You look like the Atomic Bomb. You might give old Bernie a heart attack."

One hand goes to her hip while the other flies around in explanation. "I was literally steps away from getting on a plane to Vegas for a girl's trip, and then I came here straight away. I only brought my Vegas party girl clothes. They'll just have to do."

He shakes his head and gets up out of the chair. "Well. If you get tired of looking like you belong on a street corner, there's Bella's boutique down on Third. She's got some more comfortable things to wear. I'll bet your feet are going to be killing you by the end of the day in those 3-inch heels."

She shrugs her shoulders stubbornly. "Thanks for the reminder that male chauvinism still exists, but I'm sure I'll be fine. Who's Bernie?"

He frowns. "You want me to apologize for being a red-blooded male, 'cause that ain't gonna happen." He sniffs. "As for Bernie, he's the man who lives above the café. Didn't you read the list your mom e-mailed you?"

Green eyes stare back at him, all defensive. "I've been busy just trying to get here on time. This was all very last minute."

He sighs. "Your mom put a lot of work into that e-mail. Maybe you can read it later when you *find the time.* Anyway, as I was saying, every morning Bernie comes down at 7 and has his oatmeal and Chai tea and reads his morning paper. Then Ms. Blue comes in and she..."

She holds up her hand. "I don't need the 4-1-1 on every elderly person who stops by for tea and crumpets. I'm sure I can handle it."

He throws up his hands in defeat. "If you say so. I guess I'll go off to my writing corner and let you handle things."

She jangles her car keys noisily in his face. "You want a ride?"

"Nah. I think I'll walk."

Against her better judgment, she follows along behind him. They wander down a few side alleys, and she's shocked to see they're already at the café. "This isn't the route in my phone. It says three minutes driving time."

He laughs. "GPS doesn't know everything."

Her eyes narrow at his bold statement. "Whatever you say, and for your information, these are 4 ½-inch heels, not three."

He tosses his hands in the air. "Well excuse me. I never claimed to be a shoe salesman." He unlocks the cafe and holds the door open for her to walk in.

She scoots behind the counter, eyeing all the chairs on the tables. "Why are all the chairs upside down?"

He sets them up and answers as he walks along. "Your mom does things a certain way."

She rushes to the open kitchen in her heels, and he holds in a laugh at the sight of her slip-sliding on the tile floor in her ridiculous shoes. "Fine. Whatever," she responds in what appears to be her favorite, flippant response, "Where's this oatmeal I'm preparing, and the tea?"

Alex approaches the counter with a smirk. "Are you saying you want my help?"

The front door rattles, and an old man in faded blue jeans rolled up at the bottom, a red and black flannel, wool socks, and Birkenstocks sandals, walks in. "For Pete's sake, unlock both the doors. I about jammed my *blasted* thumb trying to open that dad-gummed locked door!" He steps up to the counter, and slaps down a five-dollar bill. "Where's my oatmeal?" His voice booms, rattling his thick, black-rimmed glasses perched on the end of his nose.

She slides down the counter to stand in front of him. "You must be Bernie."

He looks her up and down. His eyes bug beneath his magnifying lenses. "Who in the Sam Hill are you?"

"I'm Ali, Maggie's daughter. Pleased to meet..."

He waves his hand. "Yeah, yeah, now we've met." He makes a show of staring at his wristwatch. "It's 7:05 and I have no oatmeal." He sniffs the air. "I don't smell any tea in the making either."

Ali looks pointedly at Alex, who throws up his hands, an irritating gesture she's become very familiar with in the short time they've known each other. She turns away from Bernie and puts her hands together, pleading. Alex waltzes behind the counter, rummages through cupboards, grabs a packet of oatmeal, and empties it in a bowl. Next, he grabs a measuring cup, fills it twice with hot water from the water stand in the corner, and pours it on the oatmeal, which he then hands to Bernie with a packet of yogurt-covered raisins and snack peanuts. "Here you are, Bernie. I'll just get that tea started."

He turns away, grabs a tea kettle from a cupboard below, fills it half full of water, sets it on the stove, and flips the gas flame on. She watches all of this with great attention as Alex turns back to the old man. "What's the world look like today?"

The man snaps open his newspaper, folds it in half, and gets to work on the crossword puzzle. "Zip it, Alex. I'm busy."

Alex gives her a bold wink, reaches over her shoulder, and crowds her as he grabs a flowery teacup on a high shelf. She stills and waits for him to move; irritated that his touch gives her butterflies. "You could've just asked me to move," she mutters.

He turns back and shrugs, as if the close encounter meant nothing. "Time is of the essence." He whips open a drawer, grabs a tea bag from a box, weights it down in the cup with a metal spoon before pouring boiling water on top. "Here you go Bernie, your tea." He turns back to open the fridge, grabs a small container of half-n-half, and sets it on the counter as well.

She narrows her eyes at the two men. "Wouldn't it be a lot faster to microwave the water in the teacup?"

Bernie lifts the teacup carefully. His blue eyes sparkle and shine behind his thick lenses. "It's all in the preparation and presentation, dear. That's what makes a good cup o' tea."

Alex grabs her elbow and pulls her to the back room. "Okay, now. Your mom left a few lists so you'd have references."

She wrenches her arm from his firm grasp. "Great. Just let me have them. It'll save us both a lot of time."

"I wasn't done yet. There's more to know than what's on the lists," he argues.

"May-be, but I'd like to read over the lists first. If I have questions, I'll ask."

He stares back at her, amazed that he's still coherent. She's tall and blonde with a gorgeous complexion, a perfect tan, and yet seemingly unaware of the effect she has on men. She'd pass for an angel if it weren't for that mouth of hers and her bossy demeanor. He tries to give her advice one last time. "You know I'm all for empowered women, but there's a big difference between confidence and being too stubborn for your own good."

She gives him an exasperated look. "Just show me where the lists are."

He shrugs. "Suit yourself. They're in the top drawer beneath the café phone."

She marches back into the kitchen, whips open the drawer, and smiles at her mom's polka dot three-ring binder. She opens it, grabs a chair as she scans spreadsheet after spreadsheet of menus, schedules, and numbers. "Oh, boy." She heads for the backroom, opens the refrigerator to find the casseroles and cinnamon rolls labeled and ready in the pans. "Thank you, Mom," she whispers with her eyes closed for half a second before grabbing the pans and taking them back to the kitchen to turn on the oven.

Things are going well as guests trickle in a few at a time. Ali slips into a somewhat comfortable groove, but then glances at the clock on the wall that tells her two hours have passed. A small, dark-haired lady walks in with two big dogs. She rushes around the corner to cut her off. "Excuse me, you can't bring those dogs in here. This *is* a restaurant."

The lady smiles kindly despite Ali's abrupt nature. "You must be Ali, Maggie's daughter."

"Yes. And you are?"

"I'm Amber, and this is Silas and Maddy. They usually spend a few hours here every day while I work at the church or for the church, wherever I'm needed."

Ali looks over at Alex, who seems unphased by two giant dogs sitting and staring up at Ali. "What are they, Great Danes?"

"Yes, but they're very well behaved. You'll hardly notice they're here."

"I don't know. Big dogs make me uncomfortable," she says, and hates the tremble in her voice.

Alex looks up from his laptop. His gaze zeroes in on Ali. "Jason didn't." Before she can even come up with some sort of clever response, he turns back to Amber, whistling. "Silas, Maddy, come." The giant dogs get up, march over to him, and lay down on the floor at his feet. "Good boys," he praises them, and Ali feels strange when she wishes he would talk to her that way.

Her face burns with embarrassment over his comment

about her ex-fiancée. She wonders just how much her mother told Alex about Jason.

Amber smiles and gives Alex a friendly wave. "Thanks! I'm off to the nursery. I get to love on the babies today."

Alex raises his coffee cup. "Have a great morning. We'll be here when you get back."

four

Ali decides to ignore Alex and the two Danes. She heads back to the kitchen to start on lunch. She scans her mom's recipe for her special meatloaf and mashed potatoes and takes note of the salad dressing to be prepared as well. She takes a deep breath. It's been a while since she's been in a kitchen. "No big deal, it's just like riding a bike." Her phone buzzes, and she glances down at the text message. "Why aren't you answering my calls? I'm worried about you —Jason."

She pockets it, muttering to herself. "If you were so worried, why'd you run off to Europe, ending our wedding plans, not bothering to tell me until the last minute?" She looks up, irritated to find she had an audience, as Alex stands at the counter, looking uncomfortable. "Eavesdrop much?" she accuses.

He tugs at his collar. "Ah, no. I was going to ask if you wanted any help in the kitchen with the lunch crowd coming in soon is all."

"It's only 9:30, I think I'll be fine."

"Actually it's 10:30, and people around here eat at 11."

The bell rings over the café door again, and a grey-haired couple walks in. Alex turns around and takes the man's lidded coffee cup from his outstretched hand. "Give me a few minutes, Marvin. I'll fix you right up."

The lady steps up to the other side of the glass case, watching Ali intently. "You must be Ali."

She gives the grey-haired lady a little smile. "And you are?"

The lady chuckles. "Oh, I'm Becky. I'm friends with your mom. We love sharing pictures of our kids."

Ali nods in understanding. "That's nice."

Alex hands the cup of coffee to Becky. "There you go. That should hold Marvin over on your walk."

Becky smiles at him. "Thanks." She turns to her husband. "Marvin. Here's your coffee. I'll get Silas and Maddy."

Ali looks alarmed. "What are they doing? Those aren't their dogs."

Becky turns back and grins. "Marvin loves to walk Amber's dogs, and it's good exercise for my heart. It's a win-win." They walk out with Silas and Maddy. Becky turns back, waving. "See you in about an hour."

Ali shakes her head. "It's like a three-ring circus around here. Can you *please* help me? I've barely started peeling the potatoes, and this knife isn't doing so hot. I can't find a peeler."

He sneaks back into the kitchen. "You know what? It's your first day, so give yourself a break. Just let me come around."

She jabs a hand on her hip. "You help my mom a lot?"

"Not in the kitchen, no. But this is her business, and she's been doing it for a long time. I bet you don't need any help at your regular job. Which is?"

She slams a cupboard in irritation, looking for a potato peeler. "You make a habit of prying into people's lives?"

He opens another drawer and grabs a peeler, holding it out. "I was only making conversation." He gives her a wink. "Guess if you won't tell me what you do for a living I'll have to use my imagination," he says as he lifts one eyebrow and makes a show of looking her over in her flashy dress.

She snatches the peeler and leans over the trashcan with the potato. "So you're a writer?"

He answers as he grabs ingredients with the speed of a short order army cook, mixing the meat, eggs, and crackers in seconds. "Yes. My first book kind of took off, which was nice, because it gave me some time to relax a little before starting my second one, and that's why I'm here. I was driving through, and I stopped at this café and it just kind of spoke to me, so I stayed, and I've been here about a year."

She looks at him with skepticism in her eyes. "Just like that? You uprooted your whole life for a year on a whim?"

He looks puzzled, but then a charming smile lights up his face. "Yeah. I'd been working in a factory, and I kept waking up in the middle of the night with this idea, and it wouldn't go away, and so I started writing, and it just kept coming, and before I knew it, it turned into a book, and the rest is history I guess."

"So there's no one waiting for you back home?"

He gives her a wink. "Is this your way of asking me if I'm available?"

She ducks her head, but not before he sees the blush in her cheeks. "No, no. Don't be ridiculous. I'm sure you know I just got out of a serious relationship." She looks him over, taking in his polo shirt, corduroys, and tennis shoes, wrinkling her nose. "Besides, you're not my type."

He loads eight bread-loaf pans in the over-sized oven before walking slowly toward her. He stands up tall to look down at her. He scratches the back of his neck, flexes his biceps, and crowds her. "Yeah, probably not. The last time I checked, I haven't ditched any women on the way to the altar," he growls out the words before he walks away, shaking his head.

Ali's red-faced and stunned at how quickly he broke down her walls. She blinks away tears of hurt that quickly turns to irritation. "You going to help me with the potatoes or what?"

He wheels around slowly and moseys back toward her. "Since you asked so *nicely*, how can I resist?" He steps up beside her, scoops up the peeled potatoes, and then turns away to whip out the cutting board on the opposite counter. He starts slicing, but turns back, bumping into the back of her. "You need to grab the big potato pot." Her nerves dance when she feels his warm breath on the back of her neck.

She ducks away from him. "Where is it?"

He spins away from her to get back to peeling. "I think it's in the back. You can't miss it. It's huge," he calls out.

She heads into the back storeroom and scans the shelves and floors. "I'm not seeing it," she announces.

"Check your mom's office," he yells back at her.

She shakes her head, walks to the very back of the café, and opens the office door. She's shocked to see a very young, very pregnant girl sitting at the desk with a laptop. "Hello?"

The girl looks up. She doesn't answer at first. Her eyes are wide open as she takes an earphone from her ear. "What?"

"I said hello. Who are you and why are you in my mom's office on her computer?"

The girl frowns. "I'm Talia, and I'm doing my online high school. Your mom lets me do schoolwork back here."

"Why aren't you in school?" Ali asks.

"I kind of dropped out because I'm pregnant, but your mom talked me into continuing my education online. She took me up to the high school and got me enrolled in classes and everything. It's kind of hard to focus at my mom's house, so I stay here during the day." They stare at each for about a minute. "Can I help you?"

Ali is embarrassed. "Um, no. I didn't mean to grill you. I was just looking for the potato pot. I'm sure it's not back here, but I couldn't find it out there, so."

"It's in the supply closet." Talia points to a closed closet in the room.

"Oh. Well, thanks." Ali crosses the room to open the door. She's surprised to see a giant pot in the middle of the floor. "I don't suppose you know why she has it *back here*?"

The girl giggles. "Your mom worries about weird stuff. She said she keeps it back here so no one will walk off with it. Like anyone would want to steal a giant soup pot. Can you imagine someone trying to walk off with that? It'd be like someone trying to walk off with this," she points to her protruding stomach.

Ali giggles awkwardly at the girl's humor. "You've definitely got a point. No, I can't. I better get back up front. Alex's helping me with lunch."

Talia smiles. "Alex? He's so dreamy. And he's soo nice."

She laughs nervously. Talia hit the nail on the head. "Dreamy? Alex? He's alright."

The girl purses her lips. "Just wait until you see him without a shirt on. Then you'll know what I mean. The man is *beautiful*. I just love his dimples when he smiles."

Ali shakes her head, looking at Talia's full tummy. "You need to forget about men for a while." She slaps her hand over her mouth, embarrassed. "I'm sorry, I didn't mean..." there's a long second of silence.

Talia saves them both from further awkwardness when she laughs out loud. "You're probably right...but, there ain't no harm in lookin'." She gives a saucy wink. "Besides, he's Greek too. If he's the closest I ever get to seeing those islands, I think that'd be alright."

Ali shakes her head again. "If you say so." She strides back up the hallway with the big soup pot and hands it off to him. "You take this heavy thing. I'll get the potatoes ready."

He grabs it by the handles. His fingers brush hers. Heat shoots up her arms. She glances at him, trying to read his expression, but his attention is elsewhere. "It's past 11. Did you call Bernie?"

"Why would I call Bernie?"

"To tell him to take his pills. And where is Amber? She should be here by now. Silas and Maddy are going to get anxious."

She can't help but smile at his worrisome brow. "Chillax, old man. Dogs can't tell time. Amber will probably be here any minute. Besides, they're not back from their walk yet." She scans the stickie notes on the wall above the counter. "Where's Bernie's number?"

He opens the drawer by the phone, pulls out a little black book, and opens it up to the "B's", pointing. She dials the number. "Hello, Bernie? It's Ali from the café. Did you take your medicine yet? Oh, she did. Well, good. No. Lunch isn't ready yet. I'm working on it now." She hangs up the phone. "Evidently, my mom already called him."

He gives her a wink. "Sounds about right." He sets the big pot of water on the burner. "We've got to hustle. The lunch crowd will be coming in any time now."

She gives him a stare and throws up her hands. "I'm trying, but you keep interrupting me."

He just smiles back at her. "Well, hop to it then."

five

More and more people file in the door, and Ali's stress level goes through the roof, despite her practicing her deep breathing exercise as often as she can. She stares at the boiling pot of potatoes in the pan, poking them with a fork, irritated when they're still too firm. "Can this stove get any hotter?"

He gives her a wink. His easy manner infuriates her. "Perfection can't be rushed. Just move your mind on to something else." He whips open the fridge and pulls out the garlic, milk and sour cream. "Here, prepare the garlic while you're waiting. It'll feel good to smash something."

"What's that going in, and where's the garlic masher?"

"It goes in the potatoes," he says as quickly as he drops a garlic clove on a cutting board. "Look. All you do is take a chef's knife with a wide blade, lay it sideways, and push down with the palm of your hand." He demonstrates before he holds up the knife. "Voila. Smashed garlic."

She grabs the knife angrily and copies his movements as she talks. "Aren't you just a smooth know-it-all, mister improvisation..."

He smirks. "I'm not a know it all, but I know how to save a few dollars here and there. You never know what you'll discover unless you try to see things in a different light." He taps her nose. "You might just be surprised."

She leans away from him, wrinkling her nose. "Your finger smells like garlic."

He smells it. "So it does."

She looks past him at the customers seated at the tables. "Oh, my gosh! They have no drinks. Where's our waitress?"

He looks around the room before his eyes land back on her. "I guess you're *it* today. Amber must have gotten hung up with a church thing."

She shakes her head furiously. "Seriously? Isn't she supposed to be here at a certain time? Isn't that *her job*?"

He gives her a look. "Did you not read *anything* your mom left for you? She's a volunteer waitress. She doesn't get paid."

Ali throws up her hands, grabs the notepad, and wheels around to face him again. "We're numbering these tables ASAP. That's the only way I'll make sense of taking orders." She marches out of the kitchen to the first table, calling out to him, "Don't let my potatoes boil over!" He watches her with admiration as she darts between the tables, scribbling away on her little pad. Before too long, she's back with drink orders scribbled inside of circles. She steps up beside him. "I hope we have tea, lemonade, and water, because that's what they all ordered."

Although he's 6'2", she almost looks him in the eye in the highest pair of heels he's ever seen, and he can't help but notice she wears them so well. "Did you make the lemonade and the tea?"

Her green eyes flash back at him. "Had I known, I would have..." He chuckles, and she slaps his shoulder. "You've already made them."

He points to the six big coolers lined up in the back storeroom. "The red is tea, and the blue is lemonade. The water comes from the tap." He picks up her tiny notebook. "I'd try to help you out, but I can't make heads or tails of what you scribbled on here." He looks down at it again. "Purple shoe-ties? Gray overalls?"

She looks at him like she'd like him to wither right in front of her. "That's what they're wearing. I don't know people's names here, but I recognize distinctive clothing choices." He chuckles as his eyes scan her list. "Now what's so funny?" she demands while she tries to snatch her make-shift meal orders from his dodging hand as he looks her over with a heated perusal.

"So for you, we'd just write down Vegas Show Girl."

She tosses a dish towel at him. "Ha, ha, very funny. Come on, help me fill these drink orders, please."

He drops the notepad on the counter. "Fine."

A brown-haired lady approaches the counter. "Think we can get some salads and rolls going out here?"

Her words threaten to be Ali's undoing as she turns to answer the woman. "I'm doing my best, lady. I'm sorry. It's my first day."

The lady surprises a trembling Ali by rounding the corner and stepping into her workspace. "Don't you worry, hon. I know my way around a kitchen." She whips

open the fridge, yanks out a few bags of rolls, and tosses them on a few pans. She throws them in the oven above the meatloaf. Then she grabs the heads of lettuce and a few vegetables, makes short work of them, and tosses them into bowls before pouring a little Ranch dressing on them. She heads back out to the tables of customers. "I'm Bonnie, by the way," she sings out as she walks back in, slapping her hands together. "Your salads are out." She glances at the oven. "Oh, shoot. The rolls!" She grabs an oven mitt, pulls out the rolls, and drops them in a few baskets before she goes around the restaurant, distributing one to each customer.

Ali's surprised to feel a tear roll down her cheek. "I'm Ali. And thank you, Bonnie, you're a lifesaver."

The bustling lady snorts a little snort. "I'm a retired lunch lady and a farm wife. We know how to pitch in."

Ali looks over at Alex pouring the glasses of tea and lemonade. She feels so inept so she gets busy delivering drinks to the tables. She finishes just as a buzzer goes off in the kitchen. She races back in, but he beats her to it, shutting off the oven. "You finish your potatoes and let me handle the meatloaf."

She grabs a fork and stabs at the potatoes. She's pleased when they fall off her fork. She starts to pick up the pot, but it's steaming, and it's huge. She sets it back down. "Help, please. I'm afraid I'll burn myself."

Alex stops what he's doing. "Oh, I didn't think of that. Grab the huge drainer under the sink and put it in there so I can pour these potatoes." She runs over and tosses it in right before he gets there. He strains with the effort of holding the huge pot out in front of him. "Stand back."

Soon enough, she's got the potatoes back in the pot. She mashes them as fast as she can while steam creeps up her arms, coating her face with sweat. She rubs her forehead on her forearm. "Ugh. Who knew potatoes could be so steamy? This feels disgusting."

He leans up against her, whispering. "Mush, mush."

She laughs out loud. "How much sour cream and milk?"

He looks back. "I don't know, I'd just wing it. You'll know when it's right."

"Seriously? I need a measurement; this isn't how I cook." Her voice grows shrill.

"Calm down, woman. I was kidding. Put the whole tub of

sour cream in along with three sticks of butter, and a half cup of milk. And don't forget the smashed garlic."

"Three sticks of butter?"

"You asked me for your mom's recipe. Don't disappoint the people now."

"Fine. This is definitely comfort food."

He laughs. "Well, you don't have to eat it."

She snorts. "Heck yes, I'm having some. I think I've earned it."

They prepare the plates. Alex, Ali, and Bonnie serve all the customers lunch. They sit down for a few minutes, but he clears his throat. "You might want to go around and see if anyone needs drink refills."

Ali gives him a glare. "My feet are killing me."

He smiles, gives her the once over, and stops at her shoes. "Ready to lose those killer heels?"

She grimaces as she starts for the tables. "Nope. I'm fine."

He shakes his head, muttering to himself. "Stubborn woman."

six

Lunch is finally over, and the tables are clear. Amber shows up somewhere in the middle of it. Ali's amazed as Amber flies around the room, cleaning as she goes. It isn't long and the lunch dishes are all clean.

"Wow. Thanks a lot! Are you sure I can't pay you?"

The dark-haired lady with friendly brown eyes laughs at her question. "You did. You watched my babies, Silas and Maddy. They're holy terrors if I leave them at home, but I've got to have time for Bible study and helping out where I can as well."

"So you trade dog sitting for waitress hours?"

Amber gives a decisive nod. "Yep." She turns to her dogs, who are still camped out in Alex's writing corner. "Silas, Maddy, come." Ali smiles as she watches the little lady walk out the café door flanked by her two giant dogs.

She turns to Bonnie, who lingers. "Thanks again. How can I repay you?"

Bonnie smiles a toothy grin. "It's nothing. I'm just happy to help. I miss the bustling around. Today was nice. Besides, I got a free lunch out of it." She knocks on the counter. "So long, you two. I'll see you around."

Alex looks down at Ali's feet. "There's no one here. Give your arches a break."

"Marvin and I are still here. We're almost done with our Scrabble game," someone calls from the back corner.

Alex answers before Ali can. "No worries, Becky. Go ahead and finish. We've got plenty of time."

Ali looks down at her toes. She shakes a foot as if to wake it up. "Fine. But if these shoes come off, they're not going back on."

He laughs at her warning. "If I have to carry you home, lady, you're goin' over my shoulder like a sack of potatoes."

She smiles. "I don't think so." She tiptoes back to the office, trying not to startle Talia. She's surprised to see her sound asleep on the little couch. She walks back out and whispers to him. "Talia's sleeping."

He frowns slightly. "I don't think she gets much sleep at home. And she's probably worn out. Pregnancy wears on the body."

She looks hard at him. "How would *you* know?"

"I have a *sister*. She has *children*. Man, you're cynical."

She's not ready to admit she's wrong. "Well, I don't know you from Adam. You could have a kid or two out there."

He stomps back to his corner. "You're unbelievable. All I've been is nice to you today, and you go and say something like that."

She shrugs her shoulders, worn out. "Just like a man to get mad at one little thing I say and stomp off in a pout."

She opens the fridge and looks for something to eat, as lunch time left no leftovers, but everything is labeled for the café. She shuts the door hard. He pops back around the corner. "Something wrong?"

She remains in front of the fridge. "No. I'm just starving, but everything in there is assigned. I can't have any of it."

He leans back on the counter and crosses his arms over his chest. "How about I go get us something to eat? We deserve a little break."

She plops down on a chair. "Is that allowed?"

He grins. "Is what allowed?"

"Can you bring food from other places in here?"

He glances around and raises his eyebrows. "Who's going to know?"

"I don't know, I was just..." She stops at the sparkle in his eye. "You really like to tease, don't you?"

He shrugs. "You're so uptight, you make it too easy."

She takes a deep breath and stands up straight. "I am not uptight. I just like things a certain way. I need order. I like rules. I don't like guessing." She plops down in a chair. "Okay, maybe I'm a little uptight."

"Can I order yet? Ike's grill will shut down in about ten minutes."

She sighs. "Yes, please order."

He picks up the phone. "Yo, Isaac. What you makin' today?" He turns to her. "You eat paninis?" She nods. "Are you a vegetarian?" She shakes her head emphatically back and forth. "Alright, we'll take two of your daily specials. I'll be over in about fifteen." There's a pause. "No, and no. Maggie's daughter. She's visiting." Another pause, as he looks her up and down before turning away from her. He cups a hand over the phone. "I'd say about a five, maybe a six." Another pause. "Sounds good. Bye."

He steps to the side and wipes down the counters with a rag absentmindedly as she stares at the side of his face. "Did you just rate me to your friend on the phone?"

He shrugs his shoulders. "I don't know, maybe."

"And you said I was a five or a six." Her voice is full of irritation.

"Maybe."

"That's really rude. I'm definitely a seven or an eight. Lots of people have told me so."

He laughs out loud. "You're so easy to tease. Isaac knows me. He knew what I was doing. Man, I got you good."

She glares back at him. "Just for that, you get to wipe down all the tables again, with bleach water."

He picks up the bucket of water and the rag and bows deep. "Just call me Cinderfella." He walks away whistling.

She turns away from him and tries to hide her smile. "I've smiled more today than I have in months." She whispers mostly to herself. She looks back at him. She shakes her head. "It's probably just because I'm not working and I'm away from the city and everything."

She hears a throat clear in the direction of her mom's office. "You keep tellin' yourself that."

She catches Talia out of the corner of her eye. "You're a sneaky little thing," Ali scolds half-heartedly.

Talia laughs out loud. "I ain't been called little in a long-as...a long time."

Ali watches Talia climb onto the bar stool slowly. "Do you have names picked out yet?"

Talia nods. "Yep, but it's a surprise. I ain't tellin' no one."

"Do you know what you're having?"

She smiles and shakes her head. "Nope. That's a surprise, too. For me and everyone."

Alex plops the bleach water down in front of Ali, making her turn her nose up. "Why didn't you dump it?"

"I gotta go grab the food." He looks at Talia and points. "You stay right there, girlie. I'll be back soon."

Talia hugs the table, lays her head down, and moves one hand to settle on her stomach. "This little one sure likes to kick, so I don't get much rest these days. I've about run out of room."

Ali feels a little uncomfortable. She's not used to pregnant women. "When are you due?"

"Oh, in about three weeks. Your mom didn't want to leave me here, but I told her the baby won't come 'til she's back. At least I hope."

Ali gives a little sigh of relief. "That's good. I don't know a thing about babies."

Talia makes a face at her. "Didn't you ever babysit?"

The girl's question makes her feel foolish. "Not really."

"I sure have. I started watchin' my mom's when I was seven or eight, 'cause she worked lots of hours. Then my aunt-y moved in, and pretty soon I was watchin' hers. You'd think with all that baby and kid watchin' I wouldn't be so anxious to have my own, but these things happen I guess."

Ali is concerned at her choice of words. "What happened?"

Talia gives a little laugh. "Oh, you know. A tall, brown-eyed boy with gorgeous lips lookin' all grown and starin' at me, makin' me feel like I'm all that. When we were together, no matter where we were or what we were doin', he made me feel like I was his whole world. I ain't never have anyone treat me like that before. It was sooo nice."

Ali's eyes narrow. "Where is he now?"

Her lip quivers just a little. "Oh, he don't know about this baby. I didn't tell him."

Ali plops down beside her. "Why not? You don't need to go through this alone."

She shakes her head. "He has big dreams. He's all excited to join the Air Force, and I couldn't hold him back. He didn't make me do anything, anyways. It was his last night before he was leaving, and he was willing to wait for that...but I wasn't." She looks sideways for a few seconds. "And now, I can't take his dreams from him."

Ali sits in silence, thinking. "But what about *your* dreams?"

She smiles sadly. "Oh, I don't have any, really. My mom and my aunt-y need me to stay close to home so I can babysit, so I figure, what's one more?" She looks away and watches the couple walk out the door. "Bye, Becky," Talia calls out.

Becky turns, smiling. "Bye, Talia."

seven

Alex walks in and spreads out their supper. Talia hops up. "I'm gonna go home now."

He turns to her. "Nonsense. You're eating supper with us, right Ali?"

She looks over at Talia, who looks all uncertain. "Right. Sit down and have some real food. You can't survive on Cheetos and beef jerky. I saw what you had in the office. Your baby needs some vegetables."

He shakes a drink at her. "Besides, I got you your favorite all-natural lemonade from the bookstore on the corner. Abby flagged me down. She told me she's been holding that lemonade for you all day."

Talia slaps her head. "Oh, shoot. I forgot to go by her place today."

He slaps a book on the counter. "That's alright. She sent this with me. She said you can return it whenever you're done."

She slips the book into her backpack and takes a long drink of lemonade. "Thanks."

He slides a box of food at her. "Now sit down and eat."

She opens it, her eyes lighting up. "All of this is for me?"

He taps the box. "Yep. Every last bit of it. Isaac sent you extra broccoli even. He said it's good for your baby's brain." He turns to Ali, who opens up the other box. "I thought we could split it."

Her face is full of doubt. "*I don't know*. I'm pretty hungry."

He laughs and pulls out another box. "I figured as much. That's why I brought you one of Abby's signature coffee cake muffins. They're ginormous and scrumptious, too."

Ali smiles. "I can smell it already. Let's dig in."

The table's quiet for a few minutes with everyone feeding their hunger. Talia glances over at Ali. "So what's the story on your man? I can't believe anybody'd leave you."

She gives Talia a kind smile. "Thanks. We met through mutual friends, and we just sort of clicked. We like the same things and have the same interests, but I guess he got bored. He proposed and then things kind of went downhill from there. Everything got more and more strained between us, and he started having more nights out with the guys, but I didn't think about it because my work keeps me pretty busy, and it was nice to have a boyfriend who didn't nag me about my long hours on the job." She fiddles with her earring and leans on her elbow resting on the table. "But then he went on this last hoorah trip to Europe with his buddies, and he just never came back."

Talia swallows her food with big eyes. "Well, I say good riddance. It sounds to me like he just don't want to grow up. He's probably afraid of commitment." She eyeballs Ali again. "You sure he didn't meet anyone over there? Men always be doin' that sort of thing."

Ali coughs mid-bite, her eyes watering. "No. Jason would have told me if he had found someone else."

Alex clears his throat. "Did he invite you to go to Europe with him?"

Ali rolls her eyes and looks at him indignantly. "No, he did not. It was a guy's trip. And even if he had invited me and I didn't go, would that be a reason to end an engagement?"

He taps his fingers on the table. "Relax. I wasn't implying anything. It was a question. Don't blame his bad behavior on me."

"I'm not. I just get tired of people trying to find a way to blame me."

"Isn't that what you were just doing?" He answers quietly.

She looks down at the table. "Maybe. I've gone over our conversations a thousand times, trying to make sense of where things changed, or if I should have seen from the beginning things would end this way, and I still don't see any warning signs."

Talia gets all excited. "Ooh! I know. Did you Facebook stalk him?"

Alex and Ali turn to her. "What?"

Talia laughs. "You know, like check out any of his ex-girl-friends to see if this is a pattern for him."

Alex shivers. "Is that what you girls do these days? It's intimidating enough to try and talk to a girl, and now I think I'll think twice before Facebook friending any woman. That's just wrong."

Talia gets all defensive. "Hey. How else am I gonna know if a guy's lyin' to me?"

Ali stares back at her, but Talia's attention is on her food. "You ask him."

Talia taps the table. "Girl, you think a guy's gonna tell me he's lyin'?"

Ali turns to Alex and grabs his arm. "You talk to her."

He chokes on his sip of water before shaking his head. "I think I know when I'm outnumbered."

The door chimes. A petite, green-eyed, brown-haired girl

comes in, followed by a tall, brown-haired, hazel-eyed boy with dark curls going every which way. Alex looks at the two of them and back to Ali, shaking his head. "I still can't believe you are all blood relations."

The girl runs over to Ali, and they squeal, hugging each other. "Parks!"

"Ali! I can't believe you're home. When did you get here?"

Her sister looks at her funny. "I came in late last night."

Parker's mouth falls open. "You were here last night and this morning? I didn't hear a thing."

The boy sits down and steals a few fries off Ali's plate. She smacks his hand. "Conner!"

He answers. "Hey, Ali." His voice cracks just a little.

She stares at her little brother. "That's all I get?"

He grins back at her. "I'm fourteen now."

She gives him a grin and slips on her heels. "I'm still taller than you."

He stands up, and they're nose to nose. "With heels on. Take 'em off."

She gives him a hug. "No way."

Parker flops down in a chair beside Talia. "Hey, Talia. I sure miss you in art class. We're getting ready to start decorating for the Valentine's Day dance, and we miss your mad drawing skills."

Talia's face lights up. "Thanks. Remember the year we got in trouble for a too revealing cupid? That was so hilarious. I thought Mr. T's head was going to blow up."

Parker giggles. "I'd forgotten about that."

"So what's this year's theme?" Talia asks.

"It's 'Calling all Crushes'."

Talia nods her head enthusiastically. "That's cu-ute. You could do like a retro telephone theme, or something with Orange Crush. That might work."

Parker taps Talia's hand with hers. "See? That's why you

need to be part of the decorating committee. I could totally talk to Ms. Smitz for you. She'd love to see you again."

Talia shakes her head. "I don't know. The new principal doesn't really like me being around."

Parker claps her hands. "It's all after school! If home-school kids can play sports with us, I don't see why you can't be part of our decorating committee. In fact, just say the word and I'll go to the board tomorrow about it."

Conner looks over at Parker. "Oh, no. Not another cause, Parker."

Parker stands up with her hands on her hips. Her shoulders are about the height of the high-top table they all sit at. "Conner, it's for a good reason. There's nothing wrong with asking for a change when it's needed."

Ali and Conner exchange a look before they both start laughing. Talia pipes up. "Everyone stand back. Congress-woman Parker has the floor."

Parker smiles big before turning back to Talia. "What do you say? It might be a good distraction while you're waiting to pop out a little Talia."

Talia laughs. "How do you know it's a girl?"

Parker gives her friend a wink. "I just have this feeling." Parker wheels back around to face Alex and Ali. "So, this dance needs chaperones, and I think it'd be epic to have a famous writer and my favorite Vegas show girl sister! What do you guys say?"

Ali punches Parker's shoulder. "Very funny, Parks. I was on the way to Vegas when Mom called. I couldn't say no."

Conner smirks. "That's a relief. I was wondering why you were dressed like a…"

Parker turns on him, one eyebrow raised. "Like a what, Conner? What were you going to say?"

Conner throws up his hands. "Nothing, sister. Nothing at

all. Certainly, nothing that has a *hint* of sexism in it. Calm your little *Moxie*-quoting feminine heart down."

Parker and Talia lean into each other while putting up hand signals with two fingers as they stare wildly at Conner. "Rebel girllls," they sing out.

Conner plugs his ears and hums to himself in response.

Parker slowly turns back to Ali and Alex. "So you'll do it?"

Alex smiles at Parker. "Count me in. I'm not up for your persistence if I refuse."

Ali frowns at him. "Pushover."

Parker focuses on Ali. "Please, Ali. It'll be so much fun. You can revisit your old high school. And maybe you can even be the DJ? Playlists and Bluetooth speakers make it so much easier now."

Alex coughs. "Do they still *allow* One Direction?"

Ali makes a face at him. "And what's on your Playlist, Mr. Cool?"

He winks. "The Beatles, Pearl Jam, Norah Jones, some Bruno Mars, a little Elvis, Coldplay, Maroon 5, and Lauren Daigle. I like to mix it up."

Conner laughs and covers his mouth with his hand. "The Beatles! That's like Ali's favorite band!"

Parker taps her foot. "Al-i. I'm waiting."

Ali sighs. "Fine. If your dance turns out totally lame, just remember you asked your big sister and a bookworm to chaperone."

Alex lays a hand on his chest. "Ouch, Ali. I'm wounded. We bookworms have moves, too. Just 'cause I love knowledge doesn't mean I can't rock a dance floor."

Ali giggles at the thought. She turns back to Conner and Parker, raising her eyebrows.

Conner stands up. "Come on, Parker. Let's get home. I'm starving."

"Yeah, alright. I've got a term paper to work on. So long, Talia. See you at home, Alex and Ali."

Talia looks at Alex and Ali. "Y'all just got played."

He laughs. "Yeah, probably so."

Ali sighs. "I'm tired. How much longer before today's over?"

Talia gets up, takes all the boxes and throws them in the trash. "Thanks for supper, guys. That was delicious. Hopefully, those peppers don't come back to haunt me. I've been having heartburn like nobody's business."

She hauls her backpack off the floor. Alex comes around and takes it from her. "We're done for the night. Let us walk you home."

She giggles. "It's only a few blocks."

He links an arm through hers. "Yeah, well. I'm afraid of the dark. Walk with me."

The three of them walk out; Alex beside Talia, carrying his messenger bag on one side and her backpack on the other. Ali limps along beside them on the other side in her Vegas heels. It isn't long and they're at Talia's apartment. Alex hands her the backpack and waits on the step until she gets inside.

He turns back to Ali. "Want a lift?"

"Excuse me?"

"Piggy-back ride. Do you want one?"

She laughs. "I'm almost as tall as you."

He looks her up and down and pops his knuckles. "I think I can handle you."

She steps up on the apartment stairs and removes her shoes. "Just remember you asked for this."

She's surprised when he lifts her like she's as light as a feather. They walk home in silence, and she relishes the feel of the cool night breeze kissing her cheeks and cooling her toes, as she leans her head on his shoulder, worn out.

He shakes her awake. "Ali."

She lifts her head. "Hmm."

"I'm going to put you down now."

She slides down his back. Her aching feet touch the sidewalk. "Thank you."

He steps back. His hand goes to his neck as he looks into her eyes. "Anytime." His voice is all husky and low.

She steps back, almost tripping over her feet. "Right, well, I'd better get to bed. Tomorrow's going to be another long day."

She goes to open the door, and it's yanked open. Parker sticks her head out. "Goodnight, Alex," she sings.

He puts up the back of his hand in a wave as he moseys down the sidewalk. Ali rushes past her to get inside. Parker giggles. "Somebody's got a crush on my sis-ter."

"Whatever, Parks. I'm going to take a long bath. Come keep me company in about five minutes."

"Ew. I don't want to see you in the tub."

"I'll have bubbles. We haven't talked in forever. I want to hear all about your senior year."

"Fine, but I'm moonwalking in the bathroom. You can keep all your lady bizness to yo'self."

Ali hops into the deep tub, sinks into the bath, loving the scents of lemon and jasmine floating around the room. There's a knock at the door. "Come in."

A deep chuckle on the other side of the door causes a hitch in her breath. "I don't think that's the best idea."

She flushes clear down to her toes. "I thought you were someone else. Do you need something?"

There's an awkward pause. "I thought I did. I guess I forgot. I'll see you tomorrow."

She hums to herself and sinks down to her chin.

A few minutes later the door opens, and Parker walks in backwards, holding out a glass of wine while balancing a full plate in the other hand. "I come bearing wine and cheese."

Ali squeals. "Thanks, Parks! You're the best."

"I try," she says dryly.

"Sooo... spill tea. Who's the cutest guy at your school? Who are you asking to the dance? Are you seeing anyone?"

Parker laughs. "Calm down. Has it been that long since we talked?"

She takes a sip of wine. "I'm sorry. I guess I've been busy. But I'm here now."

Parker smiles. "Yes, you are." She clears her throat. "Well, the cutest guy in our school, if you are only going by looks is probably Travis because he's got perfect hair, perfect height, big brown eyes and he dresses nice every day. But, if you're going by personality, there's a guy named Jeremy who kind of sneaks up on you because his nose is slightly crooked, but I like it that way, it gives him character. He's really smart, but he's kind of quiet, not as noticeable, but that's what makes him perfect."

Ali taps the back of Parker's head. "I'm thinking you're asking Jeremy to the dance."

Parker shakes her head back and forth. "No. I mean, neither of them have girlfriends right now, so that's a plus, but the girls in our class this year thought it might be fun to ask their crushes from like junior high."

"What?"

"Yeah. Because if they ask their junior high crush, then maybe it won't be so intimidating, and if they get rejected or whatever, then they can say they were like asking their old-school crush."

"Okay...so who did you have a crush on in junior high?"

Parker giggles. "Manuel Reyes."

"Wait. Wasn't he like the kid whose mom drove a big Harley?"

"Yeah. She was soo cool." Ali giggles at the far-off sound in Parker's voice.

"You do realize all the kids were afraid of her."

"That's what made her so cool." Parker's voice remains full of awe.

Ali pokes the back of her sister's neck. "Are you sure you didn't have a crush on *his mom*?"

Parker slaps her hand away. "Nooo. He was just super sweet to me. His lunch had two pieces of candy in it, and every day he would eat one, but he would save the other one just for me." She looks down at the bathmat, playing with the material.

Ali leans her head back on the tub and stares up at the ceiling. "Really? You never told me that."

Parker looks down and plays with the rug. "I never told anyone else either."

"Why not?"

"I guess it was just between us," she giggles. "That was the year I got the citizenship award."

"And why is that funny?" Ali's answer is a little sharp.

Parker shrugs her shoulders. "It's not, really. It's just when he first came to our school, he mostly spoke Spanish. He spent most of his time in the ESL room, and he didn't have any friends. The other boys used to pick on him because he spoke Spanish."

"That's stupid." Ali interjects.

"Well, that's boys for you."

"So, what happened to him?"

"Well, Mrs. Riggs chose me to be the model peer in his classroom, and that's kind of how we met, and that's probably what lead me to getting the citizenship award."

Ali flicks water at her. "See? It pays to be nice, Parks."

Parker turns narrowed eyes on her sister. "I'm nice to most people, but I'll call someone out if they need it."

Ali fake shivers. "Oy. Those are fightin' words." They sit in silence for a second or two. "So where is the mysterious Manuel Reyes now?"

"Oh, he's still at our school."

"Does he have more friends I hope?"

"Not really. Well, he and Talia are friends. They live in the same apartment building."

Ali glances over at her sister, trying to read her expression, but Parker's got a great poker face. "Do you want to ask him to the dance?"

She clears her throat. "I don't know. Maybe."

"Why don't you then?"

She picks at the rug she sits on. "My friends probably wouldn't like it."

"Is he a nice guy?" Ali pops bubbles in the water.

"Yeah. I mean, as far as I can tell. He's still pretty quiet. He's really into art and cars. Like he hangs out at his uncle's mechanic shop downtown."

Ali smiles to herself, remembering her high school crushes. "It seems like you've been keeping pretty close tabs on someone for not being that interested."

Her sister ducks her head in embarrassment. "Whatever. It's a small town. You can't sneeze without someone knowing."

"So why wouldn't your friends like it if you asked him?"

"I don't know. His life is kind of different from ours. He and his siblings live with their mom, and they keep to themselves."

"Well, why don't you invite him over sometime while I'm here? I'd like to meet him."

"I...I can't just do that. We don't talk much anymore. Like, at all."

"That's a shame. I guess I'll have to introduce myself at the dance." She nudges Parker's shoulder. "I've never known you to be afraid of anything, Parks. If you want to ask him, I say go for it."

Parker knocks on the side of the tub. "What about you?"

Ali's taken aback by Parker's tone. "What about me?"

"I think there's something between you and Alex."

Her cheeks warm at the thought. "What? We just met. I just got out of a relationship."

"Are you afraid?"

"No. He's just not my type."

Parker rolls her eyes. "What's that mean? What is your type?"

Ali tries to explain, though she kind of doubts her words. "I don't know. I've become more of a big city girl, and I like activities like hiking and organic health shakes."

"You telling me you did all this with Jason?" Parker accuses.

She feels kind of silly, but she's not ready to admit she might be wrong. "Yeah."

"And then Jason left you." Parker's words are so final.

Her irritation rises slightly because she walked right into her sister's trap. "Well...yeah."

"All I'm saying is, maybe Jason isn't your type anymore." Parker waits a few minutes. "Besides, you can order health food online, and if you like hiking, we have a city lake nearby where you can do all sorts of outdoor things. You can hike, canoe, or fish. It's really nice."

She pinches the back of Parker's neck. "Alright, little sister. You've made your point. I hear you loud and clear. But weren't we talking about your dance and the boys at your school?"

Parker laughs. "Yeah, but that's a short conversation. They're not that interesting."

She giggles. "*Somebody's* bitter. What about college? Do you have that figured out yet?"

Parker turns toward Ali, looking her in the eye. "I think I'll go to a junior college next year. Stay close to home and save some money. It's cheaper but the credits still transfer. I think it'd be a good transition before going to a bigger state college. I'm thinking about going into journalism."

She taps Parker's hand on the tub excitedly. "You're a writer? I had no idea."

Parker giggles. "You k*now* I'm opinionated."

She laughs. "Yep. There's no shortage of opinions in your tiny frame."

Parker traces circles on the rug. "I don't know if I want to be a writer or a journalist. I mean, I suppose I could be a journalist and then write on the side, kind of like what Alex did. It's not that easy to make it as a writer. He said he got like at least 30 rejections before someone said yes. That's a lot of "no's"."

"So you've been talking to *Alex* about your writing."

Parker's surprised by the hurt in Ali's voice. "You weren't here. Besides, he's a writer. Why are you so against him?"

Ali tries to explain herself, but she's unsure of her own feelings. "I don't know. It just seems like he's worked himself into Mom's life awful quick, and he sure seems right at home around here."

Parker crosses her arms on her chest. "Well, maybe he was filling the void."

Her anxiety goes through the roof, and she sits straight up in the tub, peeking over the side. "What do you mean? *How* is he filling the void that Dad left?"

Parker clears her throat. "Ewww. Gross. Not *that* void. The void you left."

"I grew up and moved away, Parks. That's what grown-ups do."

"I know. And we're all happy for your success. We're

proud of you. But you hardly come home anymore, and it's been hard on Mom. She misses you."

She feels defensive at her sister's words. "She never says so."

"Of course not! She's mom. She's not going to guilt you into coming home. But that doesn't mean you're not missed. It's okay. If you're happy, we're happy. I'm just saying."

She laughs bitterly. "I thought I was happy. I thought Jason was happy. I guess it's better I find out now instead of like Mom did, twenty years into marriage."

Parker crosses her arms over her chest. "Yeah, well. Look at all she's done since Dad left. She has her own business, and she has a whole new group of friends that mean a whole lot more than just face value." She giggles. "You know where she got her café name, right?"

"No. I mean, I figured it was just another part of her new forced positivity."

Parker snorts. "Not exactly. When Dad left, he was such a jerk about it. He got all cool and flippant. He was just like 'You don't fill my cup anymore.' That's like *literally* all he said before he walked out the door with his suitcase."

She can hardly believe her ears, and she wonders why she never heard any of this before. "That's all he took?"

"Yeah. He never came back after he took up with his nurse. So Mom had to go through all his clothes and box them up. She took them to the DAV. I know that had to be hard on her, but you know mom, she never said a negative word about him. She never talked about him, period. She just dropped Conner and I off at the therapist once a month and she..." her voice lowers, "she bought a gun and went to the firing range."

Her sister's words shock Ali. "What?" is all she can muster.

"Yeah. That's where she met Alex."

She leans back in the tub and stares up at the ceiling. Her mind reels. "This story just gets stranger and stranger. It's like aliens took over Mom's brain or something."

Parker sighs. "Nope. Just divorce."

Ali chuckles and flicks the back of her sister's neck with a wet finger. "Good one."

Parker smiles and stares at the floor. "Thanks. Anyways, it's not what it sounds like. Alex was at the firing range doing research on a character for his novel. They started talking, and he's the one who convinced her to channel her anger into something more positive, and I think he may have even given her some money to start up her café, but I'm not supposed to know any of that."

"But he's only been here a year. That's what he told me. Why would he lie to me about that?" Ali asks.

"He *has* only been here a year. He wasn't living in this town when they met. You are way too cynical."

Ali sighs. "I'm not cynical. I'm a realist. There's a difference."

"If you say so," Parker challenges, and Ali supposes she's referring to Jason, and she changes the subject.

"So Mom named her café what she did just to slap Dad in the face?"

Her sister giggles. "Kind of. And it's been a success, so I would say she slapped him big time. He *totally* deserves it."

"This is true. How's Conner been with all of this?"

"Oh, he has his days where he's angry at the world, but most of that has passed. Mom keeps telling him every cloud has a silver lining. I swear she could recite positivity lines in her sleep."

"Well. That's better than being ticked off forever. There's no use in spending all your time on negative energy. There's plenty to be happy about, too." Ali pauses. "This water's starting to get lukewarm, and I've got a long day tomorrow. Mom busts her *tail* running the café."

"Yeah. She learned from the best, thank goodness, because I don't know the *first thing* about running a restaurant."

Ali can't believe how much she didn't know about her Mom's new life. "Oh?"

"Oh, yeah. When she started, she didn't know a *thing* about running a restaurant. So the *terrific trio*, that's what Mom calls them—Sheila, Loretta, and Yvonne—they came and spent a month with Mom, showing her the ins-and-outs of running a business, time management, and multitasking—the whole nine yards. If you ask Mom, she'd swear to you those ladies are Einstein Bosses, and there's nothing they can't do. Anyway, after spending a month with them in the café, she came out a new woman, good to go, and she's been doing fine ever since."

Ali is so confused. "Where did she find them?"

"Apparently there's a women empowering women group online and if you are a woman needing assistance with your business, you can reach out to them for help, and that's what mom did. She's quite resourceful."

Ali thinks about her day. "Well, she has a lot of help from the community, too."

"Oh, yeah, she does. But did you know the whole schedule she's got going, how all the puzzle pieces fit together just right, that's Mom's doing too. She's the one who arranged for Amber to leave her dogs there so Marvin and Becky can walk them. Mom suggested Amber trade dog-sitting for Amber's waiting tables, and she got Talia lined up for school. Mom also told Alex to come down every day to write so he could use the free wi-fi." She pauses. "She thinks of everything."

"Gee. Is that all she does?" Ali asks in a dry tone, but her sister ignores her lack of enthusiasm and rattles on.

"Actually, no. On the mornings near certain holidays, Mom feeds all the high-schoolers breakfast in exchange for them working for free for her to bring in a crowd for her holiday lunches. Her customers love seeing the kids, and the kids can put their service on their 4-H community record and scholarship forms for community service as well. It all works out. If Mom sees a need, she does her best to fill it."

"Huh. I had no idea."

"Yeah, well. You know Mom. She's not a talker. She's a doer."

"I guess so." A few minutes go by. "So Alex loaned Mom money to get her café going?"

"I thought I already told you that; but don't say anything. He doesn't know I overheard."

"Eavesdropper," Ali teases.

Parker clears her throat. "To be a good journalist, you have to be a good listener. It's all in the details. Speaking of which, I've got a paper to work on. I'll talk to you later, Ali."

eight

Maggie's nervous as she steps off the plane. She wheels her small suitcase behind her. Her eyes scan the huge New York airport, and uncertainty fills her as she looks for Joshua. She wonders if she'll even recognize him after all these years. She rushes off to the lady's room to freshen up, feeling foolish. The crowded hallway stuns her when she exits, as she's not used to so many people. She takes a few steps backward and bumps into a very solid someone. She spins around, grabs a hold of an arm, and looks up into a very familiar set of bright blue eyes. "Excuse me...Joshua! I'm so sorry."

He chuckles. "Maggie Louise, just the girl I was lookin' for." The childhood nickname takes her back, and her heart skips a beat as she laughs.

"Joshua Dean. You were the only person who was ever allowed to call me by my middle name." Maggie studies him and sees the haunted look in his eyes. She gives him a warm hug. "How are you?" She whispers in his ear.

He doesn't answer right away. He just squeezes her tight. "I've been better. It's so nice to see you."

She takes a step back and clears her throat. "Are you ready to go, then?"

He chuckles. "Maggie, Maggie. Always on the go. I see you haven't changed much."

She grins back at him. "It sounds like we've got a lot to do."

"That we do." She links her arm with his and follows him outside. She shivers with the cold. He steps away from her and removes his jacket. "Put this on. I'm wearing a sweater."

She slips into his coat, ducks her head into the collar and sniffs. "You haven't changed your cologne."

He smiles back at her, making her blush. "You remembered." He calls a Lyft and they get in. "I thought we'd pick up lunch on the way home, if that's alright. There's a great little sandwich place not far from the apartment."

Her eyes water as she thinks about stepping into Natalie's apartment and going through her things. It's all so personal. "Yeah, sure," she answers quietly before taking a deep breath. "So, tell me about you, Joshua. What have you been up to in the last twenty years?"

He laughs. "I thought Natalie would have kept you filled in on my life."

"Nope. Believe it or not, most of our conversations did not revolve around *you*. We talked about *our* lives. Besides, I'd like to hear about your life from you," she says with a giggle. She can't believe she's flirting with him!

He clears his throat. "Well, I've done some traveling, and that's been fun. Although traveling alone isn't as enjoyable as having a companion."

She glances over at him. "Did you never marry?"

He studies her thoroughly before answering. "I guess I never found the right one."

She blushes under his intense gaze. "Well. You always were a bit particular. No one is perfect."

He's still looking, and she has to look away. "That may be true, but I believe there's someone who's perfect for me." His comment makes her feel all warm inside. The car suddenly feels too small.

She turns back to him, changing the subject. "Just so you know, I hope to do some touring of New York while I'm here. Do you have a favorite spot?"

He sits back a minute, thinking. "That's a tough question. There's so many. They have some great libraries and museums, but if you're into tourist hot spots; there's the obvious, the Statue of Liberty and Ellis Island."

"I've always wanted to see both of those places, but we'll see how much we can get done first. Plus, I *have* to see the top of the Empire State Building, especially with it being this close to Valentine's Day."

He looks over at her again. "*Sleepless in Seattle*."

She giggles. "Yep."

He shakes his head. "I can't *believe* that's still your favorite movie."

She throws up her hands. "Busted." She leans toward him, talking quietly. "*And* I totally want to see every street that was in *You've Got Mail*."

He takes her hand and kisses her knuckles, making her blush. "As you wish."

The Lyft driver glances in the rearview mirror. "Hey Romeo, we're here." They scan the board before ordering their sandwiches. Soon they're at the apartment. Joshua hands Maggie the food bag and takes her suitcase. "I've got this."

She follows him up the stairs. She can't help but notice his broad shoulders and narrow waist. He hasn't changed much from his high school football days.

They step inside, and she's overcome with emotion as she smells Natalie's signature scent throughout the apartment. She smiles through her tears. "She always smelled so nice."

He nods. He goes to the kitchen to pull out paper plates. "Yep. She'd kill me if she knew I was eating off a paper plate."

She laughs. "She totally would. I'd forgotten that about her." He pulls out a few wine glasses and fills them half full. He holds up his glass, and she clinks her glass on his. "To Natalie."

He gives her a wink. "To Nat."

She swallows hard as she looks sideways. A few tears roll down her cheeks. "Oh, how she hated that nickname. She used to get so mad when you'd call her that." She turns back to him and gives him a small smile.

He smiles back, wiggling his eyebrows. "I know."

She takes a big bite of her sandwich, groaning as she chews. "I had no idea I was so hungry. You don't know how good it is to eat something I didn't have to make." She takes a sip of wine. "I love running a restaurant, don't get me wrong, but this... this is heavenly."

He watches her in amusement. "They make a pretty mean sandwich."

Her eyes twinkle at him. "So, tell me, what do you do?"

"Well, I putter with computers mostly."

She wrinkles her nose. "Putter? Stop being modest and spill. I *know* you."

He leans back in his chair. "Fine. I was working at a hospital as an IT guy and I met a nurse named Jenice. She and I got to talking, and she had some great ideas about apps, but she's not tech-savvy so much, and so we got to work. I kind of created some apps for the medical field, and they were kind of useful. And now I have my own hours and I work from home mostly."

She sets her glass down. "If I'm reading between the lines

correctly, you're an independent contractor and you pretty much set your own hours and your own price."

He leans forward and shrugs his shoulders. "I got lucky. What can I say?"

She studies him. "You didn't get lucky. You worked darn hard, and this is your reward." She taps her temple. "If you didn't have it up here, you couldn't have done what you did."

He smiles sadly. "I guess. But you know, I think my parents would have traded all of our achievements for at least one grandchild."

She stares at him. "You have no children?"

He laughs. "I never married. I just told you that. And Natalie never had children, either. I guess it wasn't in the cards."

She bites her lip, but she can't keep her smile in. "Just because you're single doesn't mean you couldn't have a kid or two out there. Are you telling me you never had any relationships, because I don't believe that for a minute. I remember your high school days."

He slaps the countertop. "Maggie Louise! I never thought I'd hear you say such a thing. I was a responsible guy. I knew what I was doing."

She gives him an ornery grin, raising her eyebrows. "I'm sure you did."

His face flushes. "What was that?"

She giggles before taking a big bite. She shakes her head back and forth, grinning with a closed mouth. She finishes her sandwich and her glass of wine. "What is your goal for the apartment, and where do we start?"

He looks back at her. "My goal is to sort through all of her things and decide what to keep and what to give away. I just... I have no one to give anything to. Most of her friends were online because she was always traveling and vlogging."

She looks around the eclectic apartment. She notes all the

knickknacks from all the countries, and the stacks of books here and there, along with the beautiful photos on the walls. "I'd like to take the photos she took with me, if I could. I mean the ones you don't want. I'd like to hang them in my café."

He nods. "Sure, sure. I think she would have loved that."

She stands there longer, thinking. "Her books could go to my friend, Abby. She *adores* a great book collection. She runs a bookstore in our town. And her clothes and furniture could go to Isabel. She runs Bella's Boutique. She'd love to go through anything you don't want."

He looks over at her. "I just don't have room for most of this stuff. I wouldn't know where to start if I kept it. I want it to go to someone else who will keep it someplace they can look at it and enjoy it, you know? Like Natalie did." They stand in the middle of the room a bit longer. He claps his hands, making her jump. "Here's a wild idea! Why don't I pay someone to box up all of this, and load it into a U-Haul, and then I could drive it to your town?"

She's not sure what to say. "What will I do this week if I'm not going through everything here?"

He looks over at her. "You could go sight-seeing with me. You said you wanted to."

Her heart lifts at the thought. "If you're sure. I mean, if your schedule is open." She giggles. "I guess you just said that your schedule was open."

His eyes light up as he looks at her. "It is. I'm ready for the Upper West Side whenever you are."

She takes her suitcase off to the bedroom to find another layer of clothing. She steps out a few minutes later in her white jeans, red sweater, and a yellow scarf, complete with her brown fuzzy boots. He gives her an appreciative look of approval. "New York, here we come."

They find a Lyft driver and her eyes take in all the sights

as they drive down busy streets. She turns to him. "This is the first vacation I've had in two years. And it's the first vacation I've taken alone." She feels bad about what she just said. "I mean, it's not a vacation, I just mean..."

He squeezes her hand. "I know what you meant. I wish Natalie were here to see you. I know she would be happy you're here now."

They sit in silence again. She keeps her hand in his. Memories flood her of the night he picked her up from a party, and she wasn't able to drive home. It was the first time she'd ever drank, and she'd made a complete fool of herself. Embarrassed, she had snuck into the kitchen at the house and called Natalie's house, but Natalie wasn't there. Joshua had answered. She hadn't wanted to tell him, but he pulled it out of her, and minutes later he had showed up. When they left the party, he took her hand to lead her across the lawn, and even though she was drunk, she knew she'd never forget that night and the feel of his hand in hers.

"Penny for your thoughts?" His voice cuts through her silence. Maggie's embarrassed.

She takes her hand back. "Oh, I was just walking down memory lane. Nothing too exciting." He frowns at her secrecy, and she looks away, feeling bad.

The car stops. "West 69th Street." She hops out, looks around, and scans the building titles before turning back to him. "Where's *The Shop Around the Corner*?"

He answers. "I'm afraid it's now a dry cleaners. But we could walk a bit and see if there's another bookstore."

She nods decidedly. "Let's do it." She turns back to him. "Could we also get a cup of coffee?"

"Yes, ma'am." He takes her elbow and pulls her close. They start down the crowded sidewalk. "I bet you can quote that movie in your sleep."

She laughs. "Yep. That's the one thing your sister and I

could agree on. Our romantic movie choices. She always said that movie was what first inspired her to travel."

He stops in his tracks. "Really? I didn't know that."

She glances around at the hustle and bustle, smiling. "I guess she finally made it to New York City."

They start walking again. "She always felt bad that she didn't get to see your café."

Her eyes are wide as she looks around. "Oh, Joshua. I totally understood. I mean, Natalie's seen so many amazing things. My café is nothing compared to all this." She waves her free hand excitedly. "It's certainly not renown."

He shakes his head. "Maybe not, but she would talk about your town and the people in your café like she knew them. And she would get *so excited* whenever she got an e-mail from you. She loved hearing from your little corner of the world."

She smiles at the thought. "Really?"

He nods. "Oh, yeah. She forwarded *all* your e-mails to me."

She stops. She feels exposed when she remembers the details she put in her e-mails about the divorce. Her face heats. She stumbles over the memory of asking Natalie a time or two if Joshua ever asked about her. "You shouldn't have read my e-mails, Joshua. I sent them to Natalie."

He hesitates. "I didn't read them. I wanted to, but it felt strange. And I couldn't exactly send you an e-mail and ask your permission. Natalie used to get annoyed with me when she realized I wasn't reading them, but after a while, she just stopped asking me about them."

She stares at him questioningly. "If you didn't read them, what did you do with them?"

He gives her a little smirk. "I still have them. They're in my mysterious Maggie folder."

She leans into him, shoving him. "You're such a brat."

He nudges her back. "You love me that way." He looks past her and points across the street. "There's a bookstore."

She claps her hands. "Yes!"

He groans at her excitement. "Do I need to set a time limit?"

She sticks out her tongue. "Nope. I'm on vacation. No time frames." She starts to step off the sidewalk, and he grabs a hold of her. He yanks her against him, and she stills.

"Maggie. This is New York. You don't just cross the street wherever. Let's go find a crosswalk." His voice is hoarse. She steps away from him. She feels guarded and careless as she tries to sort out the confusing feelings that keep popping up with his touch.

"I'm sorry, I wasn't thinking." She follows him to the corner. Soon they arrived at the bookstore. She turns to him, smiling. "Ooh, coffee!" She hops in line to wait with a huge smile on her face. He can't help but grin. It's finally her turn, and she approaches the register. "Yes, I'd like one mochaccino decaf, nonfat please."

He nudges her heel from behind. "Is that really what you want?"

She giggles at the humor in his voice. "Yes."

She goes for her wallet, and he steps up. "No. This is on me, you're not going to like that coffee, even if it is a Tom Hanks quote."

She takes her cup of coffee stubbornly and starts her rambling walk through the bookstore, meandering slowly toward the mystery section. He grabs a coffee and a newspaper. He settles into a big, oversized chair in the corner. She wanders aimlessly, her eyes roving over spine after spine for a bit. With a glance, she sees Joshua hiding behind his newspaper and strides over to sit down beside him. She sips her coffee and people watches, two of her favorite pastimes.

He glances over at her. "Does it feel weird to relax?"

She smiles behind her coffee cup. "A little." She takes out her phone, feeling ornery. "Here, lean in. Let's take a selfie. I'll send it to my kids."

He leans toward her and makes a silly face. She sends it on SnapChat. He clears his throat. "Tell me about your kids."

Her face lights up. "Ali's 22, and she just graduated. She's into graphic arts and marketing. She has *excellent* business sense. Parker is a senior in high school, and she's *kind of* into journalism. Conner is a freshman in high school and he's basically into sports and girls."

He laughs. "My kind of guy."

"You could say that again," she mutters under her breath.

He frowns. "Ouch. Do I hear resentment?"

She nods her head decisively. "I think you did. I'm going to go look at more books now."

Two hours and five books later, they leave the bookstore. He steps outside, shaking his legs. "My butt fell asleep."

She gives him a look. "You could have walked around or gone to a store close by."

He looks at her indignantly. "And leave you alone in New York City? What kind of tour guide would I be?"

She looks at him expectantly. "Now where to?"

He winks at her. "It's a surprise." His phone lights up. "Here's our Lyft."

She hops in. Soon they're stopping again, and she hops out. She looks up. "Café Lalo! No way."

He comes around and takes her bag of books. "Let's go, ShopGirl."

She giggles. "After you, NY152."

He looks around, confusing her as he heads in a different direction. She follows him as he walks down to the corner to buy a rose. He turns to her. "Here, for your book." He pulls a book from the back of his shirt.

She takes it from him, smiling. "*Pride and Prejudice?* But how did you? I mean, when did you?"

He gives her a wink. "If you're going to do it, you may as well do it right." He gives a mini bow. "After you, my lady."

She takes the rose and puts it in the book, feeling all mushy inside. "Natalie, I could really use your help right now," she mutters under her breath as she turns away from him.

He steps up beside her. "What's that?"

"Nothing." She reads through the menu posted outside. "There's no meat here."

"There's salmon."

She wrinkles her nose. "That hardly counts, but I'll take it."

He leans forward, still reading. "We could split a piece of cheesecake. The Black & White is really good." He takes her elbow and leads her inside.

She looks around the café, smiling. "Sure. Why not? That sounds good to me." She lays her book down on the table between them, places the rose inside the book, and feels a bit silly.

He raises his eyebrow. "What are you going to do if someone approaches you about that book?"

She giggles. "I'm hardly sitting alone. I'm not too worried."

He leans in and gives her an ornery grin. "Would you like me to sit somewhere else?"

She makes a face of mock horror. "Don't you dare." He picks up the book and opens it. The rose falls out. She glances over at him. "Have you read that book?"

He lays the book down. "Have you?"

She nods her head. "At least twice."

"Before or after you watched *You've Got Mail?*"

She giggles. "After. You wouldn't believe how long it took

Natalie and I to get through the book the first time, but we were determined."

He taps his fingers on it. "I've watched the *Pride & Prejudice* movie, if that counts. I *barely* got through it."

She laughs. "I've seen that one at least six times."

"*Six* times? You've *suffered* through that movie six times?"

"It's beautiful! The language, the dancing, the scenery, and the music. Those trees." Her eyes sparkle.

He shakes his head. "I guess that's why God made women. *Someone* has to watch ridiculously ancient movies about stuffy men in trousers gallivanting across green pastures on their dark horses - taking long walks on gloomy mornings."

She gives a golf clap. "Bravo, Joshua. I didn't know you had any poetry in you. If only the high school football team could see you now." She glances down at the book again. "There might be a little bit of Mark Darcy in you after all."

He studies her across the table, plays with her fingertips, and smirks. "Maggie Louise. You're simply captivating." He says in a somber voice.

She blushes, takes her book back, and puts the rose back in place. She's relieved to see the young waiter show up with their food. He glances down at the book. "What's the big deal about that book?"

Maggie and Joshua look at each other and laugh out loud. He turns to the blue-eyed waiter sporting a man bun. He reads his nametag before throwing his hands up at him. "*Thank you,* Sebastian."

nine

It's late by the time they get back to the apartment, and Maggie is exhausted. She trudges up the stairs behind Joshua. "Does the apartment have a tub?"

"What's that?"

She speaks louder. "A tub. Does the apartment have a tub?"

"Oh, yeah."

"Good. A hot bath sounds wonderful right now. I'd love to wash off the airplane ride and city streets."

They walk in wordlessly. She shuffles off to the bathroom, dragging her bag of books behind her. She comes back out and pours herself a glass of wine. He smiles after her. "Books and wine, huh? Don't fall asleep in the tub."

She shuts the door, sheds everything, climbs into the hot water, and drops a bath bomb in. She closes her eyes and enjoys the scent of roses as they fill the air. She crawls into her book, sips her wine, and relaxes. Forty-five minutes later, she emerges in sweats and a hoodie. She's surprised to see him sitting on the couch with his earphones in, watching something on his laptop.

He looks at her, and his eyes go dark. She backs away, takes her wineglass to the kitchen, and puts it in the sink. She jumps a foot when she turns around to find him right behind her. "Joshua!"

He steps in and puts a hand on her waist. "Mags." Her stomach flips. She hasn't heard that name on his lips since she was seventeen-years-old and he was home from college. It was her birthday, and she was out at a dance club with Natalie. She was tired and ready to go home, as it wasn't really her scene, but Natalie had been so excited to go, so she went. Maggie had gotten too hot on the dance floor, and she'd stepped outside to get some air. She snuck around the side of the building. He'd appeared out of nowhere, staggering a little as he stepped closer.

He leaned in and said three words. "Happy birthday, Mags," before kissing her like she'd never been kissed before. His palms spanned her waist as he held her tight while his fingertips brushed her rib cage, giving her feelings she didn't know she had. As fast as it happened, it stopped. His hands dropped. One settled on her hip, gripping, while the other hit the wall beside her as he hung his head. "I'm sorry," he said, and wouldn't look her in the eye. "Go back inside. Please." He sounded so tortured.

She had put a trembling hand on his chest. She scarcely believed her brave words as she'd stepped into him, looking up. "But I don't want to."

His eyes had burned her through as he looked down at her. "Go, Maggie. This never should have happened," he growled. A very confused and heartbroken Maggie had run back inside. His kiss was the only secret she ever kept, and it was one that would haunt her, waking her in the middle of the night, leaving her wanting.

And now here he was again, after all these years, tying her in knots, as his hand slips under her sweatshirt, touching the skin of her waist while his lips graze her throat, moving upward to her jawline. "You smell so good." She's tongue-tied and frozen once again, not knowing what to say or do. She puts her hands on the counter and leans backward. He follows. His searching lips find hers. It's a slow, sweet kiss, full of longing and rediscovery. When he ends the kiss, her fingers fly to her lips. His fevered eyes roam her face. "That was a long time coming."

She shakes her head. "What do you mean?"

He looks a little uncertain. "I've been wanting to do that since the moment I saw you at the airport."

She steps sideways to put space between them. "It's late, and I need some sleep. Thank you for the wonderful day we had."

He reacts as if stung. "Right. You're welcome, Maggie." He gets out while she crosses the room in seconds. His polite tone sounds forced, and even though she knows she's the reason, it still stings.

She stares at him from the bedroom door a few seconds longer, studying him as he turns away. "Goodnight, Joshua."

He hears a touch of sentiment in her voice, and he turns back to her. "Did I do something wrong?"

Her feelings are all over the place, but she's not ready to talk. "I don't know what I'm doing here."

She closes the bedroom door, shutting him out.

ten

The next morning comes bright and early, but Ali's determined to be ready, and Alex finds her waiting on the front step in a soft tee shirt dress, wearing flats, shivering a little in the cool early morning. He approaches, sticking out his arm. "Would you like to walk to work with me?"

She stands up, takes his arm, leaning in. "Warm me up, Alex."

He throws an arm around her. "Yes, ma'am."

She takes the apple from his hand, munching as they walk along. "So tell me, where's your favorite place to write?"

"I like to write at the bakery. Watching all the people bustle about and listening to their easy conversations makes for good background noise."

"Really? I find I can't think straight if I hear people talking in the background. It's difficult to shut out their words."

He laughs. "It took a little while to learn, but I'm pretty good at it now, especially when I get on a train of thought. It just keeps going. But you're right, it just depends on what I'm writing. I also enjoy writing at Abby's bookstore. It's quiet there and I love to sit at a back table with a hot cup of coffee and a delicious-smelling muffin as I contemplate what comes next."

She laughs. "So, do you ever write of elegant old houses lost in fields of green with a charming pond nestled between a couple of giant trees, and the days of fine letter writing and horse-drawn carriages?"

He laughs out loud at her description. "I'm afraid I'm no Jane Austen."

She nods. "Well, that is a shame. I do so enjoy the music of *Pride & Prejudice*, as well as the stubbornness of Elizabeth Bennett."

He looks down at her, surprised. "Aren't you a bit young for that sort of movie?"

She glances up at him. "My mother was a lover of all things classic and romantic, especially movies with great soundtracks. I guess she passed it on to me."

He nudges her ribs. "So you prefer an old stuffed shirt like Mark Darcy over Magic Mike?"

She slaps his arm, laughing. "Definitely. How *dare* you utter their names in the same sentence?" She waits a few moments. "Of course, the perfect man would be a combination of Mark Darcy, Jim from The Office, and Joe Fox, but hey, I don't think I'm asking for too much."

He laughs out loud. "No. Not at all." He pauses. "So you're a modern-day career woman who enjoys old-fashioned rom-com movies?"

She smiles, squeezing his arm as they walk along. "I suppose so."

"That's refreshing. Some of the romantic movies young people watch today I can't make heads or tails of."

She laughs. "I totally agree." She looks ahead and nudges him. "Oh, dear. There's our first customer of the day, sitting at a patio table outside." She cups her hands to her mouth and calls out. "Hello there, Bernie."

Alex hurries to the door, turns the key in the lock, and throws the door open. She's right behind him. She rushes past him to the kitchen, putting on the teakettle and throwing Bernie's oatmeal together, glancing at the clock. The bowl rattles in front of Bernie as it hits the counter. She tosses his snack sacks at him before pouring his tea, looking all smug. "It's seven on the dot."

Bernie gives her a raised brow, growling. "You're barely on time."

She surprises herself by winking at Bernie before rushing off to view the spreadsheet for the day's menu. "Oh thank goodness, it's sub sandwich day. I just have to make a huge macaroni salad is all."

Alex sneaks into the backroom behind her. "Yes, but today's also Tuesday, which is muffin day and your mom makes them all from scratch the day of. So, let's get to work."

She peeks back at him while looking in the fridge. "You really don't mind?"

He puts out his hands. "I'm offering."

"Okay. Here's the recipe. I'll get the ingredients and you can get out the bowls, mixers, and pans, please."

"Sounds good." He heads back for the kitchen while she starts pulling everything from the fridge and cupboards. It doesn't take long for them to find a rhythm. An hour later, the kitchen is filled with wonderful baking smells as she fills the display case with freshly baked muffins. They exchange a high five through oven-mitted hands. She puts her hands on her hips, frowning. "And now, for the fun part, clean up."

He puts his head down and walks toward his writing corner. "I'm out of here."

She grabs his upper arm, giving him a squeeze. "Thanks for all your help."

He gives a small bow. "Glad to be of service."

She plays the *Pride & Prejudice* soundtrack on her phone as she cleans the kitchen. The peaceful sound of piano playing surrounds her as she works. She busies herself by writing the muffin types on the folded white cardstock to put out on top of the glass display case before re-arranging her muffins on display.

eleven

A li turns to Alex who just sat down. Her face is all lit up as she rushes over to sit down at his table. "I just had an awesome idea!"

"What's that?"

"When we have the Valentine's Day dinner here, we could do a "how we met" game. Like we could have everyone write down how they met on a piece of paper and then we put them all in a jar and then someone reads them aloud one at a time from behind the mic and everyone tries to guess which description belongs to what couple."

"That could be fun."

"Ooh, here's another one. We could have them write a funny personal story about their partner that could be read aloud and people try to guess who it is, or like they could write down a nickname their partner has. And, also, we could do a sweet game like they all write down something sweet their partner does that they appreciate so the young kids could hear about true romance."

He watches her, his eyes twinkling. "You sure know how to brainstorm. I love all of these ideas."

"Thanks. I'm going to do my best to make sure this Valentine's Day dinner night is going to be one to remember, and a lot of fun!" She claps her hands together, holding them in a prayer at her lips.

He crosses his arms, squeezing his biceps. "I totally agree."

She jumps up with her fingers on her temples. "Timeless Love!"

"What?"

"Timeless Love is the name of our Valentine's Day Dinner."

He watches her. "That's classic. Like you don't feel time pass when you're with the one you love." His voice gets quieter as he continues to stare at her. She stares right back at him.

"Exactly." She breaks his intense gaze, feeling self-conscious, writing the words down on her notepad. She taps her finger on her chin, leaning on the table. "The next thing we need to do is come up with ideas for wine and cheese and chocolate combinations."

He steps closer to the table. "If you want some help with that, I think I could get us a date set in the next few days at a nearby winery. It'd be a lot of fun, and I'm always open to new ideas."

She nods her head. "Yeah, that would be the easiest. I've never done one before. Do you think we could book it on such short notice?"

He shrugs. "Well. I kind of know a guy."

She drums her hands on the table. "Sure. Let's do it."

His blue eyes are full of warmth. "I'll set it up."

She coughs. "Be sure you tell him it's for a dinner and all."

"Don't worry. I will."

Her voice raises again. "Oooh! Also, we could serve appetizers and main entrée in white boxes, so they'd be easy to clean up."

He raises his pointer finger in the air. "Orrr, we could do red boxes. For Valentine's Day."

"True. Ooh. And we could have like Shakespeare love quotes typed out in pretty, cursive writing to put on the tables like big pieces of confetti. I love reading book quotes and movie lines about subjects. Maybe we could number them and whoever gets the most references correct wins a door prize. There's some great little shops here I'd love to visit for the door prizes."

He laughs. "You're making this into a much bigger production than your mom does."

"I'm sorry. I'm just having fun. Sometimes my brain goes on hyperdrive. Parks could help me with all of this. She's a great writer."

He smiles, tapping her hand with his finger. "If you want to put all that effort into it, be my guest."

She shies away from his hand. "Hey. Didn't you say some of the high school kids would be over to help?"

He pulls back, slightly wounded. "Yeah. You might want to make some of this into a PowerPoint, might save you some paper cutting. I bet Parker or Talia could help you with that. That's what they do."

She narrows her eyes. "Alex. I'm plenty capable of creating a PowerPoint. I'm a career woman. I think I know my way around a computer." Her voice sounds all prickly.

He lifts his hands up in surrender. "It was *just* a suggestion. Trust me, I know better than to try to tell *you* what to do."

She softens a little, looking back at him. "I like your PowerPoint idea. It would keep things a lot simpler, less scattered. The couples could just have paper with numbers on them and they could write their answers on them. I'd better get started on my noodle salad."

He follows behind her, still talking. "You'll have to get movie quotes from like every decade, you know, because you're going to have all different ages. It would be cool if you got like a couple of high schoolers to be your announcers or whatever. And maybe you could get Isaac to sing a few love songs at the beginning and the end. He's a great singer and he can play the guitar. Oh, for door prizes, I bet you could get some donations in the form of gift certificates from local businesses."

She's at the stove, getting ready to lift the pasta pot. He rushes over, picking up the huge pot and setting it on the stove. She glances at him. "I could have done that."

He frowns at her. "Do you want me to put it back on the floor?"

Her cheeks turn pink. "That'd be silly since it's already on the stove."

He stands in front of her. "Would it kill you to say thank you?"

She grabs the saltshaker, pours some in the water, and side-eyes him. "Thank you." She studies him, deep in thought. "What's your idea of a romantic movie?"

He smiles, putting up his fists. "*Rocky*."

She makes a face. "*Rocky*? Isn't that a boxing movie?"

"Yes it is, but did you *know* that Sylvester Stallone wrote the first one *himself*, and that it almost didn't get made? Can you *imagine* a world without *Rocky*? It's like the ultimate underdog movie, and *that* in itself is romantic."

She giggles, shaking her head. "You can keep your *Rocky*. I'll take *Pride & Prejudice* and *Letters to Juliet*, or any movie filmed in Italy or France."

He crosses his arms on his chest. "Wasn't *Dr. Zhivago* filmed in Russia? What about that one?"

She wrinkles her nose. "Way too old for me. Plus, it was filmed outside of Madrid, and they never get together at the end, so it doesn't have a happy ending, thus, it isn't romantic."

He chuckles, shaking his head. "How do you know if you never watched it?"

She grins. "I watched *Must Love Dogs*."

He shakes his head and turns to walk away. "I'm not sure how to exit a conversation I just got lost in, but I'm pretty sure I'm not winning this argument."

She laughs out loud, waving her pasta spoon at him. "And that's how you know you're discussing romantic movies with a woman."

"*Clueless* was the most romantic movie eeveer." Talia calls out from the office.

They turn in her direction, answering together. "Noooo."

twelve

Maggie wakes early, unsure of herself after the kiss in the kitchen last night. What did it mean, and now what does she do? There's a knock at the door, and she pulls the covers up over her slip top. "Yes?"

"Can I come in?"

"Yes."

Joshua opens the door, raising his eyebrows. "I thought you'd be up, Maggie Louise. We've got a full day of sight-seeing ahead of us if you're still up for it?" She can't help but smile back at him, when he's looking at her all hopeful.

She clears her throat, embarrassed. "Oh, yeah, sure."

He stares a few seconds longer. "Didn't you get my e-mail last night?"

She shakes her head. "No, I'm sorry. I guess I went right to sleep."

He chuckles. "Alright. Well, I'll be out here waiting. I thought maybe we could leave in thirty minutes or so. I'll take you by my favorite bakery."

She nods her head, still clutching the covers at her chin. "Sounds good."

He gives her an ornery grin. "Relax, Mags. I'm not the big bad wolf." She blushes, thinking his wolfish grin says otherwise.

"You said you'd wait on the couch. Shut the door so I can get out of bed." Realization shows up on his face, and he looks a little sheepish.

"Oh, right. Sorry."

The door shuts, and she flies out of bed, grabbing her shower bag and a fresh set of clothes before throwing on her hoodie. She races to the bathroom, setting her phone alarm. Twenty-seven minutes later, she walks out, feeling fresh and triumphant, in her favorite jeggings and long sweater with her brown boots. "I'm read-y," she sings.

He wastes no time, tosses on a light jacket and takes her arm in his. "New York is waiting."

She stops and smacks her forehead. "I'm sorry. I still haven't read that e-mail."

He turns, grinning. "Great! Then today will be a surprise for you."

She turns to him, feeling strange. "Joshua, about last night."

He clears his throat. "Maggie Louise. Today is a new day with no mistakes. What happens in New York stays in New York."

She's not sure what to say as she follows him down the stairs. Her heart sinks a little at his words. Does he really think the kiss was a mistake? She takes a deep breath and smiles as the crisp cool air kisses her cheeks. "I love sweater weather."

He laughs. "Yes. It is lovely. This winter is one of our milder winters, so that's been nice. It works just right for tourism." They walk a few blocks, and he ushers her into a shop on the corner with a line of people out to the sidewalk. She giggles, shaking her head. He turns to her. "What?"

She smiles back at him. "I don't think I've ever seen a line like this outside my café. I'm not sure old Bernie could handle it."

He shakes his head. "Is Bernie the reason your phone alarm goes off three times a day?"

She nods her head. "Yes. He's forgetful sometimes. I call him to remind him to take his medications."

He shakes his head again. "Couldn't he just live in assisted living and then someone would help him with that?"

She looks horrified. "And lose my best customer? It would break sweet Bernie's heart to move into that type of place. He's a little forgetful, but that doesn't mean he can't live on his own. The pride he takes in his apartment makes my heart sing."

He smiles back at her. "You really love the guy."

She crosses her arms on her chest. "I do. He's kind of like a father to me."

He raises his hands up. "Okay, okay. Don't get your back up." They step inside and the bell over the door rings. He looks up, spying mistletoe. He looks back at her. "May I?" She blushes, giving a little nod. He leans in, giving her a little peck on the lips. The line behind them cheer. Inspired, she reaches for his jacket collar, tugs him forward for another kiss, and he hugs her tight. After, they stand in line, and his arm remains around her waist. She leans into him. "Why is there mistletoe above the door in February?"

He smiles back at her. "Did you not see the name of the bakery?"

She glances up at the sign above the chalkboard, reading. "*It's Christmas Every Day*." She glances around, her face lighting up at the festive decorations lining the walls beneath the twinkling lights. "I love it!"

He beams. "I thought you would. I remember how

Natalie would go on about how much Christmas has always been your favorite holiday."

She can't believe what she's asking. "Did you two talk about me a lot?"

He clears his throat. "No, it wasn't like that, but whenever your name came up, I paid attention." She warms with the thought.

She scans the chalkboard. "What do you like here?"

"Just about all of it is delicious. But I think my favorite is a piece of their salted caramel pie with a Chai tea to drink."

She glances up at him. "Do we have time for that?"

He gives her a squeeze. "We're on vacation, Maggie. There's no schedule. Remember?"

She nods. "I'd love some." They get their order and sit down at the table near the window, and he enjoys watching her watch the busy street outside. She takes a bite of the pie. "Oh, my. I'm going to have to find a similar recipe and put these out at the café. Wow."

He laughs. "It's that good?"

She closes her eyes, savoring the flavor. "Definitely. I'll call it 'A Touch of New York'."

He smiles. "Sounds perfect. You've got a knack with food. Did you ever think of running a café when you were married?"

She looks up from her pie, shaking her head. "I suppose not. I was so busy raising the kids and being the perfect doctor's wife. My days were filled with hours at the gym, shopping, entertaining guests, and being friends with the right people, but surface friendships aren't at all the same."

He makes a face. "Surface friendships?"

She nods her head. "Yeah, you know. Like acquaintances, but no one you would call if you were having an actual crisis."

He looks down at his plate before looking back at her. "Sounds kind of lonely."

She nods. "I guess it was, but I didn't see it that way at the time. But, you know, I had Natalie, and that helped tremendously. I don't know how I would have gotten through the divorce without her. She was my rock."

He studies her. "So you didn't go to therapy?"

She snorts. "My ex-husband was a doctor. I was so insecure about anything I said getting back to him, I couldn't bring myself to see any health provider for therapy in those days."

He takes her hand. "I'm sorry you felt so alone."

She takes her hand back, holding it in her lap. "It's alright. I mean, the one good thing about the divorce is it taught me how strong I really am. Once you survive something like that, you realize a mistake is a mistake, but it's not the end of the world."

He studies her a bit longer. "But you were happy together, right? I mean, you would have stayed with him if he hadn't left."

She sighs. "Yes. I suppose I would have stayed with him. I thought we were in love. I was happy enough. But now that all this happened, I feel like I'm living a *real* life, a fuller life, with real relationships."

He sits back in his chair, smiling. "You're an amazing woman."

She blushes. "Thank you."

He leans forward. "So, tell me about your café. How did that get started?"

She looks around at the people sitting and enjoying their breakfast, noticing they're out the door in less than ten minutes. "Well, I was tired of living in the big city, and I was wondering how in the world I would pay taxes and a mortgage once the alimony and child support stopped, but I also didn't want to depend on my ex-husband any longer than necessary after what he did so I crunched the numbers on our house, and they were astronomical. I decided to heck with the trophy wife image. Besides, it's hard to be a trophy wife when your other half finds a younger, shinier trophy."

She pauses, staring out the window, taking a deep breath. "It was Natalie and Alex who gave me the idea of opening a café. Natalie told me I already had the baking experience, and she started nudging me in the direction of opening a business. Then I met Alex at the firing range, and he offered to help me financially, and well, the rest is history."

He frowns in confusion. "Who is this Alex, and what in the world were you doing at a firing range?"

She giggles nervously. "Alex is a writer, and he lives in the apartment attached to my house." She notices the worry on his face. "He's a *young* writer, but he had big success. We're good friends. I'm kind of hoping he and Ali might turn into something."

He grins. "Playing matchmaker, are we?"

She shrugs. "There's a first time for everything. But I would never let on. That would be a sure bet that Ali would never be interested."

His eyebrows raise. "So, you met this guy at a firing range?"

She gives a shiver. "Terrible, right? I guess I had some unresolved anger over the divorce. It didn't last long. I went there probably six times, but it was on the second time that I met Alex. See, he was there doing some character research. Neither of us care for firearms. I don't know, we just kind of clicked, and he was the one that went with me to find the right building for my café, and then he pitched in with the construction part, and together we got it business ready."

He shakes his head. "So, you basically built your business from the ground up. That's amazing. What's it called?"

She smirks. "It's called 'Fill Your Cup, Valentine'."

Joshua nods his head. "I like it."

Her eyes twinkle. "I do too, although sometimes I think about changing it, because I kind of hate to give any credit to my ex-husband. You see, those were the last words he said to me before he left."

He shakes his head. "I'm sorry, what? I don't get it."

She giggles a little more. "I know, right? At the time, I didn't get it either. He just said, 'You don't fill my cup anymore.' And then he left." She pauses. "With his nurse."

He takes the last bite of his pie and a sip of tea before taking her hand. "I'm sorry, Mags. That must have been a rough time for you."

She gives him a small smile. "It was. I did my best to hide my emotions from the kids, and sometimes I wonder if that was the right thing to do. I mean, now I think it's okay if they know I had hurt feelings or whatever, but at the time, I just wanted to be strong for them."

He gives her hand a little squeeze. "All you can do is be there for them. As long as they know that they'll be alright." There's a pause, and he makes a face. "What about the word Valentine in the café title?"

She exhales slowly. "I guess in spite of all that happened between Mike and I, I'm still a romantic at heart, and so I added the 'Valentine' on the end as a reminder there's never enough love in the world—so why not share it while we're here."

He winks at her. "Couldn't have said it better myself." He holds up his cup. "To love."

She clinks her cup on his. "To love."

He studies her. "Was it hard going through the divorce? I mean, did you feel like you fell out of love?"

She swallows hard. "It was a little strange at first, you know, 'cause we had so many of the same friends for so long. That was probably the most awkward part, dividing friendships, or whatever you want to call it. I mean, I thought for sure more women would stay on my side, since he was the cheater. When so many of them stayed his friend, it felt like they were betraying me or approving of what he did, and I guess I just couldn't understand how they could do that, and the more I thought about it, the more it ticked me off, so I just sort of shut them out. But then I felt so alone, and that was really hard; so when I made the decision to move, and the house sold so quickly, it felt like perfect timing. In some ways, I didn't feel like I was leaving that much behind."

She pauses, gazing out the window again. "As far as falling out of love, I suppose it happened in stages. I'm not going to lie. When he left, I was devastated. I felt like I'd made a lifelong commitment and it came to an abrupt halt without my knowledge. He was there one day and gone the next." She looks at Joshua again. "It's been a lot to process, but I think I have. Having the café to keep me busy and great friendships to rely on has helped a lot, too." She smiles with remembrance. "Friends like your sister. When I started looking around at smaller cities nearby, I remembered once that Natalie had told me of a quaint little town she spent a perfect day in, and something about that vlog made me want to go there, and so I did. That's where I found my future home."

His eyes widen. "For real? Natalie led you to your café?"

She nods her head. "Yep. I printed her vlog about the town, and I put it in a frame that hangs on the wall in my café. Your sister really had a way with words."

He laughs. "She sure did. I couldn't write my way out of a cardboard box."

She giggles. "Where to next, Mr. Tour Guide?"

"I'd say it's about time for a trip to the Statue of Liberty."

She takes one big bite before chugging the last bit of tea. "Sign me up."

thirteen

Ali removes the chilled salad from the freezer as lunch time rolls around. Amber's back, and this time she has her husband, Todd, in tow. She pops around the corner. Her brown eyes sparkle and shine. "I brought extra help today. He works from home, so he has his own hours."

Ali smiles over the glass counter. "Thanks."

He nods his head. "Just give me orders, and I'll follow them."

Ali passes him the notepad. "You can start taking drink orders. We've got tea, lemonade, or water. The three sandwich styles are written on the chalkboard, and the two sides are pasta salad or potato chips."

Ali checks the tables. "Amber. Where's all the silverware?"

Amber grins. "Today's basket day, Ali. Your mom's favorite. No clean up after. Everything is picnic style."

Ali's face lights up. "Works for me." She glances at the clock halfway through lunch, noting it's 11:45. "Oh shoot, I need to call Bernie." She gets out her phone and calls him. "She did? Oh, great. Alright." She hangs up, smiling, shaking her head, muttering. "Mom's still calling Bernie from her vacation."

Ali's bustling around the kitchen, wiping down counters, and Alex appears out of nowhere. She's flush up against him. Her forehead brushes his chin, and his arms reach out to steady her. The background noise of the café becomes distant, and her feet won't move. Her breathing slows. "Ali." She hears her name in her ears.

"Excuse me." Is it her imagination, or are his fingertips caressing her arms? She whips around to finish wiping counters. She feels shaken to the core. She's never felt this way before around a man. What does it mean? How can she feel so much for someone she just met, and so little for Jason who she'd dated for almost two years? His hand burns her hip through her thin tee shirt dress. She whips around, furious. "What do you need?"

His charming smile cuts through her anger. "You're standing in front of the napkins. I'm just trying to help."

She feels foolish and clumsy, moving out of the way. "You could have just asked."

"I just did."

She's furious, because she can see by the look on his face he knows he's getting to her, and this makes her all the more determined not to show it. "I'll be gone as soon as my mom's back, you know."

He looks her up and down and steps closer. "Are you telling me, or yourself?"

He walks away, all cocky and sure. She wheels around, looking for more work to do before she flings a wet dishcloth at the back of his head. Lunchtime flies by without a hitch, and she's humming with success. Everything's put away, and she's hauling the big pasta pot back to her mom's office. Talia laughs. "Girl, you've got it bad."

Ali shoves the pot into the bottom of the closet. "Excuse me?"

"You're practically singing. What's that about?"

She shakes her head, feeling embarrassed. "Lunch went really well today. No hiccups. It was great."

Talia giggles. "If you say so."

She puts her hand on her hip. "I do."

Talia throws her hands up. "Alright, alright."

Her eyes light up. "I just got another idea." She races out of the office, runs to the front counter to grab her notebook and scribbles "Lady's night" in it.

Alex waltzes over, glancing down. "Lady's night?"

She flips her notebook shut. "Mr. Snoop-y Snoop. That's none of your business."

He studies her, lowers his eyes, and smiles a secretive smile that turns her insides to mush. "Are you bringing a wild ruckus to this sleepy little town, woman?"

She leans back on the counter and stares down at her little notepad to escape his heated gaze. "I'm doing no such thing. I was thinking more along the lines of a mani-pedi night for the girls. No alcohol, as I thought maybe I'd do this for Parks and her girlfriends."

He slaps his hand down on the counter beside hers and studies his nails. "Maybe I'd like a manicure, or a hand massage." He looks back at her, raises his chin, and waves at his face with one hand. "A charcoal facial mask might feel nice, too."

She shoves his shoulder, laughing. "You're such a clown."

He grins back at her. "So, we're still on tonight for the wine tasting, right?"

She frowns. "What time is that again?"

He hits a fist against his flat hand and snaps his fingers. "I figure we can get out of here by 8 and be there by 8:30. That way, we won't have too late of a night."

Her eyes fly to his hands, remembering the feel of them on her hip, and the way they ran into each other earlier, and she gets nervous. "Um, I don't know. Maybe we should just skip tonight. I mean, I think I can do research on this, and that should be good enough."

He winks at her and steps closer until his arm brushes hers. "Are you scared to be alone with me? Do I make you nervous?"

She swallows hard. "No, not at all. I just..."

He grins in victory. "Then, it's a date." He goes to walk away but turns back. "Oh, be sure you drink plenty of water and eat something. The wine can really go to your head."

She stares at his back. "I can hold my wine."

He gives her another wink, and she hates how much she loves it. "But can you hold your wine and handle me at the same time?" he teases. Ali's only sure of one thing. She can't wait to try.

fourteen

Maggie and Joshua are stuck in a line of people on the stairs inside the Statue of Liberty, and it is slow going. She turns to him. "So, tell me some of the places you've been."

He leans against the wall. "I've been to Romania, China, Mexico, Scotland, and Tunisia."

She giggles. "Is that all?"

He grins. "Pretty much, country-wise anyway."

She studies him. "And where do you think you'll go next?"

His face gets more serious. "I don't know. Your town sounds kind of nice."

Her heart flips over. "My town?"

He studies her. "I don't know. Maybe. I mean, I can work from wherever."

"Wouldn't you miss the city?"

He takes her hand. "The city was more Natalie's speed. I've just been here for the last six months. It's alright, but I wouldn't mind a slower pace."

"What about the apartment?"

"Oh, it's paid through the end of the year. After that, who knows? Trust me, I'd have no problem finding someone to take over if I decide to move out. I've had five offers already."

Her eyebrows raise. "People are that eager to live in New York City?"

He shrugs. "It's a rat race."

A young guy a few steps above them turns around. "Excuse me, I couldn't help but overhear you might have an apartment opening?"

He turns back to Maggie, grinning. "See?"

She shakes her head, nodding. "You weren't kidding."

He turns to her. "So, if you could go anywhere in the world?"

She cuts him off. "The Skopelos islands of Greece or the Santorini islands, but Skopelos would be my first choice."

The lady behind her chimes in, as they are standing shoulder to shoulder. "Isn't that where *Mamma Mia* was filmed?"

She smiles down at her. "Yep. My favorite scene is the walk to the wedding on the hill."

He shakes his head. "You really do love romance."

She smiles back at him. "Isn't that the point of romantic movies, to fill our heads with all kinds of flowery notions, beautiful scenery, and happy endings?"

"I suppose," he grumbles.

He glances at his phone. "I don't suppose you have pictures of your travels with you?"

He hands it over. "I thought you'd never ask. All of my favorite pictures are in here. Would you like to see?" He shows her picture after picture, telling her the names of all the places, and the minutes fly by. Finally, they reach the top.

She grabs his arm and pulls him close. "Selfie for the kids."

He leans in, smiling. They turn around, looking out of the

crown. He takes her hand. "I'm glad I waited to come here with you."

She turns back to him. "You haven't been here before today?"

He shakes his head. "I've been busy, and you know, you don't really do touristy things in the place you live."

She nods. "I guess. So, all of what we've been doing are firsts for you?"

He squeezes her hand. "I like making memories with you."

She glances behind her at the people waiting in line, a welcome distraction to all of her emotions at his words. "Time's up. Now we get to start the long walk down." He studies her, not saying much. She nudges him. "What are you thinking?"

He smiles. "I was just remembering that one orange sweater you liked to wear your freshman year. It was about the color of this stripe right here." His hand brushes her chin as he touches her V-neck sweater, grazing her clavicle, and heat skitters up her neck as he sticks his hand back in his jacket pocket. "It was fuzzy and snug in all the right places. You used to wear it to all the football games with that little corduroy skirt of yours and your brown tights with those little black boots you had. I could always see you in the stands from the football field."

She blushes, looking down. "I didn't know you were watching."

He leans in, talking in her ear. "I was, Mags. I always noticed you."

She glances up, looking him in the eye. "You never said anything to me like that."

He leans back on the wall. "You were my little sister's best friend. It just felt weird."

She stares at the wall behind his head. "I had no idea."

He looks at her again. "By the time I decided to do something about my feelings, you'd gotten married."

She smiles. "Yeah. I think about it now, and I can't believe I got married at the age of twenty. All my friends thought I was nuts. Mike kind of swept me off my feet."

He puts an arm around her, leaning in. "That's because you never gave me a chance."

She elbows him playfully. "Whatever, you were a major player. You weren't anywhere near settling down."

His hand goes to her waist, and he grazes the skin just above her jeans. "I could have been, for the right girl."

She gives a delicious shiver, smiling at the thought of having his child. She shakes her head to clear it, feeling crazy. She looks to the side before turning back to him. "The past is the past. We can't change it, and I wouldn't change a thing about my beautiful children. They are my heart."

He studies her. "They must take after their mother."

She punches his shoulder. "Aren't you just the charmer?"

He studies her, looking all serious. "I mean what I say, Mags."

fifteen

Ali's frantic as she holds the fish with two fingers, dips it in the batter, and tosses it in the pan of grease that pops and sizzles, making her jump backward. "Alex!"

He moseys into the kitchen. "You *called*?"

"What if I burn the fish, or it's not cooked through, and all of these people get sick?" Her eyes are wide, and her lip trembles.

He stands there grinning with his hand on his hip. "Are you asking for reinforcements?"

She glances over at him, irritated by her weakness. "Maybe."

He picks up the phone. "Isaac, can you send someone over? Ali's flipping out on me." He hangs up the phone, giving her a wink. "Mason will be right over."

She glares back at him. "I'm not flipping out."

He gives a half bow. "You're welcome."

"Thanks," she utters under her breath. There's the sound of a bike outside, and the doors fly open. A burly, brown-eyed guy with a man bun and a beard struts into the kitchen, all smiles.

"I'm Mason."

She smiles back self-consciously. "I'm Ali."

"Alex said you'd like some kitchen help?"

She steps away from the stove. "I haven't made fried catfish before, and I'm not sure I'm doing it right. I'm afraid I'll either undercook it or burn it all to heck."

He throws a kitchen towel over his shoulder, whips on an apron and ties it in the back. He approaches the sink to wash his hands. "Why don't you get out the batter for the hush puppies? That needs to get started. I'll keep the fish going. You've got a bit of a crowd tonight."

She steps closer. "Thanks so much, Mason. You're a lifesaver."

He waves her away, giving her a friendly wink. "No worries. The kitchen is my second home." He starts the fish. "I'd do anything for your mom."

She rolls her eyes, muttering, "Does everyone in this town owe my mom a favor?"

He throws back his head, laughing. "No. We're just a tight community. We restaurant owners have to band together." He leans closer, rubbing shoulders with her briefly. "Do you have a problem with that?"

She feels bad. "No, no. It was just a question. Never mind. What do I do with this batter?"

Alex returns, shoving Mason away from Ali, sidling up beside her, all in her space, turning back to Mason. "You just fry the fish. I've got this." He turns to her. "First, you have to form the dough into balls."

She surprises herself by shoulder bumping Alex. "I know that. I'm not stupid."

Mason chuckles, giving Alex a wink. "She's a feisty one." Ali's not sure what to say, so she doesn't answer. Mason keeps talking. "So, I hear you're wine tasting tonight. You'll love it. They've got some delicious wine and chocolate."

She turns back to Alex. "This really *is* a small town. How'd he know?"

Mason shrugs. "My uncle runs the winery. His son, who is my first cousin, told me."

She rolls her eyes. "Of course." She mutters to Alex. "When we get done tonight, I'm going home to rinse off. I'm not walking into a winery smelling like a grease-fried hush puppy."

Mason laughs, takes an exaggerated sniff, and leans back with his hands in his apron pocket. "Ain't n*othin'* like the smell of fried catfish."

"Speak for yourself," she grumbles.

He stirs the big pot of green beans on the back burner. "Yep. This is my favorite night. Smells like home cookin'."

She shakes her head. "I had no idea Mom served so much comfort food. We didn't see any of this growing up at our house."

He makes a face of confusion. "Really?"

"No, sir. It was all veggie greens, white meat, and lots of fruit."

He harrumphs. "Well, I guess she's making up for it now."

Alex wipes his hands on his apron and walks over to the sink to wash up. "I'm going to see if they need any help with drink orders." He walks by Ali, lays a hand at her waist, and leans over her shoulder. "I think you're gettin' the hang of it." She blushes with his praise and the feel of his hand.

"Thanks," she whispers back softly. She continues making the hush puppy balls and Mason cooks them in between the catfish fryin'. Soon everyone's baskets are full, and supper is served. Mason stands in the back, eating his supper. She fixes up a basket and carries it back to the office to Talia. "Eat up. I gave you two helpings of beans."

Talia backs away from the computer. "Thanks."

Ali glances down, seeing Talia's swollen feet. "Why don't you lie down on the couch and I'll put your feet up."

Talia eases out of the chair and goes over to sit on the end of the couch. Ali hands her the basket and Talia rests it on her stomach. Ali grabs a few couch pillows and props Talia's feet up one at a time. "There. How's that feel?"

Talia smiles up at her. "Could I have a drink, please?"

She smacks her forehead. "Of course! I'm sorry." She rushes back to the kitchen to grab a glass of water and a lemonade and spies Parker and Conner in the kitchen. She grabs two baskets shoved off to the side, holding them out. "Here. I was hoping you two would come by."

Parker glances around. "Where's Talia?"

"In Mom's office. Her feet are swollen, so don't make her move." Ali hands Parker the glass of water and Conner the lemonade. "Could you take these to her, please?"

Parker and Conner head back with their baskets and drinks for Talia. Mason waltzes over to Ali, leaning in. "You just gave those two yours and Alex's supper."

She shrugs. "I wasn't that hungry. I don't like fried food."

Mason chuckles. "You might not, but Alex does."

Alex comes around the corner. "Alex does what?"

Mason glances at closed-mouth Ali, who's not about to admit to anything. "Ali just gave your supper to her brother."

Alex steps up in front of her with his hands on hips. "Is that so?"

She looks him in the eye, mimicking his movements. "Yeah, I did."

He smirks. "Well. I guess you'll have to make it up to me. It just so happens fried catfish is my *favorite* supper."

She looks over at Mason, who's also smirking. "Surely there's another restaurant that serves fried catfish. I'll just call Isaac."

Mason shakes his head. "No dice, Ali. This is a small

town. Isaac doesn't make fried catfish just like Maggie doesn't make paninis. That would violate the unspoken code of honor between them."

She glares at him. "Well, we'll just make more catfish then. Can't we just heat up the grease?"

Mason answers her with a small grin on his face like he's enjoying her squirming. "No can do. The fish is all gone, and I threw out the grease. You don't want that stinking up your kitchen."

She throws up her hands. "I give up. I guess I owe you one, Alex." She turns back to look him in the eye. "What do you want?"

He stands in front of her waiting, but not saying anything, as he lingers long enough to make her uncomfortable. "I'll tell you when the time is right."

Mason's eyes widen, and he walks back to the end of the counter with his basket of food, whistling.

She breaks their gaze and spins around, unable to look at Alex any longer. She grabs the big bean pot and empties its contents into a container before setting it in the deep sink to rinse it.

sixteen

Maggie and Joshua ride the ferry back in. She follows him to the sidewalk, and they hop in the Lyft ride. "Do you want to go to the ice-skating rink at Rockefeller Center? I hear it's nice."

She shakes her head. "I'm sorry. The Statue of Liberty kind of wore me out. There were just so many steps and so many people."

He nods. "True. Do you want to just head back to the apartment, then?"

She looks over at him, smiling. "Maybe we could stop at a grocery store?"

He laughs. "You want to cook?"

She nods her head emphatically. "I do. I can't believe I'm saying this, but I miss it."

He takes her hand across the seat. "As you wish, my lady."

She giggles. "What are you saying?"

He shrugs. "It's my best impression of Mark Darcy."

She laughs out loud. "Trust me. You're no Mark Darcy."

He wiggles his eyebrows. "No? At this moment, I am completely and perfectly and incandescently happy."

She smacks his hand. "You're such a cheeseball. Please stop before you ruin one of my favorite movies."

He puts his hand on his chest, looking wounded. "Hey. It took me a long time to memorize that line, and I did it just for you."

She turns to him, crosses her arms and lowers her voice, sneering. "Fredo, you're my older brother, and I love you. But don't ever take sides with anyone against the family again. Ever." She smirks at him. "How bad was that?"

He looks totally confused. "Excuse me?"

She throws up her hands. "It's from The Godfather!"

His facial expression remains the same. "I'm sorry?"

"Haven't you watched The Godfather? It's like the ultimate male movie."

He shakes his head. "I guess I haven't."

The Lyft driver glances in the rearview mirror. "Dude. Hand over your *man card*. I'm twenty-three years old, and *I've* seen The Godfather."

She giggles. "See?"

The car stops. Joshua hops out, muttering at the driver. "Here's a tip. If you want a tip, always side with the customer."

The Lyft driver frowns. "Ah, come on, man."

She turns back. "Don't worry. I'll take care of it." She turns back to Joshua. "Don't be sore. Give the man his tip. Lyft drivers gotta make a living, too."

He hits a button on his phone. "Fine."

She takes Josh's arm and steers him toward the grocery store. "Alright. Let's see what we have to work with."

She grabs a couple of frozen loaves of bread, a round pizza pan, some tomato paste, a few spices, a can of diced tomatoes, a small jar of black olives, some meat, and shredded cheese. He goes along behind her, watching as she scans the shelves, following some kind of mental checklist in her head. "You're making pizza in New York City, the best place to eat pizza?"

She shrugs. "I guess I am. I thought it'd be nice to have a night in, and if we play our cards right, we'll have pizza in the morning, too."

"Pizza for breakfast? Nothing about that sounds good."

She winks at him, waving a frozen loaf of bread. "That's because you haven't had *my pizza*."

He shrugs his shoulders, squeezing the cart handle. "If you say so."

She nods. "I do."

They get through the checkout line and wait for a ride home. She turns to him. "You know where I *live*, just about everything is within walking distance. It's rather nice."

He raises his eyebrows. "Really? Everything?"

She smiles. "Yep. If I want a cup of coffee and a good book, there's Abby's bookstore. If I need a new fisherman's sweater or a catchy sign for my café, there's Bella's boutique. If I need an oil change or my tires rotated, there's the Double-O on the corner."

He laughs. "Double-O?"

She nods, smiling. "Owen and Ollie's garage."

They get settled in the Lyft car. "Proceed."

She looks sideways. "Aw, yes. If I need a haircut, there's the "Everything's Eva" salon down on Fourth. Sunday Service is in the community church on Seventh, and if I want a break from my own cooking, Ike's Bar and Grill is just a few blocks from my café."

He considers this. "Well, what about an ocean view? You can't get that in Kansas."

She taps her finger to her chin, thinking. "No, but we've got a really nice lake with quiet shores, the perfect place to *just be.*" She leans in, whispering, "We even have a bait/kayak rental shop called 'Reel 'em In' run by a couple of red-headed brothers, Marvin and Everett."

He winks. "That's catchy. Sounds like you really do have it all."

She grins. "Well. It's certainly not heaven, but it's close enough for now."

He smiles back at her. "I can't argue with you there."

seventeen

Ali finishes cleaning the kitchen, feeling more and more apprehensive as the winery hour draws near. She jumps when Talia slips through the doorway. "What's got you all riled up?"

"What? Nothing. You just snuck up on me."

She giggles as her brown eyes light up at Ali. "I *totally* bumped into like three things on the way to you. I keep forgetting how wide I am. Your head must be in the clouds."

Alex swaggers up to the counter, winking at Talia. "She's just nervous because we have a date tonight."

Ali flushes. "It's not a date, Alex. It's a wine tasting, and it's for work."

Talia giggles. "Ooh, y'all going to get a little tipsy?"

Ali throws down her dishrag. "Alright. That's it. I'm going home and I'm staying there."

Alex looks over at her. "Don't get your back up, Ali. I'll be a perfect gentleman. Come on. Let's walk Talia home."

Ali's eyes light up when she sees Parker coming back through the door. "You go ahead. I'm going to walk home with Parker."

Conner comes in right behind her. "Hey, Ali."

"Hi, Conner."

Talia moves faster than expected, as she grabs Parker's arm before turning back to Ali and Alex with an ornery look in her eye. "Parker and Conner can walk me home. You two just go on with your night."

Conner looks back at Ali in question, but Talia grabs his arm and yanks him out the door.

Ali gives Alex a skeptical look. "Did you have anything to do with that?"

"Why are you looking at me? I was just standing here talking to Talia, just like you, and they walked back in."

She flips the lights, walks out the front door, and turns to look at him. "Are you coming? I ain't got all night."

He picks up his messenger bag from the chair. "Hold your horses."

She speed walks all the way home, not saying a word. She rushes upstairs to hop in the shower, rinsing off before throwing on the one pair of jeans she brought. She jumps around, tugging on her high rise black skinny jeans that fit like second skin. She rummages through her bag to find the pale pink mohair sweater that rests just above her waistline. She pulls out her sandals, noticing her toenails. She races to the bathroom to put on a few coats of pale pink polish.

She pulls her hair up in a loose bun, leaning in to apply light eyeshadow and mascara and finally a light lip gloss. Her favorite body mist fills the air, and she steps into it. A pair of pearl earrings calls her name as she starts for the door. Careful hands fiddle with the backs, checking them one more time before she heads downstairs toward his voice, calling out to her. "Ali, it's eight-thir..."

His words stop as soon as he sees her coming down the staircase, looking all soft and dewy, smelling like a garden rose. "I'm coming, I'm coming." Her irritated voice breaks through his reverie.

She stops on the bottom step. "Are we going or what? Because I'm not riding on your motorcycle. That thing is a death trap." No sooner do the words leave her mouth, and he steps forward, reaches for her waist, pulls her in, and kisses her senseless. Her hands find his chest, and she gives him a shove. "What was that for?"

He's surprised and embarrassed by his caveman ways. "I'm sorry. You're just so beautiful." He touches her sweater again, smirking at the dazed look on her face and the idea he put it there. "And fuzzalicious."

She is more shaken by his kiss than she'd like to admit, but she's determined not to show it. His words give her the giggles. "Fuzzalicious? I believe you're thinking Fergalicious, which is hardly me."

He tugs on the bottom of her sweater, feeling it with his fingers. "Nope. Fuzzalicious."

She eyes him, trying not to smile. "You're so weird." She takes out her car keys. "Here. You can drive the Legacy. I'll have to fix my lips in the mirror. You messed up my lip gloss."

He looks at her lips. His hand rests on her waist and he steps forward, crowding her. "I could mess it up more."

The front door swings open, and Parker and Conner walk in. She's relieved by their entrance, as he turns toward them. "Hey, guys."

Parker walks by, smirking at Alex as she goes. "Nice lip gloss, Al-ex."

He wipes his hand across his lips, still smiling. "Really? I wasn't sure it was my color."

Ali slugs him on the shoulder. "Ha, ha. Come on, let's go before we're late."

She follows him out the door and they get into the

Legacy. He starts up the car. "You're really going to like this. I promise."

She can't help but smile at the excitement in his voice. "Oh? Isn't it just like wine tasting in an old barn?"

"Just you wait and see. I'm telling you. It's killer."

She looks at him again. "Just how many women have you taken out to this barn? Should I be worried?"

He laughs. "No. The only woman I've taken there is your mom."

She whips her head sideways. "My mom? You took my mom on a wine tasting date?"

He sighs. "It wasn't a date. How many times do I have to say it? Your mom and I are just friends. She's old enough to be my mother."

She answers. "Then why did you take her out there? Was it for more *research?*"

"Why do you say that like it's a dirty word?"

"I don't know. I'm just saying some things in life are about living, not entertainment value."

"Yeah, I know. But, if you read a story, and it tugs at your heart and it makes you happy, or you find a character you can identify with and it makes you a better person but also entertains, what's the harm in that?"

"There isn't, so long as you can remember that you can't *live* in books."

He nods his head. "I hear you. You gotta have balance. You can't get sucked into the black hole of escapism because it's your comfort zone."

She slaps the dash. "Exactly."

"So, when are you going to process your break-up with Jason?"

She feels sucker punched. "Why is that any of your business?"

He shrugs. "I don't know. I just think you can't really move forward until you deal with your past."

She taps her fingers on her knees. "Why is my future any of your concern?"

He takes her hand. "Maybe I'd like it to be."

She whips her hand away. "What if I have unfinished business?"

"Are you telling me you'd take the guy back if he offered? He practically left you at the altar."

She whips around to glare at him while he concentrates on driving. "You don't know Jason, and you don't know anything about our relationship. This isn't your business."

"I know he hurt you, Ali. What more is there to know?" His words are calm and rational, and they tear at Ali, who is determined not to cry.

The barn appears before them as they round the bend down the long driveway surrounded by trees. She jumps out of the parked car, feeling suffocated. "Can we just not talk about him tonight? I just want to go in there and have a nice, relaxing time. I would really enjoy that."

Alex is torn between wanting to grant her simple, yet complicated request. He planned the perfect night for the two of them, but he can't stop thinking about what she said about Jason. He stands beside her, fuming. "Fine."

She glares back at him. "Fine."

They march up to a tall, curly-haired man with a kind smile, sitting in a lawn chair in the back of his pick-up truck, who gives them a wink.

"Alex," he says in greeting.

"Jackson," Alex responds in kind.

"It's a perfect night for catching fireflies. Now, let me tell you about the savory delights inside this basket." Jackson drawls in a country accent that Ali could probably appreciate if she weren't so fired up from the argument she and Alex just had.

"Where's Don and Connie?" Alex asks, cutting Jackson off.

Jackson grins. "My folks are up at the house. They're settled in for the night. I'm the welcoming committee now." He gives Ali another ornery wink before turning back to Alex. "Looks like you've got your hands full," he says with a smirk.

She snatches the basket and papers from Jackson's hands. "Thanks. I know the drill. I'm sorry, but we're in a bit of a hurry," she says and starts to walk away.

Jackson looks closer at Alex, who stands there glaring at her retreating form. "Lover's quarrel? That's no way to start the night."

She spins and turns on Jackson. "He's not my lover!"

Alex's gaze drops to the ground. "Not even close," he mutters beneath his breath.

Jackson looks at the both of them, shaking his head. "Well. This should make for an interesting night. Alex, if you need anything, just text my cell. And let me know when you leave."

She's already back to stomping toward the big barn in the distance. "Thanks, Jackson. Will do." Alex answers as he takes off after her.

"Gotta watch out for them Post girls. I hear they've got a wicked bite!" Jackson calls out after their retreating forms before he laughs out loud.

Alex jogs to catch up with Ali who strides across the grass. "Do you know where you are going?" he says as he jogs in front of her just in time to open the barn door.

She smells hay and fresh earth. "Are there animals in here?"

"Most of the time, but not tonight. Jackson moves them out until we're done." He scurries up a ladder into a loft area.

She follows closely behind, handing up the basket. He sets it down before he stands up and grabs a lantern that rests off to the side. She grabs the other one. He grabs a pitchfork stuck in a bale of hay. "Come over and hold the light up would you?"

Curious, she does as he says. He flips a lock up above and shoves the big door in the roof sideways. She smiles as she looks up at the stars. He sits down on the pile of quilts stacked on the wood floor between the hay bales and opens the basket.

She plops down beside him, observing. She reaches out to help, and he swats her hand away. "Be a good guest."

She scoots away from the basket, spying a pillow. She flops down on her back, staring up at the stars. "Wow. I don't think I've ever seen such a sight."

He gazes at her face in the moonlight. "Me, neither."

Her eyes fly to his and he looks away, getting back to his preparations. He pulls out a couple of plastic cups, filling them half full with wine. "Now, my apologies, because we only have one type of wine tonight. However, Jackson did his best to make sure he chose the smoothest wine, and that it goes well with every piece of chocolate, meat, and cheese."

Her eyes check out the plate, and there's no mistaking the appreciation in her smile. "Ooh, gouda. And Swiss. I love them." She picks up a piece of chocolate. "Salted caramel. It's the bomb!"

His face falls a little. "So you've done this before?"

Her face softens. "Not here, and nothing like this," she offers in a softer voice.

His face falls some more. He doesn't know how to take her. "I know it's just an old barn in the middle of a pasture but give it a chance."

Her eyes light up. "It's perfect. Really. It's just the right amount of stillness in the moonlight." She picks up her wine glass, holding it up. "Here's to old barns and good wine."

His face relaxes as they clink glasses. "To old barns and good wine."

She turns to face him. "So. You know everything about my family already. What about yours? What's your dad do?"

He chuckles. "He's a corporate lawyer."

She's floored. "No way. What?"

"I swear it's the truth. He works at a huge firm, and so do my two brothers."

She ribs him. "So, there's more of you?"

He laughs. "I'm afraid so, but I'm the best looking. Believe me, I've asked around."

She giggles at his answer. "What about sisters?"

He smiles. "I have one. She's married, has three kids, lives in the city. Her husband is a CPA. They move about every three years, or every time he gets a promotion."

She studies him. "So, you're like the odd one out."

He nods. "Pret-ty much. First, I was a blue-collar worker, and now I'm a writer."

"What about your mom?"

He smiles. "Oh, she gets me, well better than they do anyway, which is good because my dad likes to blame my 'creative streak' on my mother."

She takes a bite of chocolate. "So, you're a momma's boy."

He wrinkles his nose. "Hmm. I wouldn't call it that necessarily."

She laughs again. "Then what would you call it?"

He shrugs. "I don't know. Don't you have a parent you're closer to?"

She gives a little laugh. "That's easy. My mother."

He nod. "Makes sense. I've met your mom. She's kind of great." He pauses and glances at Ali. "I'm not too sure about her daughter, though. She's got some pretty hard edges."

She sobers. "It's called self-preservation."

He sticks out his hand. "Truce. I call a truce."

She takes his hand, shaking it. "Truce."

He releases her hand slowly, grazing her palm, sending shivers up her arm, but he keeps talking. "My dad's job allowed us some nice trips and nice things, but I kind of like the simple life, I guess."

"So, do you think you'll ever go to college?"

He laughs. "I did. Did I not mention that?"

She shakes her head. "No, you didn't."

"Well, I already went. I went to school full time and worked at the factory at the same time."

"That sounds like a lot."

"Yeah, well. My dad didn't like it much. He couldn't understand why I wanted to pay my own way when he offered to do it for me. I guess I'm just stubborn."

She smiles at him. "There's nothing wrong with hard work."

He holds up his glass of wine. "Thank you." He drinks it down. "So, that's pretty much me, in a nutshell."

"I'm assuming you graduated?"

He chuckles. "Oh, yeah. I got a teaching degree. Secondary education English teacher, right here."

She smiles. "I can see that. You're definitely a people person."

He takes a bite of cheese, looking away. "Well. I got through student teaching, had my first job lined up and everything, and I just couldn't do it."

"Why not?"

"I don't know. My heart wasn't in it, so I went back to the factory and six months later I started writing."

She clears her throat. "What about girlfriends?"

He gives her a wolfish grin, turning her insides. "What about them?"

"Surely you've had a few."

He runs a fingertip down her forearm. "Not any to write home about."

She swallows. "Why not?"

He sighs. "I don't know. I guess you just have to meet the right one."

She stares up at the stars. "How do you know?"

He scoots around to sit behind her and rests his hands on her hips. "You just do."

She puts her hands on his. "It must be nice to feel so sure."

He grips her hips just a little, touches his chest to her back, and whispers in her ear. "I've never been surer of anything in all my life."

She leans forward a hair. "Slow down. This is all going way too fast. I mean we barely know each other."

He leans away, planting his hands on the floor behind him. "What more is there to know?"

"I don't know. I was with Jason for a year and a half and we..."

"What?"

"Nothing."

"It's not nothing," he insists, while trying to hide his frustration. "Finish your sentence."

"We never talked like this." Her voice is quiet.

"You say that like talking is a bad thing."

She gets all flustered, and so she turns on him, going after his lips, and pushing him to the floor. Her hands start to roam.

He grabs them. "Slow down, Ali," he says, repeating her words back to her.

She feels embarrassed, but she's determined. "Isn't this what you were hoping for?" she taunts.

He shakes his head. "No. Not like this."

"Why did you bring me out here, give me wine, chocolate, and a night under the stars, then?"

He stares up at her face, shocked at his own words. "Trust me, that would be nice, but it's not the right time. I came out here to get to know the you when you're not at work. I wanted some alone time for just us."

She climbs off him, feeling clumsy and exposed. "I'd like to go home now," she whispers. He reaches for her hand, but she evades. He lies down on the other pillow. "I said, I'd like to go home now," she repeats in a quiet, firm voice.

He smacks the floor beside him. "I heard you, but I'm not ready. Why don't you lay beside me and watch for a falling star? You can make a wish."

She lays back down slowly, turns her back to him, and looks up at the stars out of the corner of her eye.

They lay there a little while in silence.

He clears his throat. "Did you know your mom almost shot me once?"

"Too bad she missed," she muses before breaking out in giggles.

He chuckles beside her. "What a thing to say."

She lays still, waiting for him to elaborate, but he doesn't say any more. Minutes drag by. She flips over onto her other side, staring at him. "Are you going to tell me the rest of the story?"

He smirks at her. "Only if you want to hear it."

She sighs. "I just asked."

"Okay. So I was writing this thriller on a secret agent, and I knew nothing about firearms, like zilch, because we grew up sheltered, and we don't hunt, or whatever. So anyway, I got all excited, and I went and bought a Glock and a pistol and started going to the firing range. Believe me, that's the *last* place you want to tell anyone you're a writer. Needless to say, they were not impressed. I think the fact that I was a writer scared them more than the thought of all the bullets flying around. There was this one guy, Jim..."

"Alex. You're getting sidetracked," she scolds.

"Oh, yeah. So, I'd been going there a while, and one day this little woman shows up with spit and vinegar in her eye. She may not have known anything about guns, but her anger was her weapon."

She can hardly believe his words. "My mom? Really? She hid it so well. I never saw that in her e-mails or Face-timing."

"That's 'cause she brought it all with her to the firing range. Trust me, your mother was a walking grenade."

Her stomach tightens at his words. "Okay, okay. That's enough about my mother's rage. Then what?"

"So, the first time she was there, I just stood back and watched her fumble around in front of the instructor, Errol, because it was his job to help. But the second time she came, she was all tears and so broken down, I couldn't stay away. So, I walked up to her and tapped her on the shoulder, and she whipped around with that pistol of hers all cocked and ready, her finger on the trigger. I hit the ground so fast." He stops talking, joyfully watching her expectant face.

She grabs at his shirt sleeve. "And then what?"

He gives her a knowing smile. "Oh, you know your mom. She just started talking to me like we were old friends, and before too long, it felt like we were. When she stopped coming to the firing range, I missed her. So, I went looking for her in the little town. She wasn't hard to find."

"I hear you helped her start her café," she comments, and he wishes he could read her tone better.

"Yeah." His answer sounds a little guarded.

She continues to study him. "Why?"

He frowns slightly. "One, that's between your mom and me. And two, that's what friends do. They help each other."

She makes a face. "But what do you get out of it?"

He throws his hands out to the side in frustration. "Friendship. Happiness for my friend's success."

She watches him. "That's it?"

"Yeah."

"And that's enough?"

He makes a face. "Just what are you implying? Do you think your mom's turned into Mrs. Robinson or a raging cougar? I mean I know I'm irresistible and all, but..."

She giggles before giving him a shove. "Eww, you pervert."

He chuckles. "I'm not the one that started down *that road*. That was all you."

She sighs. "Give me a break. You know as well as I do in today's world it's not as easy to find people with no secret motives. True hearts are hard to find."

Her answer doesn't sit well with him, and his next words come flying out. "Ali. *You* ought to know that kind of love. Your *mom's* the one who showed it to me."

She feels defensive. "I do. I mean, I have. But she's *my* mom."

He stares up at the stars. "Exactly. Because she's your mom, you should know better than anyone her heart never stops growing and giving. She once told me you can never have too many friends or family, and it took me a while, but now I believe her."

She looks out at the night sky. "Now *you* sound like a Hallmark card."

He chuckles. "That's your mom. She's as kind and sweet as a Hallmark card."

She turns her head sideways, looking at him. "Are you sure you're not in love with my mother?"

He takes her hand and places it on his heart. "I know who my heart belongs to—a woman who dresses like a Vegas showgirl in the kitchen and drives me crazy with her fuzzalicious sweaters."

She's blushing again. "You really are a writer."

He chuckles. "I don't know about that, but I know I'm important to your future happiness. I can feel it."

Her fingertips buzz over his heartbeat, and she looks him in the eye. "Are you sure enough for the both of us?"

His steady gaze rests on her face. "I am for now."

eighteen

Maggie and Joshua carry the groceries up the stairs, and she makes herself at home in Natalie's kitchen, washing the pizza pan, and searching through the cupboards for pans. She tosses the loaves of bread in some warm water to thaw. She tosses the cold things in the fridge. Then she searches the drawers for a rolling pin. She looks over at him sitting on the couch. "Do you cook?"

"I can make eggs and toast."

"Is that it?"

"Pretty much. I eat a lot of takeout or salads. I make a pretty decent salad, or anything else that doesn't require an oven or stovetop."

She giggles. "What about grilling?"

He stands up, twisting back and forth, then raising his arms high. "I am a grill master. That is one thing I know how to do."

She laughs again. "Well, that's reassuring."

She looks around nervously.

"Maggie. What's wrong?"

"I have twenty-five minutes and nothing to do."

He raises an eyebrow at her, motioning to her with his finger as he plops back down on the couch. "Why don't you come over here." Her insides turn to mush, and her knees feel a little weak as she looks at him, remembering the girls that were always at his house, and she can't help thinking now *she's* that girl. "What?"

She giggles nervously. "Nothing. I was just thinking."

His stare turns heated. "About what?"

"About all your girls." She tries to keep a straight face, but it's hard.

He makes an incredulous face at her. "What?"

The way he looks at her makes her feel all insecure, but she trusts her memory, and she knows she's right. Even though she wants to, she can't let it go. "Don't pretend that you don't know what I'm talking about. It's not like I didn't spend half my time at your house growing up, and that was just before you left high school. I can't imagine what's happened between your college years and now."

"You don't need to remind me of your high school years. I was there. It was pure torture," he states. She makes a doubtful face at him, and so he continues. "You don't believe me? I could probably name every crush you've had from middle school on."

Her face flames. "You *listened* to my personal conversations with Natalie about boys?"

He grins unashamedly. "I sure did. I kept waiting to hear my name."

She sputters. "I wasn't about to tell your sister I had a crush on her brother."

He hops off the couch, advancing. "So, you *did* have a crush on me."

She rolls her eyes. "Yeah, along with half the cheerleading squad and every girl in every class in our school."

He stops in front of her. "Maggie."

"Yeah."

"You're not fifteen anymore." That's the only warning she gets before his mouth finds hers, and her world explodes like fireworks. She grips the countertop behind her with one hand to steady herself, but the other is in his hair, tugging just slightly as his hands twist the back of her shirt. He pulls away, looking stunned. "Whoa. I didn't expect that."

Her lips are pink and swollen. "Should I be flattered?"

He jams his hands in his pockets, rocking back on his heels. "I just, I just thought one kiss would be enough."

"Enough for what?" she asks, because she has no idea what he's talking about.

"To settle things."

She looks at him like he's nuts. "What?"

"I'm not saying it right. What I mean to say is that I thought I had unresolved feelings from our kiss when we were young, and I thought if I kissed you again, that might make things clearer, but it didn't."

She tugs on her shirt. "It didn't?"

He steps up, lifting her chin. "No, it didn't. I just want to kiss you more." He lowers his head, going in all gentle and soft, leaving her feeling cherished as she stands in his embrace, resting her cheek on his chest. "What is happening?" he asks in a voice full of wonder.

She sighs. "I don't know."

nineteen

Maggie stays a while longer, listening to Joshua's heartbeat. She feels like she's on the edge of losing control, and so she turns to her security blanket, pushing away from him to make some space between them. "Tonight, you're going to learn how to make pizza."

He makes a face that says that's the last thing he wants to do. She ignores. "Really?"

"Yes. Honestly, I can't believe you're forty-five-years-old and you don't know how to cook."

"I haven't had to," he protests.

She lays a hand on her hip. "If you can read, you can cook."

He looks around. "Where's the recipe?"

She laughs, tapping her temple. "This one is up here, so I'll help you. So, the first thing we're going to do is brown the hamburger." She hands him the skillet, dumping a tube of meat in the pan. She hands him a rubber spatula. "Always use a rubber or plastic spatula, never metal. It ruins the pan."

He nods. "Noted." She turns away from him, dumping things in a bowl. He peers over her shoulder. She swats at him, but he persists. "What are you doing?" he asks, and his breath hits the back of her neck, driving her crazy.

She shoves him away. "Tut, tut. This is my magic sauce. Super-secret ingredients. Look away." He sneaks another peek. She shoves him harder. "I'm serious. Look away." She pauses and smells the air. "Your hamburger is burning!"

She turns back to the stove, and the tube is frying. "You, um. You have to break it up. It won't fall apart on its own. Give me that." She takes his spatula and starts dividing the meat. "Just like that. Now you do it."

He smiles over at her. "You're doing just fine."

She makes a face at him. "No. You're not pulling that trick on me. The 'I can't do it right, so you just do it for me' trick. Get over here and cook your own hamburger."

He pouts a little. "Fine. But I want points for this."

She laughs at his bringing sports analogy into the kitchen. "Points? What kind of points?"

"I don't know. Whatever kind there are. I want them," he demands, and she can't help but find him adorable. She stands on tiptoe, kissing his cheek. "Thank you."

He turns sideways, looking her up and down, growling. "You can do better than that."

She steps in, feeling challenged and saucy, remembering how many times she watched him from afar, wondering what it would be like to be his girlfriend, to kiss his lips, to be able to reach out and touch him; and now he's right in front of her, like a dream. Her eyes follow her hands as her knuckles graze his jawline.

Her fingers rest on his broad shoulders, and finally, she grips the back of his neck just a little. Her one hand returns to caress the whiskers on his cheek before leaving the lightest of thumbprints on his bottom lip. She tugs him down slightly, pressing her lips to his, and he backs her against the counter once more, taking over, but she pushes back, challenging.

This time when they separate, he's the one shaking. "Mags. Where'd you learn moves like that?"

She trembles. "I was married for twenty years."

He steps back, shivering. "Married women don't kiss like that."

She smiles, feeling confident at the wonder in his voice. "I guess I know a few tricks."

He turns back to the hamburger, grabbing his spatula. "If you kissed Mike like that, I don't know why he ever left you."

She steps up beside him, feeling uncertain. "I didn't." She reaches in front of him, and he moves away. "I need to turn the heat down." She reaches for the spatula, taking it from him. "We've managed to burn all the hamburger."

He looks down at her. "That's not the only thing that's burning."

She giggles nervously. "Calm down. We're both adults here."

His hands graze the skin of her lower back, teasing. "Yes. That much is true."

Her heart races and she answers breathily. "That's not what I meant."

His wandering hand grips her hip through her jeans. "What do you mean, you never kissed Mike like that?"

She shrugs as she reaches down to brush his hand from her hip. "I just didn't. He didn't like me to dominate, in any way."

He takes the spatula from her hand, setting it in the pan. He spins her toward him. "He didn't know what he was missing."

She flushes and turns away from him to finish cooking the hamburgers. "Maybe it's just you. I've never done that before."

His eyes grow big. "You could've fooled me." She looks offended at his comment. "Did I say something wrong?"

"No. Not really. It's just, well. I've only ever known Mike." She tries to focus on the hamburgers, but her mind is somewhere else.

He steps to the side, leaning on the counter, watching her face. "Really? You never had other boyfriends?"

She shakes her head. "Not like that. I had a few, but we weren't serious."

"And you didn't, after? No wild divorcee flings?" She feels small at the tone of his voice, but she quickly becomes indignant.

She wrinkles her nose. "You men are all the same. You think the way to get over a relationship is to find someone to sleep with, like casual sex is the answer to everything."

He throws his hands up. "Ease up, Maggie Louise. Stop yelling at me. I'm not Mike."

She waves the spatula at him. "No. You're not. At least he could make a commitment to a woman. He stuck around for twenty years."

He stomps his foot. "Maybe so, but he also left you."

She's still angry, even though she's pretty sure most of her anger is misplaced. "For the record, Joshua, casual sex isn't my thing." She gives him a hard look. "Never has been, never will be."

He looks away. "Got it. Loud and clear. I think I'll take a walk."

She focuses on the food on the stove, determined not to watch him walk away. "I think that's a great idea."

twenty

Ali removes her hand from Alex's chest, but he catches it in between them, locking his fingers with hers. "Ali."

"Alex."

"Stargaze with me, please."

She shivers in her sweater as the night breeze races over her. He scoots closer to her until they're shoulder to shoulder, and she can't help but notice he's as hot as a heater. Five minutes go by and she can't stand the silence. "Alex."

"Shhhh. Let's play who can be the quietest."

She giggles. "That's a kid's game."

He looks over at her, scowling. "What's it going to take to shut you up?"

She sticks out her tongue. "I don't do quiet."

He reaches over with his other hand and holds her lips together. "Try."

She moves away and flops onto her back. Pretty soon, she glances over at contemplative Alex, who stares up at the sky like he sees something she can't. She buries her face in his sleeve before curling into his heat, throwing one arm and leg

128

across him, moving closer to rest her face in his neck, her curves fitting into the side of him.

"Ali." His voice is hoarse.

"Hmm."

"What are you doing?"

"I'm cold."

"You could lay under a quilt."

"Hmm mm, but you're warmer."

He chuckles. "You enjoy torturing me, don't you?"

She sighs into his neck, and he shifts slightly at the feeling of her hot breath on his neck. "Just watch the stars. I'm going to take a warm and toasty nap."

"How am I supposed to concentrate with you all mashed up against me?" His voice sounds strangled.

She nuzzles his chest with her nose. "Figure it out, stargazer-man." He wraps her in his arms, and she snuggles in even closer. "That's more like it."

He lays there as long as he can stand it, before shifting slightly trying to move away, but she chases him until she's all curled into him again. "Ali! I saw a shooting star," he speaks soft and low into her ear, and his chest rumbles.

She turns to look into the night sky before turning back to him, smiling sleepily. "I guess I missed it. You going to make a wish?"

"I already did."

"And did it come true?"

He smiles up at her leaning over him. "Given time, I think it might."

She lays her head back down, whispering. "What did you wish for?"

He chuckles. "I can't tell you that. Then it won't come true."

She moves around until she's laying on top of him, resting her chin on his chest. "Spread out your arms."

He makes a face at her. "Why?"

"Just do it."

He puts his arms out straight. She scoots up until her chest is level with his; stretching her arms out as far as they'll go, aligning her fingertips with his palms. He smiles up at her. "We're a perfect fit."

She ducks her head down to lie in the crook of his neck, placing her lips there, soft as a whisper, breathing in his scent. "You make a great pillow."

twenty-one

J oshua walks up the stairs. The foreign smells of bread baking and tomato sauce simmering waft through the walls to greet him. He walks in the door, immediately alarmed by the couple sitting at the table, talking animatedly to Maggie. The young man hops up, sticking out his hand. Joshua takes in his stained tee shirt, the bandana on his head and his cargo pants. "What's up, man? I'm River, but people call me Riv, and this is my girl, Amber." He holds his hand out, waiting.

Joshua grabs a hold, shaking hands. "I'm Joshua and I see you've already met Maggie."

The man nods his head. "Dude. Her cooking is like a whole other dimension. It's transcending."

Joshua nods in agreement, holding back his grin. "Yes. That's the word I've been looking for this whole week." He picks up a glass of wine, holding it high, looking at Maggie. "To Maggie and her existentialism." He gives her a bold wink, and Maggie turns toward the sink to hide her happy giggles.

There's a knock at the door, and Maggie spins around.

Joshua raises his eyebrows at Maggie as he goes to answer it, peering through the keyhole, spying an elderly Hispanic couple in the hallway. He opens the door. "Hola. I am Sylvia. Aqui esta mi esposa, Domingo," the lady says in a friendly voice.

Joshua turns to Maggie, who suddenly stands at his side, putting her hand on her chest. "Me llamo Maggie. El se llamo Joshua."

Sylvia's face lights up as she looks at Maggie. "Habla espanol?"

Maggie shrugs her shoulders. "Mas or menos."

River calls out from his seat on the bar stool at the island. "Yo hablo espanol, Sylvia. Maggie, I can totally translate if needed."

Joshua stands back, letting Maggie do her thing that she does so well.

Maggie waves at the two of them. "Vamanos," she says with a grin.

The couple steps in. The man wanders around the room, looking at Natalie's pictures on the walls, spying her only selfie by a waterfall. "Mira! Ella esta Natalie!"

Joshua nods his head. "Yes, she's my sister."

Domingo looks questioningly at him, and Maggie answers while pointing at the picture. "Ella esta hermana de Joshua."

Domingo's brow furrows. "Donde esta Natalie?"

Maggie glances at Joshua before placing one hand on her heart and the other on Joshua's chest. "En nuestros corazones."

Domingo nods his head in understanding before throwing an arm around her shoulders. "Lo siento mucho."

Maggie leans into his hug, shedding a few tears. "Gracias." She looks over at Joshua as she pulls away. "You could turn on sports."

Joshua turns on the TV, drawing River and Domingo into the living room. Maggie turns to Amber and Sylvia, clapping her hands. "That's better. Get those men out of here. Now here's what we're going to do. Amber, you're going to make the cake balls, and Sylvia, you're going to help me with this horchata. I've never made it before."

Maggie checks her sauce. She pulls the meat from the skillet, tossing them into the pan of sauce. She gives it one final taste before turning off the heat, putting the lid back on while she prepares the dough. She tosses the meat sauce on followed by some veggies and lots of cheese. Then she rolls out the second ball of dough, spreading it over the top of the pizza before tossing it in the oven. Amber claps her hands. "Double-crusted pizza. My favorite."

Sylvia hands Maggie a small cup, and she tastes the horchata, smiling. "It's perfect." Sylvia smiles, giving her a nod. Maggie glances over at Amber's plate of cake balls. "You're quick."

Amber smiles, ducking her head. "Thanks. My mom's a caterer. I kind of grew up doing this sort of thing."

Maggie's eyes widen. "Are you serious? I'm not sure I want you eating my food. I think I'm a little intimidated."

Joshua sneaks up behind Maggie, hugging her waist. His eyes light up as he addresses Amber. "Don't let her humility fool you. She runs a café. She's totally up for tonight."

Maggie blushes, shoving his hands away. "Let's start supper. Everyone take a hand." Soon they're standing in a circle. She closes her eyes. "Dear Lord. Let us love. Let us laugh. Let Your loving kindness rule in our hearts." She squeezes Joshua's hand. "Amen."

They all say "Amen." Joshua's eyes fly open, looking around. "So, did Maggie catch you in the hallway with an invite?"

River laughs. "No. I found a note on my door."

Joshua's confused. "A note?"

"Yeah. It was an invitation to your place tonight for supper, so I asked Amber if she wanted to go, and she was like cool with it, so here we are." He digs a stickie note from his pocket, slapping it down on the table.

Joshua picks it up, reading. "Good food. Great conversation. Dinner at 27B. Be there or be square." Joshua laughs. "Maggie, what kind of message is that?"

Maggie shrugs. "I don't know. I was trying to think of something catchy, but not too lengthy."

Joshua pockets the note. "Fair enough."

River studies Joshua. "Your sister was an awesome vlogger. I was so psyched when I found out we lived in the same building. Amber and I, we do like mini road trips and make like little videos. We totally watched every one of Natalie's on her site. We try to kind of capture her style."

Joshua nods, his eyes tearing up. "She would have loved knowing that. She was an awesome sister."

River sips his wine. "I'm sorry, dude, if I'm bringing up memories."

Joshua looks at him, smiling. "Nah, man. It's okay. It's nice to hear stories about her."

Sylvia takes a drink of her horchata. "Your sister took a very special gift from me to my sister down in Ecuador once. I ran into Natalia in the hallway, and I didn't know she traveled. We were talking about family, and she told me about you, and so I told her about my sister who was sick, and I wanted to send something to her for her birthday, but I was afraid to put it in the mail. It was a very special necklace from our mother, and it got me through some hard times, and I wanted my sister to have it, but I didn't want it getting lost in the mail. Your sister told me she was going to Ecuador in a couple of weeks. I couldn't believe it. She told me she would find my sister and give it to her, and she did."

River's eyes are wide open, and he sits very still. "Natalie found her and gave her the necklace?"

Sylvia's eyes tear up as she nods. "Si, es verdad. She gave her the necklace, and she sent me a picture of them together. My sister passed away two days after she met Natalie." Sylvia holds her phone up, showing them a picture of a little woman lying in a bed, clutching her necklace. "With Natalie's help, I was able to Facetime my sister. I got to talk to her one last time. It was a very special day for me."

Maggie takes Joshua's hand. "Sylvia. Thank you for sharing that memory with us. I just got goosebumps."

The dinner continues, and the conversation flows with the wine. Toward the end of the dinner, Sylvia looks at Maggie and Joshua. "How did you two meet? I love those stories."

Maggie laughs and leans away from Joshua. "We are not together. Natalie was my best friend growing up, and so he was my best friend's older brother. We are just friends."

Sylvia looks confused. "Are you sure? You seem so good together."

River nods his head. "Yeah, I can totally see you guys meshing. There's something there. I can feel it."

Joshua nudges Maggie's foot under the table, being ornery. "Maggie, here, used to have a crush on me in our younger years."

Maggie kicks him back. She turns to Amber, looking for an ally. "Joshua was a senior stud, and I was a lowly freshman. He was very popular with the ladies, and I was hardly noticeable." She forces a grin she doesn't feel. "Besides, he was too busy staring at the cheerleaders from the football field." She stops talking. She's embarrassed by the bitterness in her tone. Part of her knows his popularity wasn't his fault, but the other part, the part that wanted to be seen, feels wounded.

Joshua's hand finds her knee, giving it a squeeze and her cheeks turn pink, as he winks at Sylvia as he clears his throat. "Maggie played in the band. They always sat right behind the cheerleading section. Maggie sat in the front row, and if I looked really hard, I could see her perfect little lips playing on her flute. She would always sit so straight and tall, and her fingers would race up and down the keys. She was so serious. It was utterly adorable."

Maggie swats his hand away from her knee and jumps up. "That's enough of that. I'd say it's about time to clear the table. I can't wait to try the dessert Amber made."

The dinner guests take their plates to the sink, and Amber brings the plate of cake balls to the table, while Sylvia pours little cups of horchata to go around. Maggie smiles over at Sylvia. "How did you two meet?"

Sylvia takes Domingo's hand and lays her other on his arm as she looks into his eyes. "Domingo and I were neighbors growing up. He was my brother's best friend. My brother got a little mad when we got together, because Domingo spent more time with me when he found out I cared for him, but my brother didn't stay mad for long. We are all friends now."

"How about you, Amber? How did you and River meet?"

Amber blushes but doesn't say anything. River jumps in. "It was kind of like the Bridget Jones story, except she stayed around after."

Maggie shakes her head. "I'm sorry. Which one?"

River nods his head, eating another cake ball. "The Patrick Dempsey one. You know, we were at like this giant RockFest, and everyone was tent camping, and she wandered into the wrong tent, and one thing led to another, and then she just stayed there. We've been together ever since."

Amber smiles a little smile. "I knew he was my soulmate the moment we kissed. I could just tell."

Joshua nudges Maggie's foot again under the table. "I guess when you know, you know." He stands up, clearing his throat. "Before you leave, I'd like you to feel free to take something of Natalie's if it speaks to you. I know she'd love for you to have it."

twenty-two

Ali and Alex leave the barn and he drives her back to her mom's house. He's confused to see a shorter, stockier, black-haired man sitting on the house steps as they drive up. Her eyes widen. "Jason?" She hops out of the Legacy and walks toward him. "Jason. What are you doing here? Shouldn't you be in Europe?"

He steps forward and reaches for her hand, but she backs away. "Ali. We need to talk."

Ali hears footsteps behind her, and she's immediately annoyed when Alex stops beside her. "Hello, I'm..."

Jason cuts him off, crosses his arms across his chest, and spreads his feet wide. "I know who you are, *Alex*." He says Alex's name like a curse word.

Alex raises his eyebrows. "I guess we've met then. Ali, you ready to go in? It's kind of late and we've got an early morning tomorrow."

Jason's watchful gaze turns to a glare when Alex touches Ali's arm. She turns to Alex. "You can go in. I'm fine."

Alex drops his hand. "I think I'll stay here."

Jason steps closer, but Alex stays where he is. "Whatever

Ali and I have to say to each other doesn't concern you," Jason all but growls.

Alex doesn't budge an inch despite Jason's words of warning. "I think I'll just make sure Ali is alright."

Jason turns to Ali, his gaze softening. "I wondered if I could stay here tonight. I just got to town, and it's kind of late to find a hotel."

Alex clears his throat. "I know a few people I could call. It's no problem."

Jason frowns and Ali tries hard to hide the grin that sneaks out of her at Alex calling his bluff. Jason's eyes remain on Ali's. He makes his puppy dog look she used to love so much, but now she finds it rather pathetic. "I drove all day and night to get here. I'm really tired, and I'm short on cash after my vacation."

His excuses ring in Ali's ears. "And how is any of that my problem?" she demands.

Jason stares at the ground, looking unsure of what to say.

"You can stay with me. I have an apartment. It's got plenty of room," Alex offers.

Ali turns to him and grabs his bicep. "That's a great idea. I'm kind of tired, so I'm just gonna leave the two of you to it." Ali rushes past Jason, shuts the door, and flips the lock.

She turns around and almost screams when she spies Parker sitting in the dark corner in the recliner, her face lit only by her Nook screen. "Hey, Ali," she says in her strange little voice she reserves for scaring the crap out of her siblings at the most opportune times.

Ali almost jumps out of her skin as she searches blindly for a light switch on the wall but finds nothing. She's too shaken from leaving Alex and Jason outside. "Parks. Stop lurking in dark corners like a creeper. What are you doing up?"

Parker stands up. "I couldn't very well go to bed with my

sister's ex-fiancée camped out on the steps. Talk about awkward." She pauses for effect. "But then again, I couldn't let him in either."

Ali's thoughts race, and she muses out loud. "What is Jason doing here, and why did he come back without telling me?"

Parker grins. "I don't know, maybe because he's jealous?"

Ali glares at her sister. "And just what does he have to be jealous about?"

Parker giggles. "Maybe I posted a pic or two of you and Alex, and maybe Jason saw it. It's not my fault if Jason creeps on my Instagram and Facebook."

Ali whips out her phone and scrolls through it. "Parker. Why would you do this?"

Parker raises an amused eyebrow. "*Dude*. It's been on there for at least three days. Don't you check anything?"

Ali tosses a hand on her hip, staring Parker down. "*Dude*. I've been so busy with the café. I haven't had time to look at your posts. Speaking of which, Alex and I are planning an epic Valentine's Day dinner for all the couples. It's going to be classic. It'll totally top Mom's dinners, so like maybe Post the crap out of that instead of buttin' into my love life."

Parker grins an ornery grin. "Your love life is fun to mess with; and why you hatin' on Mom?"

Ali looks down at her feet. "I'm not. I'm just having some fun. I shouldn't have said it that way, but it's going to be Boss."

Parker puts her hands on her ears. "Please stop using what you think is cool teenage language. That phrase is so last year."

Ali giggles, pointing her finger at her sister. "Nailed it."

Parker giggles, holds up her phone, and shows Ali a picture of her and Alex having a discussion with each other.

"I *nailed* you. Seriously though, look at the way you two look at each other. There's definitely something there."

Ali sighs. "Parks. He's a small-town boy. I don't like small towns."

Parker makes a face. "Whatever. He's *so not* small town. He's a big-time writer. He's been places. He's imaginative. He's here because he chooses to be, not because he's stuck here with no other choice."

Ali rolls her eyes. "Of course, you'd stick up for Alex. You never liked Jason."

Parker shrugs her shoulders. "I gave Jason a chance. I've been social media friends with him for a year now. I even liked some of his posts. But yeah, I'm going to totally stick up for Alex. He's been here for *all of us.* He helped Mom get the café going. That was huge." Parker gets up, walks over to stand in front of her sister, and raises her pointer finger in her face. "Name one negative thing about Alex since you've met him, just one."

Ali stands there in silence, trying to think.

Parker grins. "Ha! That's what I thought." She marches upstairs in triumph, raising her hand in the air. "I'm on Team Alex, who *doesn't* leave girls at the altar."

Ali stomps her foot and raises her voice. "He didn't leave me at the altar!" Her hands go to her head. "I can't think anymore tonight. I'm going to bed. I gotta get up early tomorrow."

Parker calls down to her from the top of the stairs. "Goodnight, Ali-Cat."

Ali giggles before answering. "Goodnight, Parker Posey."

Conner calls out from behind his bedroom door at his two sisters. "For the record, Alex has my vote. Jason's a Cowboys fan. That's a total deal breaker."

twenty-three

Maggie and Joshua clean up the kitchen in silence. He takes a deep breath. "I think I'm ready."

She's surprised by the weight of his words. "Ready for what?"

"Ready to watch Natalie's videos that I haven't seen."

"Oh?"

"Yeah. I would wait until the end of the month to watch all of her videos for that month. It sounds silly, but it's just what I liked to do."

She takes his hand, kissing his knuckles. "Alright. Let's do it."

They sit down with his laptop, and he opens up her vlog, and there stands Natalie, big as life, with her highlighted hair pulled back in a ponytail and nothing on her face but sunshine. Her blue eyes sparkle in the camera as she rock-climbs a huge boulder on the side of what looks like a small mountain. "It's a beautiful crisp morning in Utah this morning. Notice behind me the magnificent sunrise. It's an awesome way to greet the day. Just me and nature hanging out together.

"When I get to the top, I'm going to enjoy a perfect cup of coffee and perhaps see a lizard or two sniffing the violets. Thank you for tuning in with me this morning, and wherever you are, may you start each day refreshed and renewed, healthy and happy to be alive. Until next time, this is Natalie, signing off."

Maggie laughs. "She sure loved life."

He touches the screen. "Yes, she did." He turns to her. "Sleep with me tonight?"

She leans back, irritated and excited at the same time. "Excuse me?"

He shuts the laptop. "I didn't mean it that way. I mean, will you lay beside me? I just want to hold you close." She takes his hand and leads him to the bedroom, thinking this is not one of her best decisions. They kick off their shoes and lie down on the bed, laying shoulder to shoulder. "Well, that was an interesting supper table tonight."

She turns her head to face him. "How do you mean?"

"I don't know. I just mean, I never would put any of us together in a group outside of this apartment. There's different ages, different cultures, a possible language barrier..."

She nudges him and feels a side of her daughter, Parker, popping out. "Think outside the box. Just because we're not all the same, doesn't mean we can't have a nice time together. Did Domingo look uncomfortable to you?"

"No. I guess not," he muses.

"Did River or Amber?" Her voice grows louder and more animated.

"I see your point. Calm down." He laughs. "You're one of those bigger table people, aren't you?"

She crosses her arms on her chest. "If that's how you see it, yes. I prefer to think I'm one of those who don't turn people away people. A person can never have too many friends." Her voice is soft, low, and slow, but there's no mistaking the measured firmness in her words.

He reaches over, grabs her hand, and tugs it down between them, holding it. "That's what I love the most about you, Maggie. Your big heart." He chuckles, shaking his head. "It's like you brought a piece of your work to New York."

She blushes, feeling defensive. "If you hadn't met Domingo and Sylvia, you never would have heard that incredible story about Natalie. I still have goosebumps." She rubs her arms with her hands.

He nods. "I suppose you're right."

There's a moment of silence between them, and then she turns on her side to face him. "Did you mean what you said at supper about the band sitting behind the cheerleaders?"

He chuckles, blushing a little. "Mostly, yes."

She shakes her head. "And all this time I thought you were staring at Kristi in her short skirt."

He laughs. "Guilty as charged. A guy'd have to be blind not to see that her shirt was two sizes too small and that her skirt was a whole two inches shorter than everybody else's."

She giggles, elbowing him in the ribs. "I knew it!"

He throws up his hands. "Give me some credit. I never went out with her."

She eyeballs him hard. "That's 'cause she only dated college guys. Everyone knew that."

His pride stings. "She tried to date me a few times. I turned her down."

She snorts. "Yeah, like that really happened."

His face is incredulous. "It did! If you don't believe me, I'll message her right now and you can see." He gets his phone out and starts typing.

She lunges over him and grabs at his phone. "You're texting your mother. You don't even have Kristi's number."

He smirks at her. "Yep. And you're sprawled across me. I'd say I'm winning."

She scoots off him and pokes his ribs. "You're such a guy."

He smirks at her. "You were totally jealous just now. Admit it."

She flips over on her side, facing away from him. "Whatever."

He does the same, bumping her butt with his. She smacks at the back of him. "What was that for?"

He sniffs and clutches his pillow. "You're being childish, so I gave you a childish response."

She pokes at his shoulder again. "You lied to me about having Kristi's number. You started it." She giggles again. "Maybe I'll just give Justin a call."

He squeezes her hand and growls. "Don't you dare."

She giggles harder. "Justin was harmless. He couldn't hurt a fly."

His jaw clenches. "I saw how he looked at you when you weren't watching. He was no angel."

She laughs out loud. "The same way you looked at me? The guy never tried a thing. I kissed him first."

His face heats up. "You kissed Justin?"

Her voice quiets in response. "Josh. You were in college. It was like a month after you had kissed me, and I just wanted to know if..."

"If what?"

"If it would feel the same..." The air grows heavy between them.

"And did it?"

She hesitates because she doesn't want to answer, but he turns toward her enough to stare her down. "No."

She glances at him, wanting to punch him in his smirking mouth as he winks at her. "I'd say my lips are pret-ty memorable."

She laughs out loud, trying to lighten the mood. "You wish."

He turns over on his back, reaches over and snatches her cell phone, and holds it up as he lays his head next to hers. "Selfie!"

She reaches out to grab her phone as the flash goes off, blinding her, and she instinctively turns toward him. He sends the snap to Ali before dropping the phone on the bed between them. She playfully punches his shoulder. "Why? Now my daughter will think something is going on between us."

His face turns serious. "Would that be so bad?"

She stares at the ceiling. "I don't..." Her phone goes off, and she opens the snap to Ali's face big on the screen, her mouth shaped like an O. "Way to go, Mom! Totally crushin' your Crush!!"

He laughs out loud when he reads it. "I *like* her."

Maggie's head is filled with confusion, while her heart is filled with excitement. She turns away once more, trying to sort it all out.

He curls along her backside, wrapping his arm around her, holding her tight. "Goodnight, Maggie Louise."

twenty-four

Ali wakes up the next morning before her alarm clock goes off. She's a nervous wreck when she thinks about Alex and Jason staying in the same apartment. How did her life become so complicated, so fast? She races through her shower and throws on her last clean outfit: a pair of shiny black hotpants and a striped button-up with three-quarter length sleeves. She laughs as she slips on the bright red wedges, wondering once again why she let her friends talk her into a Grease outfit for Las Vegas. She pulls her wet hair back into a bun again, applying some bright red lipstick to match her heels.

She races downstairs and runs to the kitchen for a cup of coffee. Conner's sitting at the table, eating cereal, which he starts choking on as soon as she turns the corner. "What are you wearing?"

Ali's focused on the coffee pot, as she races across the room, dumping it to fill the filter and start a new pot. "I'm Sandy, from Grease."

Conner clears his throat. "I get that, but why?"

Ali spins around. *"I was heading to Vegas."*

Parker speaks up from her corner of the room. "Yeah, but this isn't Vegas."

Ali wheels around in frustration. "I have no other clothes! Seriously! Go to school already."

Parker turns to Conner. "Come on, let's go before we're late picking up Manuel and his sister."

Conner's face turns red. "I guess he can ride shotgun."

Parker smirks at him, but he doesn't say anymore. "If you're sure." Conner gives no answer. "See you later, Ali." Parker calls as she and Connor run out the front door. "You've got company." Parker hollers across the house.

Ali nibbles on a PopTart, while waiting for her coffee, when Alex and Jason enter the kitchen. Jason's eyes just about pop out of his head. "Ali. What are you wearing?"

Alex doesn't say anything, just plops down in a seat at the table and gives her an appreciative grin.

Ali mostly ignores Alex, telling herself she won't blush as she looks over at Jason, reiterating her point like a broken record. "*I was heading to Vegas.*"

Jason's face is clueless. "Las Vegas?"

"Yes. Las Vegas. Apparently, that's where jilted girls go with their ex-fiancée's girlfriends to get away," Ali answers drolly before she turns away, pouring herself a to-go cup of coffee, adding some milk before snapping on the lid. She spins back around, cup in hand, all smiles as she looks at Alex. "Are you ready to go to work, Alex? I imagine Bernie's waiting."

He hops up, smiling. "Certainly."

They head for the front door with a frowning Jason in tow. Ali steps out into the chilly morning, leaning into Alex, who throws an arm around her. She gazes into his eyes. "I wonder what's on the menu today."

"Well, it's Wacky Wednesday, so it's hard telling."

Ali giggles. "Wacky Wednesday?"

Alex nods. "Yep. One time, your mom made confetti pancakes and decorated the café with balloons. Another time she made banana splits for breakfast and decorated the tables like it was the 1950's. A-nother time, she made pork and beans and she put it on a piece of toast with a tomato on top. She said it was an English breakfast, and she played Pride and Prejudice all morning on the wall with a projector she borrowed from Isaac. Oh, and she served everybody tea in fancy teacups."

She squeezed his arm. "That sounds like so much fun."

He openly grins. "Your mom *is* a lot of fun." He chuckles. "I'd have to say my favorite was the day she served bacon and egg biscuits with honey. She decorated the walls with the animals from the movie *Babe* and then she dressed up like the farmer."

Her eyes light up. "I think I like being Sandy for a day." She leans into him, batting her eyelashes. "It'll be swell. Will you be my Danny?"

He laughs and glances back at Jason. "I think Jason would make a better Danny since he's got the thicker hair and bright blue eyes."

Jason kicks a rock behind them. "No, thanks. That sounds dumb."

She looks back at Alex. "He doesn't want to play. What do you say, Alex? Will you be my Danny?"

Alex stops in front of the café door, shuffling his feet. "Aw geez, Sandy. I don' know. I guess, but only if you'll wear my T-Birds jacket."

She laughs and claps her hands before grabbing his jacket collar. "Danny, you're the best. I'd love to!"

Jason walks between them to go inside. "You guys are idiots."

Bernie shuffles in behind Jason. "I'd have to agree. Where's my oatmeal?"

Ali runs to the kitchen, almost tripping in her little red wedges. "I have seven minutes, Bernie. Hold onto your shirt." Minutes later, a breathless Ali sets Bernie's oatmeal bowl in front of him, tossing in his nuts and raisins, leaning sideways, and sticking out her hip. "Not bad, huh?"

He raises a thick, white eyebrow at her. "My tea?"

As if it's magic, the teakettle whistles. Ali runs to its beckoning call, pouring it over the tea bag in the teacup. She gets him a metal spoon and a little milk. Jason watches all of this. "Wouldn't it be easier if you just used the hot water from the stand?"

Ali and Bernie look over at Jason, speaking together. "It's all in the preparation."

Ali turns to Bernie, giggling, and Bernie smiles back at her, stirring his tea. Jason grunts from his corner. "You guys are so weird."

Alex slips around the corner into the kitchen. "Have you decided what to make for Wacky Wednesday breakfast?" he asks Ali with wiggling eyebrows.

She snaps her fingers. "I've got it! Peanut butter banana bacon shakes OR mimosas with ladyfingers."

"Hmm," he growls out, doing his best Elvis impression, curling Ali's toes. "I love it!"

She smiles back at him. "We could totally use the umbrella decorations and the bacon strips."

Talia waltzes out of the back office, and Jason's eyes bug just a little. "Who is this?"

Ali spins around. "Hi, Talia. How's your morning going?"

Talia eyes Alex and then Jason. "Not as good as yours," she teases.

Alex frowns at Talia's words and walks to the back. "I'll just go get the decorations."

Ali calls after him. "Thanks, Alex. Don't forget the tape." She turns back to Talia. "Talia, this is Jason."

Talia's smile disappears along with her look of appreciation that was pointed in his direction. "Jason? As in the guy who left you at the altar?"

Jason's frown returns. "It didn't happen at the altar."

Talia puts a hand on her hip, stands sideways, and stares him down. "You know what you did." She stares at him for a few more seconds. "Mmm hmmm." She turns away with a big smile for Bernie. "Good morning, Bernie."

Bernie gives her a quiet nod in answer, but his blue eyes remain on Jason.

Talia waddles back to the office.

Ali gets in the fridge and pulls out the bacon. She turns on the oven, and soon the smell of frying bacon fills the air. Bernie sniffs. "Ain't nothin' like the smell of fryin' bacon. Man, I miss the days before low cholesterol and no salt diets."

The door jingles and Becky walks in. Ali's confused. "It's awful early for you to be here, Becky. Where's Marvin?"

Becky holds up her phone. "Alex texted me."

Alex walks out, holding cardboard bacon strips. "Thanks for coming, Becky. We need some ladyfingers, and I wondered if you'd go buy us some, please." He walks over to the register, opens it, and takes out some cash. "That should cover it."

Becky palms it and walks toward the door, until she sees Jason. She stops a few feet from him. "Hey, aren't you Jason?"

Jason looks confused. "Yes, but how did you know?"

Becky shakes her head at him and frowns as she waggles a finger at him. "You know what you did." She says and walks out the front door.

Jason turns on Ali. "Did you tell *everyone* our business?"

Ali throws up her hands. "No, I did not. This is a small town, and mom has a lot of friends. Apparently, word got around."

Alex walks up to the both of them. "Jason. There is one way to keep rumors from spreading."

Jason glares at him. "What's that?"

Alex grins triumphantly. "Don't be such a jerk."

Ali's face turns red, and she goes back to the blender, happy to have something to keep her busy. Alex gets back to work on the decorations.

Ali's phone goes off, and she sets it down, smiling. "Alex, did you tell Conner about the peanut butter bacon shakes?"

Alex gives her a conspiratorial wink. "May-be."

"Remind me to save one for him," she says.

She finishes frying all the bacon, then pulls out the blender. "Now, for the fun part. I love making milkshakes."

Jason frowns. "Do you know how many calories are in that shake?"

Alex scowls in Jason's direction. "Then don't have one."

Jason glares at Alex. "Are you like a waiter?"

Alex looks him in the eye from across the room. "May-be."

Ali giggles, and Jason gets mad. "What's so funny?"

She starts to answer the apparently angry Jason. "He's a wri—"

Alex cuts her off with the raising of his hand. "I work here. I help Maggie, and since she's gone, I've been helping Ali."

She looks at Alex in question. She doesn't say anything more but wonders why he's not telling Jason what he does for a living.

The door opens. Amber walks in with Silas and Maddy, who immediately start growling at Jason. He squirms on the high stool.

Ali smiles at the two dogs. "Amber. You're here early."

"I know. I hope that's okay. The church secretary called in sick today, so I need to go fill in."

Ali nods. "Alright. We'll call you if we need anything."

Becky walks back in with the ladyfingers. "Hey, Amber. Just the girl I want to see. Marvin and I are taking a drive to a nature trail today. Could Silas and Maddy go? We're taking the van. They'll have plenty of room."

Amber smiles huge. "If you're sure. They'd love that. I wish I could go, but I need to work at the church today."

Becky pats her hand. "I understand. Maybe another time we can all go." Amber walks out the front door. Becky gives a little whistle. "Silas, Maddy. Come." The Great Danes walk out with Becky, growling again as they walk by Jason, who hugs the bar.

Ali turns to Jason. "That's weird. They've never done that before."

Jason gives an uneasy shrug. "What are they doing in here, anyway? I swear, this place is like a three-ring circus."

Ali snaps her fingers. "Thanks for the reminder. I've got to get those mimosas done." She turns away, busying herself once more, and soon the first customers walk in the door. Breakfast flies by, with many compliments for Ali on her creativity, and a few questions about where the Wednesday movie was. Ali feels bad that she didn't have it ready.

She picks up the phone and dials Isaac herself. "Hey, Isaac, it's Ali. I'd like to borrow your projector, please."

"Sure, Ali, as long as I can get a peanut butter shake and a mimosa with a few ladyfingers. They sound delicious."

She laughs. "It's a deal. I'll send them down with Alex." She turns to summon Alex, but he's already standing down the counter from her. "You need me to run some drinks to Isaac in return for borrowing his projector for the day?"

She winks at him. "You've got it. Now we just need to figure out what movie we're showing tonight."

He smiles. "We could run Dr. Zhivago and decorate the walls with trains and serve train food."

She wrinkles her nose. "Like hot dogs?"

He crosses his arms. "Yes. *OR* we could do hot dogs, turkey and swiss sandwiches on wheat with individual chip bags and a fruit bowl. We could serve boxed wine and cans of beer along with tea and water, of course."

She scrunches up her nose. "You're *determined* to make me watch Dr. Zhivago."

He looks all innocent. "*It's a classic.* I'm telling you, Ali, you'll have a lot of happy customers."

She lets out a sigh. "Fine. Let's do it."

He stares at her, and she stares right back at him as if spellbound until Bernie knocks on the counter. "The shakes?"

Her chin lifts and her hands fly. "Oh, right. What was I thinking?"

She pours two to-go cups, tosses some bacon in a Ziplock bag, and spins back around to hand them to Alex, who's suddenly standing very close. She's immediately flustered. "Here you go."

He takes them and walks wordlessly past Jason, who doesn't hesitate to needle her as soon as Alex's gone. "You two got awfully close awfully quickly."

Ali's feeling defensive. "It hasn't been *awful* at all. It's been rather nice."

Jason sneers. "Just how *close* are you?"

"None yo' bizness," Talia pipes up from the back office.

Ali walks over to the doorway and sticks her head in. "Thank you, Talia, but I can handle my own."

Talia gives her a look of disbelief. "If you say so. Just so you know, I'm right here."

Ali shuts the door quietly before returning to the kitchen and Jason. "Alex and I are friends, but Talia's right. It's not your business."

Jason gets up and approaches Ali in his familiar way, crowding her at the sink. "I miss you."

Ali's back is up. "Did you miss me *before* or *after* Parker posted pictures of me and Alex?"

Jason looks caught. "What does it matter? So I didn't like seeing you with another guy. What's wrong with that?"

Ali's a little flattered, but she's not about to give in. "Jason, you broke up with me. Did you think I would just stay single forever?"

He sticks out his lip and pouts. "I don't know. I didn't think you'd find someone so soon, though."

She shoves against his chest, but he doesn't move. "Jason. Since you broke up with me, you have no say in who I date or when I date. You made that decision, not me."

He slaps the counter, and she flinches. "I know, but I'm here now."

"And not wanting me to date other guys is not a reason for us to get back together," she says with a glare. "It's definitely not a good foundation for a meaningful relationship," she states as she stares him down with a look of warning he's never seen before.

"I said I made a mistake," Jason insists, but he doesn't sound too sorry.

She studies him carefully. "Maybe it wasn't a mistake."

His face turns red, and he looks away, clenching his jaw. "We'll just see about that."

She sees an opening, and she slips out from between Jason and the counter. She's relieved when she sees Alex walk back in the door with the projector.

Alex catches the look of relief on her face. He wants to know what happened between her and Jason, because the air is charged, but he can see by the look on her face she's not ready to talk.

twenty-five

Maggie wakes up the next morning, startled to feel an arm around her, but then she remembers the night before. She turns her head slowly and spies Joshua sound asleep beside her. She rolls out of bed sneakily, rushing off to the bathroom. She treads lightly across the floor, not making a sound as she leaves his bedroom to venture into the living room, where she walks slowly from picture to picture, taking in the moments that made up Natalie's life. The pictures are filled with beautiful scenery and exotic places, and Maggie smiles as she pictures Natalie in every one of them.

His door creaks open, and he steps out of his room. "What're ya doin'?"

She turns to him, wiping a tear away. "I'm just looking at all the places Natalie's been again. She certainly loved her life."

He shoves his hands in his pockets. "She really did. My parents always wondered where we got our wanderlust, as we both did our share of traveling."

She smiles, thinking. "It's hard to say. All I know is being friends with your sister was never boring. She was so imaginative, and she just had this way about her. She didn't have time for the drama that a lot of girls loved, you know? We *never* fought, because I just couldn't fight with her. She was too much fun to be around. She had her ideas and her goals, and she didn't get caught up in the stupid stuff that so many high school girls do. And she never cared about social status. She wanted to be everybody's friend. She wanted to enjoy life, and she did."

He throws an arm around her, pulling her in to his side. "You were her best friend. She loved everything about you, too." He gives her an extra squeeze. "Everything except your mega crush on her older brother," he teases.

She pokes him in the side. "Rewriting history are we?" she teases him back as she looks at Natalie's picture on the wall once more, feeling inspired. She turns to him standing behind her. "We should go camping."

He smiles. "O-kay," he replies, not sounding too sure.

She nods in a decisive manner. "Yes, we should go camping! We can pack enough food for 3-4 days and we could go to the park with all the waterfalls, and hot air balloons, and hiking. I want to see some scenery and take some great pictures. Do you have a tent?"

He laughs. "I know Natalie did. We could use her tent."

She clears her throat. "Do you have a car?"

He smiles. "No, but we could take her Jeep Wrangler." He pulls up an app on his phone. "It might be pretty cold. Did you bring any long underwear?"

She shakes her head. "I didn't think of that."

He points to the bedroom. "I bet you can find some decent thermal wear in her things. She wore that all the time on her trips. And grab a hat and gloves while you're at it."

She heads for Natalie's bedroom, taking a deep breath before opening her dresser drawers. Maggie feels silly, but she can't help but speak aloud. "Well, Nat, I'm trying a page from your book. I'm grabbing life by the horns so to speak, and I'm stepping out of my comfort zone. I'm going camping with your brother. I'm sure you knew how I felt about him, but you were kind enough to keep that one to yourself. I hope you approve. I wish you were here so I could talk to you." She digs around, finding a pair of thick socks. "Aha. These might be a little tight, but they'll be warm, and they have some give."

There's a knock at the door. "How are we doing?"

"I think I found some things I can use."

"It should be decent during the day. It's the night that's going to get cold. Do I bring one sleeping bag or two?" Joshua's question pings off her insides.

She blushes. "Bring two."

He shrugs, giving her a wink. "I had to try." He glances around the room. "I think there's hiking boots in here, too." She reaches into the closet, pulling out a pair. "Got some. It's a good thing we wear the same size of shoe."

He drops a duffel bag on the floor. "I thought we could put our stuff in here."

She walks into the bathroom, eyeing the shampoo. "This is more complicated than I thought."

He winks. "It'll be alright. We'll just take a box of granola bars, a loaf of bread with peanut butter and honey, and a bag of apples and oranges—things like that. I've got plenty of protein bars. We can grab a 24 pack of water on the way out of town, too. I bet I can find a place that has electrical outlets. I believe it's called glamping."

She grins at his choice of words. "Now you're talking. If I go a day without texting my children, they might think something happened to me."

She bags up the bathroom supplies and pushes them into the corner of the duffel bag before grabbing a deck of playing cards off the end table. She goes to the kitchen and pulls out the two pieces of leftover pizza, microwaving them.

"Come have a slice of pizza with me." He returns to the table and sets two cans of Coke down.

"If you're eating pizza for breakfast, why not have a can of Coke?"

They pop their tabs at the same time, pick up their cans, and knock them together. She meets his eye and smiles. "Here's to a grand adventure."

He gives her a wink. "I'll drink to that."

twenty-six

Ali rushes to the spreadsheet after squaring away the breakfast dishes. It's completely blank. "Alex!"

He pops around the corner a few minutes later. "Yo."

"There's nothing written down for lunch. What do I do?"

He goes over and opens the fridge, scanning the contents. "You're kinda bare bones in here. Me thinks we were supposed to grocery shop."

She wrings her fingers worriedly. "What'll I do?"

He plops down on a high bar stool. "We could do tuna salad on hearts of romaine and serve it with a side of crackers and grapes and carrots—go for a healthy lunch day."

She claps her hands excitedly. "I like it!" She grabs the glass trifle bowl. "I could whip up a layered angel food cake with strawberries and whipped cream in here for a light dessert." She looks at him, pleading. "Do you have time for a grocery list?"

He smiles. "Write it down and give it here. Just call me Speedy Gonzales. I'll be back in a flash." He winks at her, and she blushes as she ducks her head to write her list.

She hands it to him, making eye contact. "Thank you."

As soon as Alex walks out the front door, Jason returns to the counter. "I can't believe you're *flirting* with a waiter."

Ali stares back at Jason, wondering where all his charm went. "He's sweet and kind. We work well together."

Jason steps closer, watching Ali closely. "He sounds like a great best friend, but not a boyfriend." She backs away and grabs a dishrag. She starts wiping down the counter for something to do, not giving Jason a response, so he tries again. "What are you doing here, anyway? It looks to me like he can manage this place without you."

She shakes her head. "I made my mom a promise." She looks him in the eye. "Unlike you, I keep my promises."

He frowns. "How long are you going to hold that against me? I got scared. I ran."

She stares at him. "What were you so scared of Jason? Me? Or having to grow up."

He sits down, pouting. "I don't know. Europe and the guys were just so easy. They made me feel free, not pinned down. We stayed in youth hostels and wandered around, eating good food, meeting fun people..." He pauses. "It was a really good time."

She stops wiping the counter again, watching him. "Did you even think of me when you were over there?"

He doesn't meet her eyes. "Yeah. I thought of you a few times. When I saw something really beautiful, I thought to myself, Ali would *love* to see this."

She sighs. "No, Jason. Did you think of me when you flew to Europe, and three days went by and I heard *nothing* from you, and then when you finally answered me, all you answered was we were through? Did you think of me any time after that, or just when you saw me with Alex on Parker's Facebook page?"

His face looks confused. "I just told you I thought of you, Ali, but I was busy. I was in Europe."

She holds his gaze. "And I was here—wondering what *I* did wrong, or where *we* went wrong, but I'm beginning to see the only mistake I made was choosing you. I want marriage. I want a family. I'm done waiting for you to decide. It's over."

Jason reaches for her, but she backs away. "Ali. Give me another chance, please. Now that I know what it's like to be without you, I won't make the same mistake twice. I need you."

She wants to believe him, but there's something holding her back. "Jason, if we were really meant for each other, you wouldn't have let me go so easily. I'm not the one for you, and you're not the one for me. I can't go back to what we had because it's broken. If I took you back, I'd always be wondering when you were going to walk out again. I won't do it."

He stands up, staring at Ali. "I'll wait, Ali. If that's what you want me to do, I'll do it. Just tell me how long."

She shakes her head. "It's not about me punishing you, Jason. That's not what I'm saying. You broke my trust, and you can't undo what you've done."

His fists clench. "This is about your pride. That's all this is. You won't take me back because you're so damn stubborn, and it's just stupid. We were good together. You know we were."

She crosses her arms over her chest. "If we were so great, Jason, why did you *leave me?*"

"I already told you, I got scared," he protests.

Talia marches out of the office with her hand on her hip, pointing at Jason. "Boy, you a broken record, and I'm tired of hearin' yo' excuses. You need to get grown and flown, *now*. Go on." She points to the front door, staring him down.

Jason throws up his hands. "Fine. I'm gone."

"Bye, Jason." Ali mouths softly after his retreating form.

Talia shakes her head back and forth, tsking. "I thought

he'd never leave. I's 'bout to bring him some cheese to go with his pathetic whine. He sure can carry on."

Ali shakes her head, glancing at her watch. "Where's Alex? I need to start on lunch. People are going to be coming in soon."

The back door opens, and Alex walks in with his hands full of bags. He sets them down on the floor. He walks back out, carries two more full paper bags in, and sets them on the counter. He takes Ali's hand, tugging her behind him. "Come here a second."

She tiptoes behind him on her red heels, trying to ignore Talia's knowing grin as they rush past her through her mom's office. "What's going on, Alex?"

He steps outside, gives her a yank, and she runs right into him. His arm clamps around her waist, holding her tight as his hand rests on the small of her back. He dips his head, finds her lips, and there's the slightest exchange of breath before he dives in, tasting her while his hand caresses her neck with the lightest of touches. When he pulls away, she's breathless, unable to speak as she leans against the building, trying to cool down under his heated stare. Slowly, words form in her brain. "What was that?"

He flashes her his killer smile, dimples and all. "A reminder that I'm interested, Ali." His voice drops lower as he steps up, laying a hand on the hip of her hot pants, gripping just a little. "Very interested."

She rests her hand on his chest, feeling saucy. "Message received. Loud and clear." She takes a deep breath. "Oh, shoot. I gotta make lunch. You can't be dragging me out here for this nonsense."

He laughs out loud. "Relax, woman. Tuna salad is my specialty. I practically lived on that stuff for four years. It's poor man's breakfast, lunch, and supper."

She wrinkles her nose. "And you still eat it?"

He laughs. "Yep. We starving artists can't afford to be particular."

She flashes him a cheesy smile. "Whatever, Mr. New York Times bestseller."

He gives her a wink. "Hey. I'll take my luck when I can get it." She turns to go inside, and his hand goes to the small of her back as he follows, giving her the shivers. "Let's go. That tuna salad won't make itself."

They get to work in the kitchen, and she can't help but smile at his happy whistling through lunch preparations while she stands at the sink, rinsing all the grapes. She glances over, watching him mix the mayo with a little bit of oil, sprinkling in salt and pepper, then dipping in a spoon to taste test. He nods, winking over at her. "I've still got it." He opens up the bags, pulls out the celery and onion, and hands them to her. "Rinse that celery please, so I can chop it."

She eyes the onion. "Not everyone likes onions."

He reaches below the sink and extracts two big bowls. "I know. We'll have onion or no onion." She hands the celery back, and he makes short work of chopping it before tossing it in a Tupperware container. Next, he opens a big jar of sweet gherkins, chops those up, and puts them in a container. Finally, he chops the onion, wiping his eyes on the back of his hand. "Darn these onions. They get me every time." He motions to the sauce. "Why don't you divide the sauce between the two bowls and start stirring up the tuna? Then we can add the celery and pickles."

She glances at the clock. "Sure, but pretty soon I have to get started on my dessert. It needs a little time to chill." She's stirring the bowl, and another thought occurs to her, and she freezes. "I didn't even put groceries on the list for tonight. Ugh."

He laughs. "Relax, Ali. I got you. It's going to be okay."

She sighs with relief. "Alex, what would I do without you?"

He turns to her, his eyes dancing. "Play your cards right, Ali, and you may not have to find out." Her stomach drops out as she looks back at him with a feeling in her gut she's never felt before. It's the delicious feeling of anticipation of what mysteries lie ahead, but at the same time, seeing her future right in front of her. "Ali?"

She blinks. "I'm sorry, did you say something?"

He grins at her, and her body hums from head to toe. "I asked if you were done stirring the tuna."

She drops the spoon into the bowl, feeling foolish. "Yeah." She turns away. "I think I'll go work on my dessert."

twenty-seven

Maggie and Joshua pile everything into the Jeep a bit clumsily, and she double-checks it all, shoving it onto the floor, making him laugh. "Relax, Mags. I think you got it."

She gives one more shove. "I just want to be sure it doesn't go flying out."

He zips up his heavy coat and tugs his hat down on his head. "This Jeep's closed in, but it's still pretty cold out."

She puts her hat on, securing the earflaps. "I don't care what I look like, I don't want an ear infection. If I'm joyriding in a Jeep, these windows are going down."

He starts it up, rolls down the windows, and turns up the 80's music Natalie was so fond of. "That's the spirit." He backs out into the street, and they drive down the road, the cold winter wind freezing their noses.

She grabs his arm. "Don't forget to buy the water."

He nods. "I won't."

They get the water at a convenience store on the edge of the city. Ten miles down the road, she gives in and rolls up her window with chattering teeth. "Maybe windows down in February isn't the best idea."

He rolls his window up and shivers slightly. "Thank goodness. I'm tough, but that wind is biting."

They drive down the road, reminiscing about high school classmates, and where they are now. He turns to her, looking all serious. "Time passes us by before we know it, Maggie Louise."

"It sure feels that way." She gazes out the windshield. "But you know, I wouldn't change a single second of my life. I feel pretty blessed." She looks over at him, smiling. "And the more I think about it, I'm leaving my café name the way it is. It may have been inspired out of spite, but the community I live in has shown me time and time again the kind of love I need in my cup, and it's overflowing."

He reaches over and squeezes her hand. "I'm happy for you, Maggie." He takes a deep breath. "If you've got room at the table for another chair, I'd like a seat."

She catches her breath. "What are you saying?"

"I'm saying I'm seriously considering moving to your town. I want to date you, to be around you. Losing Natalie has shown me the importance of prioritizing what matters. Even though we've just met again, you matter a great deal to me, and I'm not ready to let you go."

She keeps a hold of his hand, answering softly. "Okay."

He lets out a breath he didn't know he was holding. "Okay."

Her eyes watch the signs. "Ooh, a café with homemade pie. Can we stop?"

He signals as he exits the highway. "Why not?"

The café is quiet, and they find a table by the window, taking small bites of pie, and sipping their coffee. She looks up at him with a thoughtful expression on her face. "I can't believe you've never been engaged."

He looks down at his pie, fiddling with his spoon. "Why do you say that?"

She shrugs. "I don't know. You're an attractive guy. You're personable. I can't imagine there weren't a few girls who had their eye on you."

He gazes out the window. "I don't know. I kind of caught the traveling bug, and I lost track of time working and saving for the next big trip. I guess I just didn't make enough time for that."

She sips her coffee. "That makes sense."

He looks back at her. "You wouldn't trade any of your years for a week in Scotland, driving through the countryside, getting lost in old castles and churches, wondering in fields of green, waiting in your tin can car on the wrong side of the road while long-haired cows cross in front of you?"

She giggles. "What a picture. Tempting." She sets her cup down. "But no, I wouldn't."

He takes her hand. "What about now?"

Her heart skips a beat. "What do you mean?"

"We could take a trip somewhere together. I'd love to go to Scotland with you. Or England. Anywhere."

She looks uncertain. "I don't know. That's a big trip. It takes planning. I don't even have a passport."

He leans back in his seat, studying her. "That's alright. We've got time."

Maggie takes another bite of her pie and wishes she felt as sure about things between them as Joshua does.

twenty-eight

Ali's Wednesday lunch crowd comes in just as she's washing up a few dishes. She and Alex have got an easy rhythm going, and even though it's a lot of rushing around with the absence of Amber being at the church for the day, they manage to keep every drink cup filled and prepare every order. They grab a few seconds in the kitchen, huffing, and puffing. Ali winks at Alex. "Good call on cold food for lunch. I can't imagine if one of us had to be on the grill."

He laughs. "That would have been more challenging for sure."

She smiles as some of her customers drop their dishes in the soapy tub just behind the end of the counter. She raises an eyebrow at him. "Did you put that tub there?"

He shrugs his shoulders. "I figured we could use all the help we can get today."

She smiles as she runs the register. "Thank you. Come again."

He calls out an announcement. "Tonight's special movie is Dr. Zhivago. Spread the word. You will receive Train Car food service. All aboard."

She looks at him in amazement, laughing as she shakes her head, putting her hands on her hips. "You really are something, Alex Cirillo."

He rushes over and clamps a hand over her mouth, whispering. "I only go by Alex. I try not to advertise my fame."

She moves backward, away from his hand. "I'm sorry. I had no idea. If it was me, I'd be so excited to tell everyone I'd written something."

He shrugs. "I don't know. It was kind of exciting at first, and I did kind of toot my own horn, but then I kind of stopped doing that, because it also feels like you're inviting people to walk through your closet or something. It's kind of hard to explain." He clears his throat. "Ali. You have a customer."

She looks away from him. "Oh, I'm sorry Bonnie."

Bonnie grins as she looks between the two of them with her eyes sparkling. She waves her hand. "That's alright. I'm in no hurry."

Ali takes her check and puts it in the register. "You have a good day, Bonnie."

She checks everybody out at the register for the next half hour while he clears the tables.

Jason moseys back in the cafe and sits down. Alex stops beside his table. "Lunch is over," he announces.

Jason doesn't move. He eyes the shelves behind the glass. "I'd like a piece of pie and a glass of iced tea."

Alex whips out his tablet, pen at the ready. "What kind of pie?"

Jason leans forward, rests his elbows on the table, and answers in annoyance. "Whatever kind there is."

Alex just grins as he looks down at him. "We have blueberry pie, cherry pie, peach cobbler..."

"Anything is fine." Jason cuts him off.

Alex taps his pad of paper. "I'm afraid I'll need you to be

more specific, unless you want to pay for five pieces of dessert and an iced tea."

Jason pounds his fist on the table. "Fine. I'd like a piece of apple pie."

Alex looks over at Ali. "Any apple pie left?" His voice is way too joyful in Ali's opinion.

Ali narrows her eyes at him, willing him to tone down his cheeriness. "Nope."

Jason growls out. "I'll take cherry then."

Alex looks at Ali, and she shakes her head. Alex answers. "I'm afraid we don't have cherry either, sir."

Jason whips his head to look at the empty shelves behind the glass. "*What do you have?*"

"We have a dinner roll, but we're out of iced tea." Alice answers quietly.

Jason looks back up at Alex. "I guess I'll take bread and water."

Alex scribbles it down noisily on his pad of paper. "Bread and water it is, then."

Jason snorts. "I ordered two things, and you have to write them down?"

"Just doin' my job," Alex answers joyfully as he slaps the paper down in front of Ali with a wink. "Take care of that for me, darlin'."

She fills a cup with ice and water and places the last dinner roll on a plate. She walks out from behind the register to set them down in front of Jason, then walks back to the kitchen, ignoring his staring.

Alex comes back out to the dining area to finish wiping down the tables. "I'll get those train decorations up, and then we can glance through the box and see if there's anything else we can use," he calls out to Ali.

Ali nods. "I think I'll start on my Valentine's Day dinner quotes for the PowerPoint when I get a few minutes."

"Don't forget to put a Rocky line or two in there," Alex answers.

She laughs. "I'm leaving that one to you."

"Yo, Adrian," Alex calls back in a deep voice.

Jason nibbles on his dinner roll, eating as slowly as possible, watching Alex move around the room with ease. He waits impatiently for Ali to return to the register, but she doesn't. Alex walks by, picks up his empty plate, and wipes down his table. He looks down at Jason. "Don't worry about the cost of the roll. It's on the house."

Jason shoves his chair back, stands up, and stares Alex down, but Alex doesn't flinch as he stares coolly back at him. Jason's fists clench at his sides. "She's not staying here much longer, you know. She'll return to her job and her home, and I'll be waiting there for her."

Alex gives him a maddening smile. "We'll see about that."

Jason turns around and heads for the door. He stops with his hand on the doorknob and looks at Alex again. "She will."

"Have a nice rest of your day. See you at home," Alex calls out.

Jason turns the doorknob and flings the door wide.

Ali frowns at Alex from behind the register. "Can I trust you two not to put a hole in the apartment wall tonight?"

He turns to look at her with a caught look on his face. "I thought you were in the back office."

She snorts. "I was, but you two aren't exactly quiet."

He grins. "I guess I shouldn't poke an angry bear."

She sighs. "His feelings are hurt, Alex. He'll calm down, eventually. It might take a while. You might want to keep your distance is all. I don't think he'll take a swing at you, but I don't know."

He frowns. "I certainly hope not. I don't like to fight, but I know how to defend myself."

She grins. "Is that so?"

His face turns serious, and he pats his flat belly. "Yeah. You think 'cause I'm a writer, I'm soft in the middle? I've got abs of steel, baby. I can take a punch."

She giggles in response and hopes her face doesn't betray her thoughts of Alex and his flat stomach.

twenty-nine

Maggie and Joshua drive until they reach the park. He heads into the office, doubtful he'll get a balloon ride, but he figures it's worth a shot. The man behind the counter looks like he's closing things down for the day as Joshua approaches. "Hi. We kind of drove up on a whim, and I was wondering about the possibility of a hot-air balloon ride tomorrow?"

The guy's face lights up. "That'd be perfect. I got a few last-minute cancellations, and I was pretty disappointed. How long do you want to be up?"

He grins. "How long do you have?"

"Well. Since I got two cancellations back-to-back, you could have both time slots. You'll just have to pay for both."

He gets out his card and tosses it on the counter. "Sounds good to me. What time do we meet you and where?"

The man smiles and runs his card through the attachment on his phone. "Meet me here at zero-six-hundred tomorrow morning."

Joshua likes his no-nonsense style. "Say, do you have any recommendations for a good place to camp... I mean glamp?"

The man laughs. "Oh, sir. There's no glamping in these parts, but there is spectacular scenery." He hands Joshua back his card, winking. "Just a thought... I'm also an ordained minister if you have any ideations of a really memorable hot-air balloon ride."

Joshua gives a nervous chuckle. "Thanks, I'll keep that in mind." He goes to walk out, but the man stops him.

"About that camping spot... I know a few good ones. There's a few nearby, but if you want to sleep close among the trees and hear the rushing river, you'll have to go a ways in." Joshua steps back to the counter and writes down the directions on a piece of paper.

Joshua walks back to the Jeep and hops in. He turns to Maggie. "Good news! We have a hot air balloon ride first thing in the morning." He puts his hand up for a high five, and she hits it. "Bad news is there's no glamping and we will have to be here at 6:00 a.m.."

Her smile doesn't change. "It'll be a beautiful way to see the sunrise."

He smiles at her agreeable cheerfulness. "Not much gets you down, does it."

She laughs. "I'm on vacation in New York and I'm riding in my first ever hot air balloon ride over a beautiful state park. Who can complain about that?"

He puts the Jeep in gear. "Well, when you put it that way." He backs out slowly. "Next question. Do you want to camp close to the office or drive a little farther in and camp by the river?"

She smiles. "Let's drive a bit. It'd be nice to see more of the park. I think we'll know our camping spot when we see it."

He nods. "That's a great idea."

They take off down the road, and she oohs and ahs over the trees and the hills, and the views, making him realize how much nicer it is to travel with company. She looks over at him. "Do you camp much in all your traveling?"

He laughs. "I've never been brave enough to camp in a foreign country, but I've camped some here in the U.S."

She looks out the window. "I haven't camped since I was a girl. Every summer we'd go camping. Well, you know. A few times Natalie went with us."

"Yep. I remember her going on about it when she got home. She had so much fun."

She smiles at the memory. "It was a lot of fun. I always wanted to do that for my three, but Mike wasn't much for camping."

He looks over at her, frowning. "It's never too late to start new traditions."

She pats his arm. "I suppose you're right."

He turns at the sign, heading down the winding road, pulling off. She turns to him. "The sun is setting faster than I thought. We'd better get the tent up while we have some light."

He unloads the gear, and they rush through the trees toward the sound of the water. She steps into the clearing, clapping her hands. "This is it! It's perfect." He sets up the tent quickly with practiced precision, giving her instructions as they work together. He double checks all the corners to be sure it's secure. They race back to the Jeep and grab their bags, locking it up for the night. She giggles as they race back to the tent, climb inside, and zip up the tent flap to keep the bugs out. She shivers with excitement, giggling. "I feel like a kid again."

He laughs. "Keep moving. We're not done. Get your sleeping bag out and lay it down. I'll get mine."

She makes short work of her task. She digs out a jacket and throws it on. She grabs another pair of sweats and throws those on, along with a heavy pair of socks. She jumps inside her sleeping bag, pulls it up around her, and lays her head on the pillow. "I'm ready for bed."

He laughs at the sight of her burrowed in up to her chin. "Not hungry?"

"Not hungry enough to crawl out of my warm nest. Our café food will last me 'til morning."

He climbs into his sleeping bag in his clothes. She looks over at him. "Aren't you cold? You don't want to wear your coat and heavy pants?"

He chuckles, sending shivers through her. "I'm hot blooded. I think I'll be alright."

She shrugs her shoulders and gives a little shiver. "Okay." She picks up her phone, texting.

"Bernie?" Joshua teases her.

She sets it down. "No. I'm telling my kids goodnight. They can't believe I'm camping."

He glances at his watch. "It's a little early to be calling it a night."

She turns over, trying to get comfortable. "I'll be up early, so I'm going to bed early. I enjoy my sleep. Goodnight, Joshua."

He reaches out to her, snagging a finger or two. "Goodnight, Maggie."

thirty

Ali and Alex get the decorations up. He helps her prepare the hotdogs an hour before supper time. He shows her how to wrap them and put them in the roaster to keep them warm. Next, they get out the turkey sandwich fixings. She laughs out loud when Mason swaggers in, wearing his signature apron and a striped conductor hat. He pulls another from his apron pocket and hands it to Alex, who promptly tugs it on his head.

The usual Wednesday night crowd shows up, along with Isaac, who steps in to get the movie projector running. Ali turns to Alex. "I think we did quite well with arranging the tables so everyone could view the movie."

He nods in agreement. Minutes before start time, Conner, Parker, Manuel, and Manuel's little sister walk in, startling Ali, who grins at the four of them. "Hey! Did you come to watch the movie?"

Conner wrinkles his nose. "Not exactly. We came to serve."

She claps her hands. "Even better."

Manuel looks Ali up and down and glances back at Parker. "That's your sister? Miss hot pants?"

She clears her throat, embarrassed. "I was *going* to Vegas."

Manuel throws up his hands, grinning. "*I'm* not complaining. I'm Manuel."

He sticks out his hand. Ali shakes it, looking over at Parker. "I figured."

Manuel grins at Parker before turning back to Ali. "Nice to meet you."

Talia waddles out of the office. "Manny? I thought I heard you out here."

He gives her a nod. "Oh, hey, Talia."

Talia gives him an ornery grin. "What're you doing here?"

He shrugs. "I'm helping out."

Talia puts a hand on her hip and gives him a look, razzing him. "Since when do you help out?"

Manuel frowns at her for calling him out. "Since now."

Ali steps between them, looking at the four teenagers. "I'm sure you know the drill. Start with the drink orders and then we get the food orders. It's pretty straightforward. There are two food choices, and if you look, I've numbered the tables to minimize the confusion."

Conner looks over at Alex. "Couldn't you have chosen a movie like Lethal Weapon or something?"

Alex shakes his head. "Nope. Dr. Zhivago's a classic."

Conner gives him a look of disbelief. "If you say so."

Ali catches Parker and takes her off to the side. "Did you see Jason today?"

Parker shakes her head. "No. But I wasn't really looking for him. Why?"

"No reason. He was in here earlier, but I haven't seen him in a while. That's all."

Parker nods. "Alright. Well. I guess I'll get to work."

Alex looks at Mason and Ali. "Come on, kitchen crew. Let's get to it."

Time flies as they fill the orders, and Ali relaxes a little as she watches the four teens dash around delivering the orders. When all the tables have been set, she sits down at the small table behind the counter, takes a bite of her turkey sandwich, and relaxes. She whispers to Alex, sitting next to her. "This is nice."

A little while later, the four teens sneak off to the back office with Talia, and soon they're all laughing. Ali gets up and sneaks a peek around the corner. Her heart lifts as she sees them playing cards. Talia catches her eye. "Ali."

Ali says nothing, giving a little wave before heading back to the kitchen, plopping down in the chair once more. She looks over at Alex. "Where's Mason?"

"Oh, he left. He was headed back to Isaac's. They're working on some new sushi recipe tonight."

She watches the movie as she eats more of her sandwich. She looks over at Alex, who's staring at the screen. She leans in, whispering. "What's your favorite part of this movie, anyway?"

He smiles back at her. "The End."

She laughs out loud, and a few diners turn around to look at her. She quiets down, whispering again. "Why did you make me watch it, then?"

He gives her a deadpan look. "It's a classic." He answers in a dry tone.

She looks down at the table as she chews another bite, contemplating. "You just wait, Alex. I get the next movie choice, and I'm going to get you good."

His eyes light up, but his mouth has no smile. He's all serious. "You promise?"

His intensity gets to her, and she has to look away.

She finishes her supper, and Alex gets up, taking their

dishes to the sink. He returns to sit beside her, taking her hand and intertwining their fingers. He scoots his chair over until they're sitting hip to hip. She turns to him, feeling uncertain, but he gives her a reassuring smile. "Let's just be, Ali. How about that?"

She turns back to watch the old movie on the wall, leans her head on his shoulder, and she can't help but notice how much he feels like home.

thirty-one

M aggie wakes in the night, startled to hear noises outside the tent. She glances at her phone. It's 1:00 a.m. She tosses and turns, trying to get back to sleep, but she's too afraid of what's possibly outside; and she's freezing. After lying awake for half an hour, she crawls out of her sleeping bag and tries to sneak in with Joshua. She's halfway in and halfway out when he gives her backside a squeeze.

"What you doin', Mags?"

She shrugs out of her coat before fitting the rest of herself into his nest, curling up against him. "Shhh. Something's outside. I got scared and I'm cold."

He chuckles and wraps an arm around her. "I'll keep you safe and warm."

She reaches over and grabs her pillow, putting it beneath her head. She settles into him and closes her eyes, listening to the rhythmic sounds of his breathing, feeling relaxed and cozy.

Four hours later, her alarm goes off, and she wakes with a start. She turns over, grabbing her phone to hit the snooze button. He automatically follows her, keeping his arm around her waist. She feels a nuzzling on the back of her neck. "Brr. Your nose is cold!" she whines.

"Good morning, Mags. I don't know if I want that balloon ride now. Let's just stay here all day," he growls.

She sighs contentedly. "As tempting as that sounds, I've been looking forward to it since yesterday. We'd better get moving."

He holds her tighter. "Five more minutes, please."

She lays her head on his upper arm. "Five minutes." A few minutes go by and she reaches out, grabbing the granola bar box. She grabs one and opens it, taking a crunchy bite.

He tickles her belly, and she coughs and laughs, almost spitting granola everywhere. "What are you doing?"

"You woke me up with your loud eating." He reaches over, taking her breakfast and biting it before he hands it back.

She wrinkles her nose. "That one's yours now." She grabs another one from the box, opening it. She grabs a bottle of water, taking a swig. She grabs a second bottle, handing it to Joshua, who sits up in his sleeping bag.

He winks at her. "What do you think you heard last night outside the tent?"

She swats his knee through the sleeping bag. "I have no idea. Something was rummaging. I'm not used to hearing nature sounds."

He scoots out of the sleeping bag, unzipping the front of the tent flap so they can see out the screen. He pats the space beside him. "Come over here and watch the river with me."

She moves her sleeping bag over beside him, climbing back into it as best she can, throwing on her coat. They sit together in silence, eating their breakfast bars and drinking their water, enjoying nature.

He hops up. "I guess we'd better get going if we're going

to pack this up and find a bathroom before going up in the balloon."

She scoots out of her sleeping bag, rolling it up. She packs up the bags quickly, hurrying to get them in the Jeep. They take the tent down. "Do we need to take lunch for the balloon ride?"

He shakes his head. "Nope. They provide a whole picnic basket. Wine and cheese and everything - pretty fancy."

She grins. "Awesome. Sounds perfect."

Joshua's quiet on the drive, and she notices the air feels different, but she doesn't say anything. They park the Jeep and run in to use the restroom and freshen up. She takes her shower caddy to wash her face and brush her teeth. She gives her hair a quick brush through, before putting it up in a messy bun.

He meets her in the office. "Are you ready?"

She nods. "Ready as I'll ever be."

A man steps up to greet them. "I'm C.J. I'll be your guide today. We'll be taking the hot-air balloon tour that follows the river. You'll see a few waterfalls. Because you have two time slots, we can take the scenic route."

They follow him out to his Outback and Maggie climbs in the backseat while Joshua rides up front with C.J. It isn't long and they're at the site. C.J. turns to them, smiling. "Since you're the first customer of the day, you get the whole experience. Follow me over to the basket where it lies on its side." They walk across the grass, approaching the resting balloon. "First, we fill it with cold air." He turns on a fan, and the balloon fills surprisingly fast. "Next we turn on the heat." He flips the levers and two flames shoot straight up, and slowly the balloon shifts to an upright position.

C.J. climbs in the basket, and Joshua follows close behind. C.J. turns to Maggie, who's still on the ground. "If you could just grab that picnic basket of food, please." She picks it up, handing it to Joshua. He takes her hand, tugging her over the side. She's nervous with excitement. C.J. turns to them with a smile. "Now we just wait to see where the wind takes us."

It isn't long and they're in the air, soaring over the natural beauty of the state park, crossing over the bridge before drifting downward to follow the river below interspersed with miniature waterfalls as it winds between the bluffs. She marvels at the fog resting above the waters. "It's all so beautiful! Isn't creation mystical?"

C.J. nods soberly before answering. "Yes, Maggie. I never tire of the beauty of nature. I've taken numerous rides in my trusty balloon, and each time, I see a whole new picture. There's just something unique about connecting with nature from above. I feel removed at such a great height, yet the touch of the breeze on my face and the sounds of the river or a bird's cry keep it up close and personal."

They continue on, following the path of the river. Joshua stands near the edge, and there's a nervous energy about him. Maggie catches him watching her, and she gives him a smile, as she lays a hand on his forearm. "Are you alright? You look a little nervous." He nods silently, but the intense look on his face has her feeling apprehensive. He coughs before stumbling around as he goes to his knee. Her eyes get big and she touches his shoulder. She's worried he's not feeling well.

"Joshua, are you okay?" Maggie isn't sure what to do, so she turns to C.J. "Do you have a first aid kit? Do people get altitude sickness on these rides?"

C.J. chuckles as he looks past her, watching Joshua. "I think he's going to be alright."

She turns back around and Joshua's holding out a ring. "Maggie Louise Post, will you marry me?"

She looks down at the ring. "That's your mother's ring." Her eyes begin to water.

He nods. "I found it in Natalie's room. I can't help but

think she would have wanted you to have it." He waits a few seconds, clearing his throat, locking eyes with her. "Will you marry me?"

Her heart soars, and she can hardly believe her answer. "Yes. Yes, I'll marry you."

He slips the ring on her finger. He grabs a hold of the basket, getting to his feet. C.J. turns to look the other way as Joshua and Maggie share a long celebratory kiss. Joshua leans back, smiling at Maggie. "I was so nervous. I've never done that before."

She laughs, wipes a few tears away, and holds out her hand to look at the ring again. "It was perfect. I love it."

He takes her trembling hand in his. "We could get married here and now if you wanted. C. J. is ordained."

Her eyes light up. "Really?"

He grins. "Really."

C.J. interjects. "You just need two witnesses, but that can be done over Facetime."

She stands there a few seconds, thinking. She grabs his arm. "Let's do it." She turns to face him. "If you're sure?"

He nods. "Maggie, I think I've been waiting half my life to marry you. I'm more than sure."

She gets out her phone. "Shall I Facetime, Ali?"

He nods again. "That's a great idea."

C.J. pulls a book from the basket, opening it up. Maggie holds out her cell phone, watching the screen, surprised to see Ali cuddled up to Alex as they move along. "Hey, Mom, we're just walking to the café."

Maggie giggles into the phone. "Hey, Ali! Joshua and I are getting married, and we'd like you to be our witnesses. What do you say?"

Ali stops in her tracks. "When is this happening?"

Joshua leans into the picture. "Hi, Ali. It's happening now."

Alex leans into Ali's phone. "Hi, Joshua. I'm Alex. It's nice to meet you. Maggie?" Maggie's face takes over the screen, and Alex breathes a sigh of relief at her smiling face. "You're sure about this, Maggie?" Alex questions.

Maggie beams into the phone. "I've never been surer. He's coming back with me."

Alex moves back as Ali nudges her way back in, taking in the sky as Maggie holds the phone out. "Where are you?"

Maggie turns away from facing Joshua to face the phone. "I'm on a hot-air balloon ride over a state park in New York. It's gorgeous." She looks back at Joshua. "Let's get married." He nods his head. Maggie turns back to the phone. "Will you be our witnesses?"

Ali has serious doubts about such a rash decision, but she's not about to steal any of her mother's happiness. "Yes."

Ali grabs Alex's arm as he leans farther away, shaking his head. She yanks back him into the picture, stepping on his foot until he answers. "Sure."

C.J. opens his book once more. "We gather here today in the sight of God and man to join these two in holy matrimony. I'd like to begin this ceremony by reading a few verses, if I may?" Maggie gives him a smile and a nod. "1 Corinthians 13:13 And now these three remain: faith, hope, and love. But the greatest of these is love." He pauses. "What is love and what does it look like? I will now read from 1 Corinthians 13:4: Love is patient and kind; love does not envy or boast; it is not arrogant or rude. It does not insist on its own way; it is not irritable or resentful; it does not rejoice at wrongdoing but rejoices with the truth. Love bears all things, believes all things, hopes all things, endures all things."

C.J. pauses before turning to Maggie. "Maggie Louise Post, do you take Joshua Charles Porter to be your lawfully wedded husband?"

Maggie looks into Joshua's eyes. "I do."

C.J. continues. "Do you promise to love him for better for worse, for richer, for poorer, in sickness and in health? Do you promise to love, honor, and obey him until death do you part?"

Maggie squeezes Joshua's hand. "I do."

C.J. asks the same of Joshua, getting the same response.

C.J. smiles at the two of them. "I'll leave you with a favorite quote of my beautiful wife of thirty years. You don't marry someone you can live with—you marry someone you can't live without. By the power vested in me by the state of New York, I now pronounce you husband and wife." He turns to Joshua. "You may now kiss the bride."

Maggie holds the phone out shakily as Joshua kisses her again. They turn back to Facetime. "We did it!" Maggie's smiling face fills up Ali's screen once more. "I love you, Ali. I'll see you soon."

Ali grins back at her mom. "I love you too, Mom."

The call ends. Maggie turns to Joshua, feeling all shy. "Hello, husband."

Joshua beams back at her. "Hello, Mrs. Maggie Porter." He puts an arm around her waist as they stand at the basket's edge, looking out at a perfect blue sky.

Maggie leans into him. "I don't think I've seen a more beautiful morning."

Joshua gives his wife a squeeze. "Yep. Something tells me today is full of promise."

thirty-two

Ali hangs up the phone, shocked. She unlocks the café door in a daze, stepping back to let Bernie in. She's on autopilot as she starts his tea and prepares his oatmeal for him. Alex remains quiet as he studies Ali's demeanor. "I cannot believe my mother got married."

Bernie slaps the counter. "It's about darn time! Who'd she marry?"

She looks up at him, surprised by his response. "She married her old high school crush."

Bernie nods his head. "Good, good. At least we know he's not a complete stranger or some kook she met online." He shakes his spoon for emphasis as he continues. "Never trust a person you can't look in the eye. That's the only way to judge their character."

Alex chuckles. "Don't you worry, Bernie. Maggie's coming back soon. We'll all get to meet him."

Ali shakes her head. "I just can't believe it. How *well* can you know someone after just a week? Not even that? She's been there four days! And she's married! That's just crazy."

Alex follows her around, hovering, putting things back in

the fridge as she takes them out mindlessly. He puts a hand on hers when she puts the gallon of milk in the dish cupboard, shutting the door. "Ali. You just put the milk in the cupboard."

"What? Oh." She opens the cupboard back up, grabbing the milk to put it back in the fridge. "I guess I'm distracted."

He takes her by the elbow and leads her to a kitchen chair. "Sit down. I'll make you some coffee." She nods silently, sitting in a chair, before jumping back up.

"I need to make breakfast. I haven't even looked at the menu yet."

He whips around, pointing with his finger, while speaking sternly. "Sit down. I've got this. It's coffee cake. I know the recipe in my sleep. I wouldn't trust you to separate salt and sugar right now."

She plops back down, resting her chin on her hand. "You're probably right about that." She holds her head in her hands. "How am I supposed to tell Conner and Parker about the wedding?"

Talia waddles out. "You two getting married? I knew it!"

Her heart skips a beat at Talia's statement. "Not exactly. My *mom* got married."

Talia claps her hands. "Way to go, Maggie. Who'd she marry?"

She stares back at Talia like she's lost her mind. "Her high school crush."

Talia puts her hand on her chest. "For reals? That is so cool. I love stories like that. Did you see the pictures yet? Are they on Facebook?"

Ali gives her a look. "No. I haven't even told Conner and Parker yet. It literally just happened. Alex and I were Face-time witnesses."

Talia smiles huge again. "I can't wait to meet him." She waddles back to the office.

Ali turns to Alex. "You and me? That would have been *some* rumor. I'm glad we got that straightened out."

Bernie chuckles, looking down at his oatmeal. "The week ain't over yet, little missy."

She blushes as she studies her hands, calling out to Alex's retrieving back as he heads to the back room. "Tell me what to do, boss. I want to help you."

"First set the oven to 375, and then you can start taking down the chairs," he calls out in answer.

She gets moving, happy for something to do as her mind runs in circles. She freezes as she takes the last chair down, looking uncertainly at Alex. He catches her eye. "Go home and talk to Conner and Parker, Ali. I've got it until you get back."

She puts her hand together like a prayer. "Thank you, Alex."

She runs back to the house in her mom's prairie skirt and flowy blouse, catching Conner and Parker backing out of the driveway. She runs up to the car, waving frantically. Parker rolls down her window. "What's up?"

She leans on the windowsill, breathing hard. "Just a sec. I need to catch my breath."

She stands up with her hands behind her neck, elbows out. She looks over at Conner, feeling bad. "I've got some news. It's not bad news, but it's different."

Parker glances at Ali's left hand. "What is it?"

"Well. There's no easy way to say this, so I'll just say it. Mom got married."

Parker shuts the car off. "What?"

"You know she went to New York to sort through Natalie's things and help her brother, Joshua, with everything since he lost his sister."

Parker nods her head. "Yeah."

"Guess they hit it off, and this morning Mom got married in a hot-air balloon over a state park in New York."

Conner shakes his head. "No way. Mom would never do that. That's just...that's like really out there."

Ali smiles, biting her lip. "I don't know. It's kind of romantic."

Conner grunts. "Ewww. Don't talk about Mom being romantic." A look of panic crosses his face. "She's coming back, right?"

Parker smacks his chest. "Of course she's coming back, *moron*. What kind of question is that? Dad's the *idiot* who left us. Mom would never do that."

Conner studies his hands in his lap. "I never thought Mom would marry some guy she knew for like three days."

Ali looks down, muttering more to herself. "Yeah, that'd be crazy."

Parker studies her, grinning again. "Who are you thinking about, Ali?"

Ali's head snaps up. "What? Nobody. I mean Mom."

Parker laughs. "Well, I guess we'll meet Joshua when they get back. We'd better get to school."

Conner looks at Parker. "Don't forget to pick up Manuel and his sister."

Parker elbows him, grinning. "Conner, are you worried I'll forget them?"

Ali shakes her head. "See you two later. I'd better get back to the café."

She turns around, heading back. Jason jogs up out of nowhere, startling her. "Hey, Ali."

Ali moves away from him, still walking forward. "Jason. I thought you left town."

"Nope. I just found a different place to stay. That apartment's not big enough for Alex and me."

She keeps walking. "Thought you didn't have any spare cash."

He frowns. "I had a little for emergencies."

She rolls her eyes. "Whatever."

He turns to her. "Is everything alright? Why'd you leave the café?"

She glances over at him. "Everything's fine. Thanks for your concern."

He's irritated at her short answer. "When's your mom coming back?"

She answers him, feeling all sorts of ornery, and a little bit lonely, but she shoves that thought away. "I don't know. She might go on a honeymoon. She just got married."

He stops. "Married! To whom? She wasn't even engaged."

She looks at him again. "Her old high school crush."

His face is almost comical. "But they haven't seen each other in years."

She stares him down, daring him to elaborate. He doesn't. "I guess when you know, you know, Jason. I've got to get to work. Goodbye," she says before marching through the café door to find Alex.

thirty-three

Ali steps back inside the café, shocked at the number of people dining. She rushes to Alex's side to help out.

"Hey, Ali. I'm so glad you're back. I was doing alright, but it sure picked up. We won't have any coffee cake left over for the bakery dessert."

She nudges him. "It's that good, huh?"

He winks. "Maybe so. I've got droves of people piling in the door. I'm sure it's got nothing to do with your mom getting married this morning."

Her mouth forms an O. "How did the word get out that fast?"

He holds up his phone. "Your mom tweeted it, and then put out an Instagram picture, which Parker then found and shared on the community website. Hence, it's all over town."

She shakes her head. "Who needs a town grapevine when you have Twitter and Instagram." She stands up with her hand on her hip, grinning. "My mom has twice the social life I have - in person and on social media."

He raises his eyebrows before looking out at the café crowd. "It's good for business, anyways."

She claps her hands. "That gives me an idea."

He takes a deep breath. "Do I dare ask?"

She smiles, nodding. "It'll take some doing and some decorating and a real team effort, but I think we can pull it off before Mom comes back home."

He moves between the tables, picking up the breakfast dishes. "You do realize tomorrow night's the Town Valentine's Day dinner, and we'll be decorating for that, and the next night we're chaperoning a high school dance." He pauses. "Of course, in between, we're serving breakfast, lunch, and dinner here."

She nods her head. "I haven't forgotten." She winks at him. "Don't you worry, I've got a few tricks up my sleeve."

He turns to face her. "Don't you always?"

She smiles. "Did you know that Isabel from Bella's Boutique is an excellent online personal shopper? She knows where all the good bargains are, and which companies deliver the fastest. She's getting me the best bang for my buck."

He laughs out loud. "Bang for your buck? Sounds like you've been talking to Bernie. That expression is older than the hills."

She acts all offended, but her heart warms at the thought of Bernie rubbing off on her. "Whatever, Alex. I'll be ready for Valentine's Day dinner. It's going to be a night to remember."

He holds up the lunch special. "In the meantime, I bet we have a small crowd this afternoon. It's fried spam and split pea soup day."

She wrinkles her nose at the thought. "You can't be serious."

He grins bigger, nodding. "Serious as a heart attack. Maggie insists on having a Minnesota lunch once a month, and this is what she makes. Every time. The one good thing is the crowd is small."

She makes a face. "Isn't split pea soup like the consistency of baby vomit?"

He wrinkles his nose. "Thanks for that imagery, but yes, pretty much."

She makes another face. "And isn't spam like twice as salty and slimy as bologna?"

He laughs out loud. "Again, thanks for the imagery, but yes, pretty much. However, if you pan-fry it, it takes a little of the disgustingness away from it."

She shakes her head. "I'll take your word for it. It all sounds perfectly awful."

He nods his head. "Oh, it is. Bernie won't even touch it, and he only has half his tastebuds left. He told me he wasn't wasting any of them on something that looks and smells like the front and back end of a Texas armadillo. I'm inclined to believe him."

She giggles. "Good ole' Bernie." She slaps the countertop. "Alright. What's the recipe for split pea soup? Hopefully, it's not something that cooks half the morning and stinks up my kitchen."

He laughs. "Give me a few minutes, and I'll find the recipe, but I'm afraid you're spot on." He opens a drawer, pulling out a recipe book.

She leans on the counter, tapping her fingers. "Do we at least have a decent dessert to go with this atrocious meal?"

He shakes his head. "Not really."

She cocks her head to the side, thinking. "How about a sweet roll with a touch of cayenne to give it some flavor? And we could slap a slice of Swiss cheese on top. You can never go wrong with bread and cheese."

He gives an approving nod. "I like the way you think. I never tire of the smell of baking bread. It's the best."

She scribbles a few things on a piece of paper before

running toward the front door. "I've got to get these groceries before I lose any more time."

He glances at his watch. "You'd better hustle. If you're not back here in thirty minutes, you'll never get that soup done in time. I'll get the water boiling in the Dutch ovens for you."

She grabs the paper and runs out the door.

thirty-four

Maggie and Joshua's hot-air balloon ride comes to an end as they touch down. C.J. climbs out and then gives them a hand. "Just let me call my wife, Audrey, and she'll be down soon to pick you two up."

She smiles at the kind, elderly man. "Thank you, C.J. I enjoyed the ride so much. It was so beautiful and peaceful. I can't think of a better way to view nature."

C.J. chuckles. "It's a lovely way to greet the day."

Joshua takes Maggie's hand. "We'd better head up to the road so we'll be ready when she gets here." They turn and start their walk up the steep incline. About the time they reach the top, an old VW van pulls up, honking. It pulls off on the shoulder, and a lady waves wildly. "Hi, I'm Audrey."

Maggie waves back. "I'm Maggie and this is Joshua."

Joshua beams. "We just got married."

Audrey smiles a warm smile. "Congratulations!"

Maggie blushes. "Thank you."

"I hear you need a ride back to your car," Audrey offers.

"Yes, please," they answer in unison.

"Well, hop in." They do, and she starts up the road. "If you feel like a little hike, I can drop you off a few miles away. There's some gorgeous hiking trails."

Maggie turns to Joshua. "I could stretch my legs a bit."

He nods. "Sounds good, Audrey. Wherever you think."

She glances down. "I see you wore hiking shoes, so I'd say you're prepared." She looks at Maggie in the rearview mirror. "I have a cooler back there on the floor full of water. Feel free to grab a couple. You don't want to be without water no matter how long or short the hike."

Maggie reaches in and grabs two waters. "Thanks."

Audrey looks at Maggie. "So, what's your story?"

Maggie takes a breath. "Well, Joshua's sister was my best friend all through grade school and high school, and he was her older brother."

Audrey nods. "Ahh. So you had a crush on him, but you were shy."

Maggie nods, smiling. "Pretty much. And he had a lot of girlfriends."

He clears his throat. "I kind of liked her too, but she was my little sister's best friend, and you know how that goes. Besides, she was a freshman, and I was a senior, and I was pretty sure our parents wouldn't go for us dating."

Audrey looks over at him. "Why didn't you ask her out after high school?"

He sits back in his chair. "She got married at twenty, so I didn't have much time to try."

Maggie looks at Audrey in the mirror again. "I got married, had three wonderful children, and then my husband had a midlife crisis and he left. So, then it was just me and my kids. It was an adjustment, but we figured things out."

He looks back at Maggie. "When my sister passed unexpectedly, Maggie came up to help me sort through everything. We got together four days ago, and it felt the same between us; for me anyway, and so I proposed today, and she said yes, and then we got married on the balloon ride."

Maggie reaches up, taking his hand. "Of course, we'll get married again at the courthouse when we get back to my hometown, to be sure everything's legal, but our married life starts today."

Audrey smiles. "That's quite a story. I just love happy endings."

Maggie smiles back at her. "Me, too."

Audrey pulls the van over. "Well, here we are. It's about a 3-mile hike back. If you head up those stairs there, and follow the trail, it'll take you by a gorgeous waterfall and some unique rock formations. You'll see lots of plant life and maybe a few lizards here and there. It's a nice jaunt."

The two of them hop out and wave goodbye to Audrey. "Thanks for the ride."

Audrey waves back at them. "Thank you for choosing our business."

They start their hike. They hold hands as they walk along. Joshua chuckles. "What's so funny?" she asks.

He shakes his head. "I would've been fine with heading straight back to our tent to celebrate our marriage."

She blushes under his heated gaze. "There'll be plenty of time for that tonight."

He laughs out loud. "Are we tent camping on our first night of marriage?"

She raises an eyebrow. "I'm up for a little skinny dippin' in the river if you are."

He grins. "You're crazy, Maggie Louise, but I'll take you up on the offer. It might feel more like a polar plunge. It's February in New York."

She giggles at the thought. "I think I'll be alright. I

happen to have a hot-blooded husband who keeps me warm."

He pulls her close, kissing her long and deep. "I'll heat you right up."

She takes a shaky step forward. "Come on, Romeo, we've got a long hike ahead of us."

thirty-five

Ali's back in twenty-five minutes, feeling quite proud of herself, until she reads the entire recipe. "Alex. Where in the world would I buy a ham bone?"

He laughs out loud. "You can't. Get those peas in the boiling water. I'll dig out a ham bone or two from the freezer. Your mom keeps them there."

She wrinkles her nose. "Weird."

He rushes to the stove, peering into the Dutch ovens. "You're timing them, right? You're only supposed to boil the peas for two minutes. Then they sit for an hour."

She lays a hand on his chest. "Chillax. I read the recipe. I know what I'm doing." A minute later, she turns the flame off, leaving the Dutch ovens to sit while she puts lids on them. "I'll cut the onion, celery, and carrots while I'm waiting." She cuts the onion, and soon she's wiping her eyes. She steps away, blinking. "I need a break, Onions make my eyes red."

He comes over, takes the knife from her hand, giving her two cold washcloths. "Sit down and put these on your eyes."

She does what he orders. "I'll be fine. It looks worse than

it feels. For some reason, onions do more than just burn my eyes." The chopping sound stops and he swoops down on her face that's tilted back, kissing her softly. She whips a washcloth off her eye. "What are you doing?"

He smiles down at her. "Enjoying a perfect pair of lips."

She reaches for his face, pulling him back in. They part as they hear a throat clearing. "Am I interrupting something?"

She blushes as she hears Jason's voice. She uncovers both her eyes. "Jason."

He crosses his arms on his chest. "I came by to let you know I'm leaving town. I guess I'll hear from you when you return."

Alex grunts. "Not if I..."

She cuts him off. "I'll walk you out."

Alex frowns at Ali as she gets up, following a gloating Jason outside.

Jason steps into the alley, waiting for Ali, who stays on the sidewalk at the corner of the building. He studies her for a few seconds. "I messed things up for good, didn't I?"

She rocks back on her heel. "I don't know, maybe."

Jason watches her carefully. "Do you think he's the one?"

Her face turns red. "I can't answer that."

Jason looks down at the ground, his shoulders slumping. "Is there any point in me waiting for you?"

She shakes her head softly back and forth. "Probably not."

He looks up at her again. "Can I get one last kiss?"

She gives him a look. "No."

He leans back on the wall. "So, I guess this really is goodbye then."

She nods her head. "Yes." She steps closer to him, talking quietly. "Jason. I would have married you. I thought we were meant to be, but now I know we weren't."

He makes a face. "What do you mean?"

She smiles. "We were good together, but we weren't great. I really believe there's someone out there for you. Someone who would keep you from going off to Europe without her—someone you don't want to be without, but it's not me."

He frowns. "You're mad at me for not taking you to Europe?"

She laughs. "No. I was never mad about you not taking me. I was hurt that you chose to leave me behind and not come back. Did it even occur to you to ask me if I wanted to join you in Europe, instead of ending things?"

He leans on the wall again. "You never would have left your family behind for me."

She shrugs her shoulders. "Probably not, but you didn't even ask me. You just assumed."

He looks belligerent. "Yeah, but I was right. You wouldn't have left them behind for me."

She stares back at him. "It could also be argued that if you knew me as well as you say you did; you'd never ask me to choose. You know how I feel about family."

He throws up his hands in exasperation. "So basically, you're mad at me about a hypothetical discussion we didn't have that would have ended up with you denying me a request that you would have refused to consider, even though apparently it's grounds for breaking up in the real world."

She nods her head decisively. "Yep. I am, after all, a woman. And you, very clearly, are a man."

He rolls his eyes at her. "Thank, God." He walks past her, barely holding in his contempt. "Goodbye, Ali."

She nods her head. "Yep."

thirty-six

Maggie and Joshua hike along in a comfortable silence, stopping here and there to take pictures of the scenery. She sits down on the rocks beside the waterfall, relaxing as she listens to the roar of the water. He plops down beside her. "I'm sorry I didn't try harder to date you in high school."

She laughs out loud. "Do you know what kind of fit Natalie would have thrown? I never would have lived that down."

He grins. "You're probably right."

Her hands fly to her face. "My dad would have marched you right back out our front door. I swear, he never had one good word to say about you."

He looks surprised. "Your dad didn't like me?"

She shakes her head back and forth. "Nope. I wasn't the only one who noticed how many girls went in and out your front door."

He looks down at the ground. "I had no idea you two were keeping score."

She takes his hand. "I'm sorry. I shouldn't give you such a

hard time." She winks at him. "Besides, my mom once told me my father was quite the lady's man in his younger days."

He guffaws. "Your father? Stuffed-shirt James Parker? Popular with the ladies? I'm sorry, I just can't see it."

She slugs his shoulder. "If we ever have children, I'm sure they'll say the same about their father. You'll probably be such a pushover."

His face turns serious. "Would you consider more children? I mean, yours are practically grown."

She blushes. "I don't know. I used to dream about what your kids would look like."

He scoots closer, hugs her tight, and growls in her ear. "We could start trying tonight."

She leans in, kissing him. "That sounds like a good way to warm up."

He stands up, grabbing her hand. "Come on, Mrs. Porter. Let's get you back to the tent."

She grins to herself as they walk along hand in hand down the trail, picking up their pace.

They work up a sweat hiking uphill, and she's relieved to see their car in the parking lot in the distance. "Finally. I can take a break and grab a granola bar."

He has other things on his mind. "Shall we tent where we were before? It was nice and quiet."

She nods her head in approval. "Sounds like a good plan to me." She follows him to the car, grabbing another water bottle and chugging it down. "I'm ready to lie down for a bit."

He puts the car in reverse, and they head back toward the forest. "It shouldn't take us long to get this tent up, Mags." He glances over at her. "Are you sure you don't want a hotel to sleep in for your first night of married life?"

She turns to him, grinning. "I'm sure. This has been a

grand adventure so far, and I can't wait to see what happens next."

He takes her hand. "Something I've been waiting years to do."

She squeezes his pinkie. "Keep talking, Don Juan."

He frowns. "You're never going to let me live down the reputation you think I have, are you?"

She sticks out her tongue. "Nope." She pokes his hand. "You're just lucky you're a guy. You know what they'd call you if you were a woman."

He throws up his hands. "I surrender, Maggie Louise Porter. Don't go all women's lib on me. You can't blame other men's opinions on me."

She leans back, laughing. "You're right, but be fore-warned, I've got a very opinionated, at times overly sensitive, daughter. Some might say she's feminist, but I say asking for equality across the board isn't feminism, it's what's fair."

He smiles over at her. "Gee, I wonder where she got her opinions from."

She smiles. "Hey. I call 'em how I see 'em."

He nods. "That's good enough for me."

He whips the car into the space, making short work of throwing up the tent. He grabs a sleeping bag under one arm and Maggie with the other, giving her a squeeze. "Come on, Mags, let's break in my sleeping bag."

She giggles. "What about the rest of our stuff?"

He nudges her inside, drops the sleeping bag and tugs at her shirt. "It can wait."

She jumps a foot. "Your hands are cold!"

His hands go higher. "Give 'em a second and they'll warm up."

He steps in, burying his face in her neck, kissing her skin. "Let the baby-making begin."

She shivers as she giggles, teasing him. "You're so romantic."

He lifts his head, nipping her lip. "You have no idea. I'm hotter than a habanero."

She giggles even harder, until he silences her with a breath-taking kiss, not letting up until she surrenders. "Lay down with me."

After, she lies beside him, staring out the front of the tent, and a tear escapes her.

He catches her wiping her eye. "Are you okay?"

She nods. "Yes. I'm just happy, but I'm also sad. If we have a child or children, Natalie will never get to meet them, well, at least not here, and they'll never get to know her. She would have loved to know your children."

He chuckles. "Yeah, she definitely could have taught them a trick or two. She was ornery."

She smiles at the memory. "Yeah, she was. I never got bored when I was with Natalie. She didn't allow it."

She starts to get out of the sleeping bag, and he wraps an arm around her. "What are you doing?"

She shrugs. "I'm getting dressed."

He pulls her close. "What's the rush? It's just us. We've got all day to be nowhere."

She curls up next to him, loving his warmth. "I guess you're right."

He covers her hand on his chest with his, kissing the tip of her nose. "I love you Maggie Louise Porter."

She gives him a peck on the lips. "I love you too, husband."

thirty-seven

Ali walks back inside, sits back in the chair, applies the washrags on again, as the smell of onion in the air still stings. "Well, that's that I guess."

He fails to hide his smile. "Oh?'

She lifts the corner of the washcloth to peek at him. "You don't look too sad that he's leaving."

He takes a bite of celery, crunching. "I'm not."

She kicks out with her foot, making contact with the back of Alex's leg. "Be nice."

He chuckles. "I'm just happy he screwed up. I'd hate to have to steal you away."

Her eyebrows shoot up. "But you would?"

He steps up next to her. "Haven't you seen *The Notebook*, the story all the girls drool over? Engaged isn't married."

She doesn't know why she's arguing, but she can't hold her tongue. "It's not married, but it's a serious relationship."

He thinks it over before answering. "I suppose, but if the guy couldn't make up his mind after six months, I think that's more than enough time to know if you were the one. I think I'm with Talia on this one—he didn't want to commit."

She hides beneath her washcloths once more. "I suppose. I don't know why he wanted to wait so long, but I agreed with him, so it's not entirely one-sided."

Alex trails a finger down her arm, giving her the shivers. "I still say if you meet the right person, you won't wait six months, six weeks, or even six days to let her know how you feel. You'll just come right out and say it."

She swallows hard. "Six days? That's nuts. How can you know what you need to know in six days? It's not possible."

He shuffles back to the stove, checking the split pea soup. "I don't know, Ali. I think you'd be surprised. There's still plenty of people who believe in love at first sight."

She laughs sarcastically. "Yeah, and they're probably the same people who believe in I'll love you with all my heart until the next one comes along."

He snorts. "Man. Someone's cynical."

She held her arms. "All I'm saying is some people just like to fall in love. They value the feeling of meeting someone new and having all the butterfly feelings, more than they value commitment."

He frowns over at her. "Not everyone is like your dad."

She props one ankle on her opposite knee. "I know, but it's hard. My mom was the perfect wife and the perfect mother. She was kind. She was generous. She was supportive. She built her whole life around our family and look what she got for it."

He answers, speaking softly. "I know; he still left. But do you think your mom has any regrets about her life?"

She removes the washcloths, looking up at him. "No. Honestly, I don't."

He smiles. "You're right. She doesn't. Your mom has every right to be bitter and ugly, but she's neither of those things. She chooses to be happy. She still chooses to see the best in everyone. She chooses to love life and the people she's around."

She throws a wet washrag at him. "Alright, you've made your point, Dr. Phil."

He laughs out loud. "I'm hardly Dr. Phil, but I'm just sayin'."

She makes a face. "What, Alex. What are you saying?"

He studies her for a few seconds. "I'm just saying, if the unexpected happens, and you meet someone, don't be afraid to let the spectacular happen."

She leans back in her chair, a slow grin forming on her face. "Spectacular, huh?"

He throws his long arms wide. "Baby, I'm all sparkles and fireworks."

She laughs. "You're somethin' alright." She looks up at the clock and alarm fills her face. "Shoot. It won't be long, and they'll be coming in for lunch."

He picks up a can of spam, pops the tab, and gives her a wink. "Guess I'll get to it, then. Ain't nothin' sexier than a man frying spam in a pan."

She steps closer and eyes the collection of slimy goo sliding off the spam onto the plate. "I beg to differ. What is that, and why does it look like it could ooze across the counter on its own?"

He laughs, pokes it with a spoon, and makes it jiggle. "That's spam gel."

She cringes, backing away. "Ho-ly toledo. There's nothin' right about that."

The door flies open, and Bernie walks in. Ali looks at him, surprised. "Bernie. What're you doing here? You usually just come down for breakfast."

Bernie winks at her and pulls a sandwich from a paper bag, before sitting down at the kitchen table in the back. "I just come down to watch people eat split pea soup. Every time I witness it, I can't believe what I'm seein'."

Alex laughs out loud. "Bernie, want some sweet bread with a touch of cayenne? It's got Swiss cheese on top."

Bernie taps the table. "Hit me big time, Alex."

She opens the oven and grabs a roll from inside with an oven-mitted hand. She plops it on a plate, slapping baby Swiss cheese on top before setting it down in front of Bernie. "First one's for you, Bernie. Tell us how it tastes."

Bernie picks it up and looks it over. "I don't usually go for sweet breads, gotta watch my waistline, you know." He takes a little bite, giving a small groan. "Ali, you've outdone yourself. I daresay this is the best homemade bread I've ever tasted. I may just have to eat the whole roll."

She smiles with his praise. "Thanks, Bernie."

He takes another bite. "Say, you got any tea? That'd go perfect with this."

Talia comes waddling out. "I'll get his tea. I need to move around a bit, anyways."

She walks by, heading for the back room and the cooler. Bernie shakes his head. "Babies havin' babies. What's this world coming to?"

Talia steps up behind him, setting his tea down hard. "I ain't deaf, old man."

Bernie side-eyes her. "Neither am I."

Talia steps up in front of him, crossing her arms on her belly. "You think I can't take care of a baby? I've already been doin' it half my life."

Bernie eyes her belly before looking her in the eye. "It's not a question of are you able, it's the fact that you shouldn't have to. Ain't no reason to rush growin' up, child. There's some bridges you can't uncross. That's all I'm sayin'."

Talia doesn't say anything as she walks away, heading back to Maggie's office.

thirty-eight

Maggie and Joshua fall asleep in each other's arms, oblivious to the cold settling in outside. Hours later, they wake up in the dark. She uses her cell phone as a flashlight as she crawls out of the sleeping bag.

She steps into her yoga pants with one leg, when Joshua stops her. "What are you doing?"

She stops moving even though her teeth are chattering. "I'm cold. I'm getting dressed."

"Aren't we doing the polar plunge?" he teases.

The weather causes second thoughts. "I don't know. I already feel like my toes are blue. If you're getting me in the water, you'd better be up in the next thirty seconds."

He jumps out of the sleeping bag and snags her hand as she struggles to step out of her yoga pants. "Let's go, Mags!"

She can hardly believe it as she follows him out of the tent in her birthday suit, shivering all the way. "This is insane." He takes her hand and they run into the stream, splashing around in the dark in the light of the moon. She shrieks as she splashes. "This water's freezing! We're cra-zy!"

He rushes her, takes her face in his hands, and places his

cold lips on hers. For a second or two, the breath between them is warm. She runs her ice-cold fingers up and down his rib cage, and he jumps back. "Woman, your hands are icicles!"

She laughs out loud as she does it again. "Can we go back to the tent, please?"

He kicks his foot out, splashing her one more time. "Last one in is a rotten egg."

She barrels into him from the side, knocking him sideways, and he goes down to one knee in the water as she runs to the grass, heading for the tent, giggling all the way. There's a great splashing behind her. He rushes her from behind, catching up to her right before she steps into the tent.

He scoops her up in his arms, holding her to his chest, growling. "That was a dirty trick, Maggie Louise. Would you be so kind as to open the tent flap for me so I can carry you across the threshold?" She shoots out an arm, pulling the tent door open, and he steps in, letting her down slowly. "You're so beautiful, and you're all mine."

She hops in the sleeping bag, pulling it around her, looking up at him. "You're not so bad yourself, husband. Now get down here and warm me up."

He grins as he climbs in to join her. "There's an offer I can't refuse."

She lies beside him, happy and tired, enjoying married life, but her mind wanders, and she can't shut it down as she stares up at the tent ceiling.

He chuckles. "You're going to stare a hole in my ceiling, Maggie Louise. What are you thinking about?"

She sighs. "I suppose I'm thinking about how you're going to fit in my house."

"What do you mean?"

"Well, we'll have to find space for an office for you, for one."

He nods. "Well, eventually, yes. But with you being gone at the café during the day and the kids being at school, I could easily work from the kitchen or our bedroom. All I need is space for my laptop, really."

She nods. "I suppose that's true, but I'd like for you to have your own space."

He looks over at her, smiling. "Thanks."

She studies him. "Do you have a house somewhere? I mean, where did you live before you moved to New York?"

He clears his throat. "I lived in Idaho. I kind of have a house on wheels."

She makes a face at him. "Like an RV?"

He shakes his head. "Not exactly. It's called living minimally. I built it myself. Right now it's parked at a buddy's place, along with my Ford 150 I need to pull it with."

She giggles. "So, it's not as cheap of living as it advertises. I mean, it has to cost something to pull that thing down the road, and Ford 150's don't exactly get the best gas mileage."

He shrugs. "This is true, but it allows me to travel more and stay longer, and I don't pay for a hotel."

She grins at the thought. "And people just let you pull up in their driveway and stay a few days."

He nods his head. "Yes, actually they do, because it's a lot less invasive than asking them if I can stay in their home."

She smiles. "This is all very cool. I'm learning more and more about you. Do you have pictures of your tiny home and your big truck?"

He laughs at her analogy. "Yes, I do, and some of them even have sunsets in them."

She puts out her hand. "Hand it over. I have to see."

He snuggles up to her as she scrolls through the photos

on his phone. He nuzzles her neck. "Now that we're married, will you be my friend on Facebook?"

She turns back to him. "You mean we're not?"

He runs his finger up and down her arm. "No. I asked once, but you ignored me."

She goes to her phone, bringing up Facebook. "There, I sent you a friend request."

He picks up his phone, shaking his head. "That was quick. I'm now friends with your daughters, and they're following me on Twitter, too."

She rolls her eyes, but she's smiling. "I guess you have their approval."

"Is that okay?"

She laughs at his question. "Sure. Why wouldn't it be?"

He shrugs. "I don't know. I've got nothing to hide."

He scrolls through her phone texts, noticing the many updates from Ali about the café. "This Valentine's day dance looks like a pretty big deal."

She shrugs her shoulders. "It is, but I can miss one year. It'll be alright."

He studies her. "Are you sure? Ali's really blowing up social media with this dinner and dance event."

She turns to him with a shy grin. "If you want to go, just say so."

He leans over, kissing her senselessly. "That was me saying so."

"Well. I guess I'll have to learn your secret language," she answers breathlessly.

He holds her tight, nibbling on her ear. "I have many secrets. I promise you'll like all of them."

She turns on her side, tracing his chest with her fingertips. "Is that so, Joshua Porter?"

He leans forward, nipping her knuckles. "Yeah, that's so."

His eyes turn hot as he looks at her. "Come here and I'll tell you one."

She looks him up and down, getting excited. "Again?"

He gives her backside an affectionate squeeze, growling low. "Give me another kiss, Mags. I'm makin' up for lost time."

thirty-nine

Ali scrubs out the split-pea soup pot, trying not to gag. "Whoever wrote this recipe for this horrible soup they call food should be shot."

Alex shakes his head. "Boy, you sure are dramatic. What are we making tonight?"

She stops for a second, contemplating. "I think I'd like to do a taco bar. I could make some queso and keep it in the crock pot. Everyone likes queso."

"Sounds good."

"Taco bar is also more like buffet style, and that should be easy enough. The only trick is knowing how much meat to cook. How big do you think the crowd will be?"

He walks to the back office, bringing out a school calendar. "It says here there's a home game tonight for the junior high, so that might bring a few extras in from other towns, but it might also make the dinner crowd smaller because most of them will be at the game."

She raises her eyebrows. "I suppose if we have leftovers we could make enchiladas or burritos tomorrow, so we don't waste the meat."

He nods with approval. "Yes. That sounds like a great idea. Let's do that." He picks up the phone. "Mason. It's taco night. Don't suppose you'd like to help us out with the meat? Great! Thanks. See you in a bit."

She glances over at him. "You just call him up whenever you need a hand, and he comes running?"

He shrugs. "Yep. That's what friends do. Isaac doesn't mind sharing him, and Mason just likes to cook."

She eyes him. "Yeah, but couldn't we just make the hamburger and add the taco seasoning from the box? I've done that many times."

He scoots over closer, talking all conspiringly. "We could, Ali, but Mason's taco seasoning is killer. He makes it himself. It's perfection."

The door flies open, and a grinning Mason walks in. "Did I hear someone say I'm perfection?"

She laughs out loud. "Boy, you've got dog ears or something."

Mason gives her a wink. "Just wait til' you try my seasoned taco meat, Ali. You won't be sorry."

She smiles back at him. "I trust you, Mason. Thanks for coming over on such short notice."

"Sure, glad to be of service. I like setting up bars. Are you serving guacamole?"

Ali looks at Alex in question. "I'll just run out and grab some avocadoes, Ali. Be right back."

Mason turns to Alex. "Be sure you squeeze them. I can't use 'em unless they're soft. Hard avocadoes won't cut the mustard."

Alex nods. "Got it. Only soft avocadoes." He rushes out the back door.

Mason glances at Ali scrubbing the split pea soup pan vigorously. "You could always boil some vinegar in that pan.

It might save you some scrubbing time, and it'd probably help with the odor."

She moves the pan to the other side of the sink, rinsing it and drying it off. "Thanks, Mason. What other kitchen tricks do you know?"

He shrugs. "You learn things here and there as you go along. Makes life interesting, I guess."

She grins. "Yep."

He winks at her again. "People can make life interesting too, Ali. What do you think of my guy, Alex?"

She blushes. "He's pretty funny."

He nods his head. "And handy, Ali. He's a fast learner, and he pitches in whenever someone needs something. A guy like that can be irreplaceable."

She hip bumps him. "I hear you, Mason. Loud and clear."

He throws his head back, laughing. "And here I thought I was being subtle."

"You 'bout as subtle as a semi-truck, Mason." Talia calls out from the office.

Ali and Mason look at each other, and they both start laughing. Mason answers back. "Fair enough, Talia. Fair enough."

Minutes later, Alex walks back in the back door, dumping a bunch of avocadoes on the counter. "Here, Mason. I hope I found some good ones. Amy helped me pick them out."

Ali's standing on the other side of Mason, watching Alex with a thoughtful look on her face. She marches over and takes his face in her hands, kissing him. Alex's face is full of surprise. "What was that for?"

She smiles at him, her eyes twinkling. "Thanks for being you."

He grins. "For the record, I'm me all day long, and I like that kind of reward."

She giggles, turning away from him, but he reaches out

his hand, pulling her back to him, stealing another kiss. "You're pretty alright, too." He spins her around, smacking her butt. "Get to work, now. That taco bar won't make itself."

She rushes off to the fridge to pull out the tomatoes and onions. She rinses the tomatoes before setting them on the cutting board. When she's done, she puts them in a container and washes the cutting board down. She looks over at Alex. "Will you please cut that onion?"

He nods. "Yep. I can't have you all red-eyed and crying at the taco bar tonight. People will start talking."

Mason turns to Ali, turning down the heat and putting the pan lid on the deep skillet of hamburger. "Ali, today you're going to learn how to make guacamole."

She raises her eyebrow. "I am?"

Mason gives her a decisive nod. "You are. It's not that difficult. You just have to get a feel for it. First, we mash the avocadoes."

She wrinkles her nose. "Can't we make this in a blender? I hate mashing bananas. They're just so mushy, and I bet avocadoes are, too."

Mason shakes his head. "You ever try to clean out a blender after you make guacamole? Trust me, it's not worth the headache."

She sighs. "I trust you. Let's get to mashing."

He hands her an avocado and a knife. "First you take off the outside."

Minutes later, her fingers are deep in green avocado, using her mashing fork to push the avocado back into the bowl. Mason gives her a nudge. "Don't forget to put a little lemon juice in. You don't want the lemon flavor, but it'll keep the avocadoes from turning brown so quickly."

She nods her head as he gives her bowl a few squirts, giving more advice. "Now what you add to your guacamole is your choice. Most people start with onions and tomatoes.

But, if you don't like onions, leave them out. You can also add cumin, cayenne, garlic, salt, cilantro, and a little jalapeno pepper if you want to spice it up, it all depends on how you want it to taste."

She looks over at Alex. "What do you think, Alex?"

He steps over. "Maybe we could make three choices: one with onions, one plain one, and one zippy one. I think there's a jalapeno pepper in the fridge."

Mason glances at Ali. "You ever cut jalapenos?"

She shakes her head back and forth. "Nope."

"Well, take my advice. Handle those things with gloves. My friend, Rachel, didn't, and about twenty minutes later, she was soaking her fingers in milk. You don't feel the burn until it's too late."

She grins. "Thank you for that helpful tip. Noted." She sets the soup pot on the back burner and pours in a little vinegar. She turns the burner on. Then she opens a drawer and tugs on some rubber gloves. She finds the jalapeno pepper in the fridge. She takes the smaller cutting board off the nail on the wall. She stands beside Alex, who chops an onion. She starts on the jalapeno pepper. It isn't long and they are both red-eyed. Tears roll down their cheeks.

Mason looks over, laughing, as he snaps a picture. "I'm totally posting this on the café website. A couple of cryin' chefs."

She looks up at him and sticks out her tongue. He snaps another picture as she mutters at him. "Brat."

Mason laughs again. "You love me, Ali."

She winks back at him. "You know I do."

Alex glances at the clock. "Shoot. Time flies when you're having fun. We've only got like twenty more minutes before it's officially supper time. You think we'll be ready?"

Mason grins. "Leave it to me, guys. I'm an expert at setting up a bar." She puts the pepper in a container, rinsing off the cutting board. She steps out of the way as Mason zips around her like a kitchen madman. He stops beside her suddenly. "Will you and Alex go grab a few long tables out of the back room? We'll just set them up in front of the glass. Just leave yourself space in front of the register. After that, get busy making the tea and lemonade, please."

She salutes him playfully. "Yes, sir."

She rushes over and grabs Alex by the arm. "Come on, let's go get the tables." He follows behind her as she rushes to the backroom, grabbing the end of a table. "This one looks good." They carry it out, setting it up. "One more." She gets to the backroom, her hand on the corner of the table. He looks at her funny, studying her face, and she touches her cheek. "What? Do I have something on my face?"

He steps forward, leaning down and kissing her breathless. "Just me."

She shoves his chest, pushing him away as he chuckles. "Ha, ha. Stop playing around. You think you're so smart."

He reaches out, touching her lips gently with his fingertips. "I love you, Ali." He watches her expectantly, and she swallows hard, because she knows what he's waiting for, but she's unable to say anything. Her heart is full, and she has so many feelings, but she's afraid to speak. She leans forward, kissing him softly. He sighs in disappointment, grabbing the table corner.

She lifts the other end, feeling nervous and inadequate. "Thanks for helping me."

He gives her a hurt look. "Of course. Why wouldn't I?" They set up the second table, and she's relieved to see her first customers walk through the door. The night gets going, and just about the time they relax, a whole new set of customers walk in, and she's relieved when Manuel, Parker, and Conner come in through the back office.

Conner posts up beside her. "Talia texted. She said things were getting busy and you could use some help."

She puts an arm around her brother, giving him a squeeze. "Thanks."

Conner nods his head, squirming out of her embrace. "What'll I do?"

She glances over at Mason. "Ask Mason. He's in charge tonight."

"Got it." Conner, Parker, and Manuel stand in front of Mason. "Where do you want us?"

Mason grins. "Parker and Manuel, you man the dining room. Conner, you're with me." Mason glances back at Ali. "This will free you up to only run the register."

She nods. "I can handle that."

Mason looks over at Alex. "You can stay on dishes if you want, Alex."

"Thanks, Mason. You know they're my favorite," Alex answers sarcastically.

Mason gives him a wink. "Thought you might like to stay close to the register."

An hour and a half later, the last customer walks out the door. She plops down in a kitchen chair, and they all sit down around the table together. "Phew. What a night. I couldn't have done it without each of you."

Alex reaches over, grabbing her hand. "You could have, Ali, but it wouldn't have been any fun."

She shakes her head, her hands trembling. "That's the biggest crowd we've ever had. I don't know how Mom does this all the time."

Conner nods his head in agreement. "I don't either."

Parker knocks on the table. "Because she's our mom, and because she loves it."

Ali grins. "This is true. I hate to say it, but I can't wait 'til she's back. For lots of reasons."

Alex frowns at her words. He lets go of her hand, getting up. "Well, I'm beat. Whoever's staying, let's finish cleaning up so we can all go home."

Ali's at a loss as she notices the change in the room at Alex's words. The room feels colder all of a sudden. She hops up to help out. Mason salutes her. "I'm out."

Conner, Manuel, and Parker rush around, wiping down the tables. They carry the two tables back to the backroom before coming back to Ali. "We've got homework. Can we go home?"

She nods her head. "Of course, thanks again." The three of them head to the back office. Talia calls out. "Ali. They're walking me home."

"Goodnight, Talia. See you tomorrow."

She glances over at Alex, who's putting the leftovers in the fridge, and she feels bad. "Are you behind on your writing because of me?"

He turns to her, smiling. "No. In fact, I've started something new."

She's confused. "Oh?"

He looks down at his hands. "Yep. Lately, I've been feeling more inspired than usual, and I'm trying to be patient, to see where things go, but you don't make it easy."

As his words sink in, Ali's emotions kick into overdrive, and she's not sure what it all means, but the intensity scares her. "Oh."

His eyes fly to her face, pinning her with his gaze. "That's all you can say, is oh?"

She leans on the counter, her knees a little weak. "What do you want me to say?"

He doesn't let up. "Say whatever you feel, Ali. Is that so hard to do?"

She's tongue-tied. "I feel like there's something wonderful waiting for me, but I'm too afraid to reach for it."

She looks at him, and he looks confused. "It's like when you're a kid, and you're just learning to swim. You see all the big kids in the deep end, and you want to be like them, but going in over your head is scary, because when you can't reach the bottom, you have no security. And you start to wonder, what happens if you forget how to swim, or you go too far out and you get too tired, and you can't get back to shore?"

He walks toward her, grinning. "I'm an excellent flotation device, Ali. You just have to grab a hold."

She stomps her foot like a child. "Don't make fun of me. I'm serious."

He stops walking. "I'm not, Ali. You're saying you're afraid of the unknown, but I think that's just an excuse. You're afraid to fall in love with me."

She clenches her fists. "You're so arrogant sometimes. You're so sure of yourself."

He frowns at the jealousy in her voice. "Ali. I'm not sure of everything. There's a lot of uncertainty in this life, but I'm sure of one thing, the most important thing."

She frowns back at him. "Oh, and what's that?"

He steps up, putting a hand on each side of her, backing her up against the counter. "I know how I feel about you, and I think you feel the same about me. You just aren't ready to say the words." He leans in, brushing his lips across hers. "I love you, Ali."

She leans back, putting her hand on his chest. "This is crazy. We haven't even known each other a week."

He kisses her again, holding her snug up against him. "When you know, you know." He steps back, slipping an arm through hers. "Walk me home? It's dark outside. You know how I feel about the dark."

She giggles, leaning on him. "Let's go, scaredy-cat."

forty

Joshua and Maggie wake up early. He goes to get up, but she takes a hold of his hand in the sleeping bag, whispering. "Wait. I want to listen to morning nature sounds a little bit, please."

He turns to her, burying his nose in her neck, growling, as his hand wanders. "Mags, I could give you a memorable morning."

She grabs his wandering hand, holding it. "Be still a minute and behave, husband. I'm recording the sounds outside." She holds out her phone, hitting the record button, and they lay there still and smiling up into the camera. He winks into the camera before he goes back to nuzzling her neck. She holds it in as long as possible, before stopping the recording, and her laughter comes flying out. "You're such a brat."

He positions himself over her. "Only for you, Mags. Only for you." He dives in, kissing her soft and slow and deep. She drops her phone.

"Husband, you are insatiable."

He moves on to her ears, nibbling. "You know you love it."

Later, she untangles herself from her husband, getting up. She climbs out of the sleeping bag. "I can't wait to get back to the apartment for a hot shower. That'll feel so nice."

He gives her an appreciative once-over. "I don't know. I like you a little wild and wooly."

She laughs, shuddering. "Well, I don't."

She makes short work of packing everything, walking it out to the Jeep. They take the tent down, and she hops in. He stands over by their camping spot. "No selfie by the stream?"

She sighs, hopping out. "Alright, fine." She marches over to stand beside Joshua, and he takes a few with his phone. She does the same. She turns to him. "Now can we go?"

He reaches out, pulling her in and hugging her close. "I love you, Maggie Louise Porter. I'm so glad I waited for you."

Her heart tightens in her chest, and she gives him a squeeze. "I'm glad you did, too." She steps back, all business. "Now, let's get this show on the road. We've got things to do and people to see."

He laughs. "Yes, dear."

She feels like a grinning fool, but she can't help but smile all the way home. They get to the apartment, and she goes tearing up the stairs. "I get the shower first."

He runs up behind her. "We could shower together and save water."

She looks back at him. "Something tells me if we do that, it won't save time."

He sighs. "Fine. You can go first."

She raises a victorious fist in the air. "Yes!"

He laughs as he unlocks the apartment door, stepping back. "Ladies first." She steps inside, heading for the shower. Minutes later, she emerges, a trail of steam following behind her, and her skin is pink with the heat. Joshua gives a low whistle. "You look like a lobster. Did you leave me any hot water?"

She does a little shimmy. "I think so. That felt soo good."

He steps into the bathroom, shutting the door, smiling as he gets a whiff of Maggie's flowery scent she left behind.

An hour later, the Moving Man Company shows up and they make short work of boxing everything up and piling it into the U-Haul. He pays them and they're out the door. She looks around at the bare apartment, a tear rolling down her cheek. "Natalie's officially gone."

He sits down on the sofa. "Yeah." He takes down the lone heavy vase with a stickie labeled "Don't Touch", from the mantle. "I have her ashes."

Her eyebrows raise in surprise. "I beg your pardon."

Joshua exhales slowly. "We never had an official service, because I guess she knew what might happen."

She sits down, frowning. "I'm sorry. I'm not following."

He sets the big, tall vase on the floor. "Natalie wrote out instructions kind of like her last wishes." He takes a folded piece of paper from his back pocket. "I've read them a few times, but I guess I just haven't been ready yet."

She holds out her hand, taking the paper from him. She unfolds it carefully, reading through it slowly. "She wants her ashes scattered over the Royal Gorge?"

He nods his head. "I'm kind of glad my parents aren't here to see this. They never would have agreed to such a request."

She smiles sadly at the thought. "Probably not."

He smiles back at her. "Like you said, Natalie was a free spirit, even after she's gone."

She takes a deep breath. "Do you feel like you're ready?"

He shakes his head. "Not yet."

She nods her head, handing the paper back to him. "Then we'll just wait until you are."

She glances at the clock. "We'd better get going if we want to get back to Indiana by 10 PM tonight."

He frowns. "I'm sorry, Mags. It looks like you're going to miss the Valentine's Day dinner."

She smiles a patient smile. "That's alright, Josh. We can still make the Saturday night dance." She hops up, grabbing the vase. "Let's boogie."

He laughs. "You're such a cheeseball."

She giggles and winks at him. "The cheesiest."

forty-one

Ali's up bright and early. She comes tearing down the stairs in her gold sparkly dress and heels. Alex is in the kitchen, patiently waiting. He raises his eyebrows at her. "Breaking out the Vegas wear again? Did you forget how bad your feet hurt that first day?"

She shrugs. "I'm at the end of my laundry pile."

He grins, holding up a long tee shirt dress with a big heart on it. "I took a chance, but I think you can pull it off. I found it at Bella's Boutique the other day. It was on sale."

She laughs out loud, ribbing him. "Only if you wear something just as cheesy."

He lays it on the table, turning away from her. "I thought you'd never ask." He pulls out a men's retro tee with a big heart on it with "Indiana is for Lovers" is scrawled across the heart in cursive. He stands up and whips off his shirt in the kitchen, leaving Ali stunned and speechless, as he goes to pull the other shirt on. He gives her a saucy wink. "Earth to Ali. Stop starin' at my hot bod and go change."

She saunters over to him, lifting up his shirt in the back, tracing her finger over his tattooed rib cage. "What's this?"

"I dream of you," he answers in a hoarse voice.

His answer is as confusing as how it makes her feel. "Excuse me?"

He yanks down his shirt, grabs her hand, and holds it to his chest, while he stares into her eyes, as his eyes grow darker. "It means 'I dream of you.'" His eyes drop for a second as he stares down at the floor. "Even though I have a writer's very vivid imagination, Ali, there were times I could not imagine my loneliness away. One night I was feeling really down and depressed. So I went and got this tattoo as a reminder to myself to never give up on finding my dream girl, my soulmate. Many nights I have lain awake, hoping that one day I would find the One, the woman I don't want to live without, and I think I have."

She's floored with emotions she's not prepared for. She grabs her dress and runs up the stairs, red-faced. She slams her room door, muttering, "He's just a man, Ali; a gorgeous specimen of a man who's a smooth talker. You've seen shirt-less men before. Get a grip."

She sheds her dress, tugs on the tee shirt dress, and is surprised by her smiling face in the mirror. She chucks the heels, grabbing a pair of flats. She flies back down the stairs, waltzing back into the kitchen. He hands her a cup of coffee, giving her an appraising, soulful look. "I thought those flats would match the dress."

Parker enters the kitchen long enough to snag a PopTart. She looks at Alex standing beside Ali before whipping out her phone and snapping a picture. "Awww, matching hearts." Ali sticks her tongue out at Parker, who laughs. "Love you too, Ali."

Ali makes another face. "Get to school, Parks." Parker laughs, running for the door. Ali calls after her. "Did you ask him yet?"

"I'm asking him today!" Parker hollers in answer.

Conner runs down the stairs. "Parker! Wait for me." He's out the door.

Alex looks back at Ali. "We're all alone in the kitchen, Ali. You know what that means." His loaded tone makes her blush.

"What?" she squeaks.

He takes her coffee cup from her hand, sets it down, backs her against the counter, and hovers over her lips, waiting. "Come on, sweetheart. Give me a little taste."

She's burning up. She gets more and more irritated by the second as he teases her. She glances at the clock. "We're going to be late for work."

He remains where he is, driving her out of her mind. His lips are right there, taunting her with his soft breath. "Bernie's a man. He'll understand," he murmurs, and her knees buckle just a little.

Ali can't believe how hot Alex is. This new side of him took her completely by surprise. She wants his kiss. So bad. But she's not about to give in. "Understand what?" she gets out.

He leans back just enough to give her an ornery wink. "Waitin' on a woman."

Her jaw clenches. "I hate you so much right now, Alex." She whispers softly before she grabs a hold of his tee shirt, tugs him forward, and kisses him fiercely. She lets him go as fast as she took a hold of him. She picks up her coffee with a shaking hand, determined to keep her cool. "Come on, Valentine, we can still get to work on time."

A stunned Alex follows her out the door in a daze. It's a quiet walk as they cover the six blocks between the house and the café. She unlocks the café door, heading for the spreadsheet, hoping breakfast isn't as complicated as her feelings for him. She reads aloud, half muttering, "Green eggs and ham? Are you serious, Mother?"

His laughter breaks the silence. "Yep. That breakfast is the kid's favorite, so I'll double the eggs."

She glances over at him. "Do I even want to know how you make ham green?"

He shoots her a killer grin. "We just put a little green gravy on it. We make white gravy and add food coloring."

"Oh."

He picks up on the nervous tone in her voice. "You've made gravy before, right?"

She shakes her head, picking up the phone. "I'm calling Mason."

He laughs at her pat answer that's become a habit. "We'd better give Mason a bonus when this week is over," he suggests.

She nods her head in agreement. "I don't care what it is, I'll pay it."

"Hello?" A deep voice is heard on the other end of the phone.

Ali tears her gaze away from Alex's as she struggles to reorient. "Oh, hey, Mason. Do you, um, have time to come make some breakfast gravy, pretty please? It's green eggs and ham day."

"Just give me a few. I'm just getting up. I want a bonus, Ali."

She laughs. "You're a lifesaver. Alex and I were just discussing your bonus, actually." There's silence. "Mason?" She turns to Alex. "I guess he hung up." She looks at him again. He stands at the counter, cracking eggs, and it's so sexy. "What do I do?"

"Go and find the Dr. Seuss decorations in the back room and start putting them up. The kids love them."

"I'm on it."

She rushes around, taping the decorations to the wall. She stops. "Where's Bernie?"

He looks at the front counter. "I don't know."

She looks up at the ceiling as if it could provide her an answer. "Should I be worried?"

Talia walks through. "I'll go knock on his door."

Ali steps into the kitchen. "I got the decorations up. Now what?"

"You'd better start pulling the ham out of the fridge. It's already cooked, but we need to heat it up. Just lay them out on cookie sheets and turn the oven to 350."

She turns the oven on on her way to the fridge. It's not long, and she has the thick slices of ham all laid out.

Talia comes back smirking with a scowling Bernie behind her. She throws a thumb in his direction. "He overslept."

Bernie stomps up to the counter, growling. "I'm 85-years-old. Can't I get some peace and quiet?" He glances in Ali's direction. "Where's my oatmeal?"

She gives him a wink. "Nice to see you too, Bernie. Let me rustle up some grub for ya."

Bernie snaps open his newspaper with a flourish. "Rustlin' grub? Where the heck do you think we live, Montana?"

She giggles at his grumbling and tosses a bowl with his sides on the counter. "Your oatmeal, Bernie. I'll just get that tea going." She sets the tea kettle on the fire before popping around the corner to peek in on Talia. "Thanks for checking on him."

Talia looks away from her schoolwork. "Yeah, yeah. What's the café in the morning without the grumpy old man?"

Bernie hollers, "I heard that, baby mama."

Talia blushes as she whispers to Ali. "Ain't nothing wrong with his hearing."

Ali giggles, walks out of the office, and turns to face a

scowling Bernie, shaking his finger. "Don't you two be whispering about me."

Her smiling face turns serious. "Bernie, I wouldn't dare."

It isn't long, and families come in through the door, their books in hand. Ali turns to Alex. "What is going on?"

He chuckles. "Janet, the librarian, opens the library on this Friday so they can all go by and grab a Dr. Seuss book on the way to breakfast."

She grins as she watches the kids setting their books down on the tables. She rushes out with her pad and pen, taking orders, giving them to Alex before she dashes off to start filling drink cups. Alex and Mason prepare the food plates and she rushes around, delivering them to the tables of toddlers and pre-schoolers flipping through the pages, looking at the pictures.

Alex goes to the back, bringing out a book. "Here."

She looks back at him. "What do I do with this?"

"You read it." He points to the dining room. "Out there. To the children."

She looks over at Mason for confirmation. "Yep. It's story hour, Ali."

She walks out to the center of the room, feeling strange. "I'm Ali, and I'm going to read now."

Everyone quiets, and the little kids look at her expectantly. She looks around the room, feeling like she might faint from stage fright, but then she looks over at Alex, and he smiles back at her, giving her confidence. She opens the book. "Green Eggs and Ham, by Dr. Seuss. I am Sam. I am Sam. Sam I am. That Sam I am, that Sam I am. I do not like that Sam I am." Ali speaks louder, changing her voice, and she's rewarded with a giggle from a little girl with dark curly hair and big brown eyes. She gives her a wink, and she keeps on reading.

She reads loud and slowly, stopping every so often,

surprised to find an enthralled audience, and this makes her feel good. "I do so like green eggs and ham. Thank you, thank you, Sam I am." She closes the book with finality, and all the children clap. She smiles back at them. "Thank you. You were all such good listeners. I hope you enjoy your Green Eggs and Ham." She walks back to the kitchen, handing Alex the book, whispering. "That was *really* fun."

He smiles back at her. "You're a natural with children."

She looks down at her shoes. "I was just reading a book." She turns away, embarrassed. "I'm just going to start getting the decorations ready for the Valentine's Day dinner tonight."

Mason makes a fist. "Yes. That means you *won't* be serving lunch today." He looks over at Alex. "Make sure you put up a sign outside that tells people to go to Ike's Bar and Grill for lunch."

Alex nods. "Will do. Happy to send business your way."

Mason wipes his hands on his apron. "Well, my work here is done. You two can handle the gravy now, right?" She looks worried. Mason laughs. "Just leave it on low and give it a stir now and then. Your breakfast crowd's about done." Mason walks out the back door, setting a plate of food down by Talia. "Feed that baby some protein."

Talia's stomach growls in response, and she pats it. "I don't know how I can be hungry when there's no more room."

He winks at her. "It won't be long and that baby will be here and you'll have a whole new set of worries."

A car pulls up outside, and Parker comes in the back office. "Eat your food, Talia. Hurry up. Didn't you get my Snap?"

"What? What's the big rush?"

"I'm supposed to be decorating for the float. But I don't want to do it without you. Let's go already."

Talia hops up, grabbing a paper bowl from the kitchen shelf. She shoves her food in it and follows Parker out the back door. "I'm going to the school."

"Got it." Alex answers.

Ali shakes her head from the register, taking another check from the customer. "It's a three-ring circus." She looks around. "Speaking of which, where are Amber and her dogs?"

"She keeps them home. They scare some of the kids 'cause they're so big," Alex mutters.

Slowly but surely, the café empties. Ali rushes around, busing tables. She puts the tub of dishes on the cart, wheeling it back to the kitchen. Next, she takes the decorations off the walls. "Dishes or tables?" Alex calls out.

She returns to the kitchen. "I'll do dishes. You've been doing them all week."

He nods. "Thanks. I'll wipe down the tables then."

She starts on the breakfast dishes, scrubbing them down in the big sink. "This is quite the community."

He nods. "Yep. They support each other." He looks up. "Hey, did you hear someone bought the building at the end of the street?"

She looks up. "Oh, yeah?"

"Yep. Some guy named Blake is opening up a western wear store. It's going to be called "Blake's Boots" I think."

She smiles. "I like it. Direct and to the point."

He grins. "I thought so, too. I heard it's like a sibling's business. He's going to like put a loft up above, and his sister's going to have like a little aromatherapy kind of shop, like bath stuff? I think it's online already. 'Very Vanessa?'"

"Siblings running a business together. That's cool," she muses and turns to Alex. "So, about this dinner tonight. We've got a lot of work to do."

He laughs at her statement. "You mean you've got a lot to do."

She frowns. "You're going to help me, right?"

He shakes his head. "You don't need my help with the PowerPoint. That's all on you."

She grins. "This is true. I've just got to time manage. I need to make my cupcakes and my special cake, but I've got a solid hour I can use for my PowerPoint."

He laughs. "Special cake?"

She raises her eyebrows. "Yep. It's going to be a surprise, but I think you'll like it." She throws herself into her work, pleased with the results. She's so involved, she jumps a foot when the back door of the office flies open, and Talia and Parker march in, handing her a bunch of big red thick posterboard hearts. "What's this now?"

Parker smiles. "Talia and my contribution to your wall decorations. Talia here is an awesome artist and I am a song guru."

Talia flips a heart around, revealing perfect calligraphy in thick, black letters. "We've written down the titles of our favorite love songs and we thought you could put them around the room."

Ali claps her hands with excitement. "Oh my gosh! I love them. They're perfect."

Talia lays them down on the table. "We've got to get back to our Love Boat Float."

"What's that?" Ali asks.

Talia winks. "You'll see in about an hour. All the floats come down the main street."

Ali squeezes Parker's hand. "Wouldn't miss it." They run out the back door, and Ali returns to her computer, adding the finishing touches, saving her word document to her flash drive. "Alex?"

He waltzes across the room from his writing corner. "Yes?"

"Do you know where I can print a bunch of copies of a one-page document?"

He puts out his hand. "Tell me what it's called, and I'll get it done at the library. She should still be open."

She hands him the flash drive. "It's called *Name that Movie* and it's for everyone to fill out tonight. So, however many you think I should get." Her face lights up. "Ooh, and could you please buy some colored paper at the dollar market? Pink if they have it."

He winks at her. "As you wish."

"Thank you."

She whips open her laptop, reading the recipe for the cupcakes. She gets to work. Once she has them in the oven, she opens another recipe for the cake. Talia comes into the back office, breathless. "You'd better get outside, Ali. The parade is coming. And take some pictures for Maggie."

She rushes outside, looking down the street. She looks at her watch. "Four minutes left on my first set of cupcakes." She stands by the front door, worrying. The timer goes off, and she runs back in, snatching them from the oven, and setting them down on hot pads on the counter. She runs back out the front door, and the parade comes around the corner. She breathes a sigh of relief, taking pictures of Conner on a float as he waves wildly, calling out. "Hi, Mom!"

Ali turns around, scanning the sidewalk, seeing only Alex, who's holding his phone up. He glances over at her. "I'm making a video for your mom, Ali. She's not here."

She feels bad. "Oh. Why didn't I think of that?"

He takes her hand with his free hand. "We've got this."

She takes a few more pictures of Conner from afar. She snaps one of the next two floats. She laughs out loud when she sees the Love Boat coming down the street, with Parker on the side dressed in overalls, holding up her sign, "Equality Matters". As the boat rolls by, she calls out, "Hi, Mom."

Alex gives her a thumbs up while holding up his phone, recording, and Ali takes many pictures with her phone. Talia stands beside Ali, waving and clapping. "Go, Seniors!" Parker blows her a kiss.

Manuel's voice comes over the intercom from his lounging spot as he ducks down, out of sight, and the float comes to a stand-still. "Welcome to Gilligan's Island meets the Love Boat meets The Office. Roll call: Dawn? Dawn?"

Parker waves to the crowd. "Present."

"Captain Jack?"

Hayden takes off his hat and waves to the crowd, his other hand holding onto the limbo stick. "Yo!"

"Ginger?" Red-headed Lexi waves a graceful hand to the crowd in her formal dress, holding onto the limbo stick with her other hand.

"The Millionaires." Cole and Mia stand, waving to the crowd, calling out together. "Help us, please. We're stuck on the island!"

The intercom booms. "And last but not least, Gilligan!"

Arlen stands up, waving wildly in his sailor's uniform, grinning like a goof. "Hi, everybody."

Alex stops the video, putting his phone in his pocket. "I think I got it."

Ali takes a few more pictures. "That's pretty cute." The float starts back up, and the boat lurches forward, heading down the street.

Ali heads back inside. "I've got to get back to my cupcakes."

Alex follows her in. "Your forms are in your mom's office. Do you need anything else?"

Ali smiles at him, and it hits her once more how much she has smiled since she's been working at the cafe. "Thanks, but not right now, I think I've got it." She loads another set of cupcakes into the oven, resetting the timer. She starts on the batter for the cake, humming to herself.

She sketches a picture of a volcano with lava coming down the sides. "Let the love flow. I love you a lava." She draws a line through her words, thinking. "You ignite me." She tosses down her pencil, frustrated. "Ugh."

He wonders through, looking down at her sketch. "What's this?"

She turns, looking at the timer. "I'm just brainstorming."

"About?"

"A catchy love phrase to go with a volcano."

"A volcano?"

"Yes. I like themes and catchy phrases."

She picks up the pink colored paper, cutting it into strips mindlessly. He raises an eyebrow. "What's this for?"

"The 'How We Met' game. They all write down a few sentences and fold it up and put it in the bowl. Then I pull them out and read them and people try to guess which couple it is."

"That's cool." He grabs another bowl. "Do I get to have a game?"

She eyes him. "That depends on what it is."

"Numbers."

Her eyes go wide. "As in what's your number?"

He wrinkles his nose. "Ooh, you perv. No. As in the number of their combined ages."

She nods with approval. "I like it."

He scoots over closer to her. "So, are we a couple tonight?"

She coughs. "What do you mean?"

He studies her. "I like to play games, Ali, but this one's getting old. I think it's time you tell me if we're together."

She shifts uncomfortably. "Of course, we're together."

He opens his phone. "You haven't added me on Facebook

yet as a friend, even." He looks at her. "Have you told anyone about me?"

She feels cornered. "Everyone here knows. And it's new. We're new. Maybe I'm not ready to share." She opens her phone, tapping the screen a few times. "There, I sent you a Friend Request." She sets her phone down. "I've hardly been on Facebook this week. I've been so busy with the café."

He looks unsure as his eyes meet hers, and she feels bad, but she doesn't know what to say. "But you'll be my Valentine tonight? At the dinner?" he asks, and his insecure tone makes her feel like she's in high school all over again.

"Yes." They go back to cutting the paper, and the timer beeps. She throws on her oven mitts, snatching another set of cupcakes from the oven.

He glances at the batter bowl. "How many cupcakes are you making?"

"I don't know, like a hundred maybe."

He snorts. "I was thinking more like fifty."

She shrugs. "If we have leftovers, we can just donate them to the school dance that's tomorrow night. That's what I'm doing with all these decorations, and since the dance is here, we don't have to move them."

He taps her forehead with his finger. "You're always thinking."

She swats his hand away. "Stop teasing me. I'm busy."

He hesitates as her words catch up to him. "The dance is here? I thought it was at the community center."

"It was going to be, but someone accidentally double booked it, so I told them they could come here. We'll just have to move the tables, but the high school boys can do that. They're hard workers. They'll have it done in no time."

forty-two

THE DINNER

Ali takes a deep breath, looking over at Alex. "You've been my anchor today. I couldn't have done this without you."

He grins back at her. "Sure you can, but I'm happy to help."

She shakes her head. "No, Alex, I couldn't. I'd have been freaking out and running for the hills long before now. There's no way I could have filled my mother's shoes without you, and Mason, and Talia, and Amber, and Bonnie, and the list just keeps growing."

He stands beside her. "It's called community, Ali. We're your village, and we're happy to help."

She smiles as she looks around the room, taking in her table of cupcakes, the glass bowls set out, and the volcano cake with frosting coming down the sides. She eyes the kitchen and the huge pot of spaghetti she and Alex made, along with the big pot of sauce. She opens the two crockpots filled to the brim with meatballs.

The wonderful scent of garlic bread lingers in the air as it bakes in the oven. Her heart lifts as the servers march through the back door in their black slacks and red heart shirts, smiling at their nametags. "Thank you all for being here tonight. Alex and I really appreciate it."

Manuel and Parker cut through the crowd. Parker's holding his hand. "I've got your announcer right here."

She beams at the two of them. "Thank you, Manuel. You'll find your table with the mic. You might want to go and do a sound check." They walk off. She turns back to the others. "It's going to be a little cozy in here. We're seating six to a table, so just be careful when you walk in between, because they will all be a little closer than usual tonight, and the lighting will be a little lower, as it's Valentine's Day dinner. The drinks are the same—water, tea, or lemonade. And I've numbered the tables. You'll see there's a little playing card in the middle with a number on it."

Mason walks in, carrying the projector. She frowns at him. "What's that for?"

He grins. "Isaac made up a video for you. It's a scroll of pictures of all the couples coming tonight from different times in their lives. I think everyone will enjoy it."

She claps her hands in excitement. "Perfect!"

Alex chuckles. "I'm afraid after tonight, Ali, you'll have to come back every year to do this Valentine's Day dinner."

The customers start coming in, and she watches them with joy as they wander around the room, looking at all the decorations. As soon as everyone's sat down, Mason starts the picture roll on the projector, and soon there is laughter and conversation, as the kids mill around, taking the drink orders.

Manuel and Parker sit at the long table against the back

wall of the restaurant. "I'm Manuel and this is Parker. We'll be heading up the games tonight. You should find two slips of paper by your plates, the pink one is for the Numbers game. The red one is for How We Met. On the pink piece of paper, write down the number of your combined ages together. On the red paper, write a few sentences of how you met. Then you will fold the papers and bring them here. I will read them off and then people can try to guess which couple wrote what. The couple with the most correct answers at the end of the night will win a door prize, courtesy of all the businesses in town."

The couples get busy, and soon they're walking up, dropping their answers in the two jars on the table. In the meantime, the servers deliver the food to the tables. Once that's done, they get their own plate and go sit at the long table with Parker and Manuel, who get up to go get their food.

Ali and Alex hang back in the kitchen, keeping an eye on everything. Supper goes by quickly, and Manuel calls out the numbers, as people make their best guesses out loud. Parker writes down the winners and their points. Manuel moves onto the How We Met game, reading out the answers, getting a few laughs here and there.

Mason projects the quotes on the wall. Manuel speaks into the mic. "The last game we have is famous quotes from movies, which are shown on the wall. Each person can fill out their own sheet, and the sheets are in the middle of the tables. If you want to play, write your name on it. There's a door prize for the winner of this game as well."

The room is quiet for a while, as everyone looks up at the wall before writing their answers down on the papers. The servers go around quietly, picking up dinner plates. Manuel speaks into the mic again. "The cupcakes are over to the side, or you may have a piece of lava cake."

Ali gets up, wheeling the lava cake on its little table to the kitchen, cutting into it with a big knife. "I'm not sure how to do this. It's layered."

Mason walks over. "May I?" She hands him the knife, and holds out a plate at a time, as he cuts it into pieces, placing them on the plates.

"I'm so glad Isaac can spare you."

Mason shrugs his shoulders. "He knows how important tonight is to Maggie."

As if cued, the front door opens, and Maggie walks in. Ali almost drops her plate as she shrieks, running out of the kitchen. "Mom! You're home!"

Ali tackle hugs Maggie from the side, clinging to her mom, who pats her awkwardly, a tear rolling down her cheek. "If I knew you'd be this happy to see me, I'd go on vacation more often."

Maggie gives her a little push when Ali's embrace doesn't let up. "Ali. I can't breathe."

Ali backs away, still clinging to her mom's arm. "I'm just so glad you're here."

Maggie's eyes widen as she looks around the room. "You did all of this?" A throat clears behind her. She turns, taking Joshua's hand, walking farther into the room. "Everyone, this is my husband, Joshua Porter." Her audience claps, and there are a few whistles as someone calls out.

"Way to go, Maggie!"

Maggie's face flushes as she turns to Joshua. "Joshua, this is everybody." Joshua gives a little wave to the crowd.

Parker strides across the room, past her mother, hugging Joshua. "Welcome to the family. I'm Parker."

Joshua smiles. "I'm Joshua. It's nice to meet you."

Conner steps up in his server's uniform, sticking out his hand. "I'm Conner."

Joshua shakes his hand. "I've heard all about you."

Ali finally lets go of her mom's arm, and Alex steps out

from behind Ali, giving Maggie a hug. "Welcome home, Maggie."

He turns to Joshua, hugging him, too. "I'm Alex. Welcome to the family."

Joshua laughs. "Thanks. I haven't had this many hugs since I don't know when."

Alex looks at Maggie. "Are you hungry? We've got plenty of food in the kitchen."

Joshua smiles. "Lead the way, Alex. I'm starving. This lady made me drive straight through. She was in such a hurry to get here."

Maggie gives Joshua a playful shove. "I just wanted you to meet everyone." She turns to the dinner crowd again, smiling. "I missed my café."

Bonnie answers. "No offense, Ali, but we missed you too, Maggie."

"Manuel. Who are tonight's winners?" Mitch calls out from a back table.

"Yeah, what's the door prize?" his brother Ryan comments.

Manuel speaks into the microphone. "The winning couple of tonight's numbers and How we Met is...drum roll please..." All the servers beat their hands on the table rhythmically. "Mr. and Mrs. J." Lynn walks up to the table. Manuel hands her a gift bag. "Your prize is a free night at the Train Station Hotel courtesy of Mr. and Mrs. MacBee."

Lynn smiles as she accepts her gift bag. "Thank you."

"You're welcome. Our next winner of the Movie Quotes is...drum roll please..." the table shakes for a few seconds. "Dee Urich. Come on down." A smiling, joyful lady in a flowery dress hops up, waving her hands in the air like jazz hands. She marches up to the table, grinning ear-to-ear.

"What'd I win?"

Manuel smiles up at her. "You've won a bag of some of

Ali's favorite romantic movies, a couple of movie tickets, and gift certificates from every business in this town. Would you like to say anything, Dee?"

Dee smiles and leans into the mic. "I'd like to say a big thank you to Ali, for putting tonight together. Ali, it's been so nice seeing you around town again, and I hope we see a lot more of you. And, thanks to all the people who helped make tonight so special. We have a very generous community that just keeps on giving. Thank you, everyone."

Manuel smiles out at the crowd. "Dee Urich, ladies and gentlemen. I couldn't have said it better myself. Goodnight." He drops the mic.

Parker scoops it up. "Manuel. I have something to ask you." The crowd hushes, and Manuel's face has panic written all over it, as Parker continues. "Will you go to the Valentine's Day dance with me?"

Manuel's face breaks out in a smile. "Yeah."

Parker lets out a breath she didn't know she was holding. "Cool."

The crowd claps again, but Manuel and Parker barely notice, as they're still staring at each other. Conner bumps Manuel from behind. "Come on, it's time to clean up." Manuel stands up, following Parker and Conner into the kitchen.

Ali takes Parker's hand, whispering. "I can't believe you asked him in front of everyone."

Parker winks at her sister. "Go big or go home, right?"

Ali laughs. "I guess."

Maggie and Joshua stick around, and it isn't long and the café is clean. Ali looks over at Alex. "Take me home, Alex. I'm beat."

Talia calls out from the office. "Guys? I think my water just broke."

Parker runs into the office. "Talia, if this is a joke, it's not funny."

Talia leans over and grabs a chair, as pain shoots through her and she pants. "I wish I was."

Manuel sticks his head in the doorframe. "How far apart are your contractions?"

Talia looks at her watch. "I don't know, like six minutes."

Maggie hollers. "Six minutes! We need to get you to the hospital. Like now."

Talia groans. "I didn't want to interrupt your dinner, Maggie."

Maggie answers. "No one's mad, Talia, but I'm not delivering a baby in this café. Let's go."

Ali tosses the keys to Conner. "Lock the café up, Conner, and go home. Please. The rest of us are taking Talia to the hospital."

Conner stares back at her. "But that's 20 miles away."

Maggie and Joshua are already walking Talia to the front door. "We're taking her in the U-Haul. The rest of you meet us there." Maggie looks back at Alex. "Drive safe. We've got this."

They walk out the door. Conner turns back to Ali. "You're not going without me. We're all in this together."

Alex nods, taking the keys from Conner. "Come on everyone, let's move."

The five of them walk down the street back to the house, and Alex gets in Ali's outback, looking over at Ali. "Do you mind if I drive?"

Ali gives a big yawn. "Be my guest."

They start down the road, and Parker sighs. "I haven't gotten one thing for her baby yet."

Manuel answers. "Well, we don't know if it's a boy or a girl."

"We could get a yellow onesie. That's neutral." Conner's comment surprises them all.

Parker smiles. "Yes. Let's run by the superstore on the way to the hospital. It's open twenty-four hours."

Ali hands back her debit card to Parker. "You can run in. I'm staying in the car. You'll need to get her a car seat, too."

forty-three

They make it to the hospital and find Joshua sitting in the waiting room. "Where's Maggie?"

"She went back with Talia. Talia said she wanted her there."

Parker picks up her phone, texting. It isn't long, and a nurse comes back, looking irritated. "Is there a Parker out here?"

Parker raises her hand. "That's me."

The nurse waves her hand. "Come on, then."

Parker hops up, rushing over to the nurse, grinning all the way.

Manuel smiles, shaking his head. "That's Parker, front and center."

Joshua sighs, leaning his head back. "You might as well get comfortable. It's probably going to be a while."

Conner's eyes get big. "At least tomorrow's Saturday."

Three hours later, at 1:30 a.m. Manuel's phone dings. He opens the message. "Welcome to the world, Valentine Talia Bleu." He walks over to a sleeping Ali and Alex, pushing on Alex's shoulder. "Hey. She had a baby girl."

Ali wakes up, looking at the picture, smiling. "Everyone's okay?"

Manuel nods. "Yep."

Ali and Alex go back to napping.

Conner looks at Manuel's phone and turns to Alex. "Can I go sleep in the car?"

Ali nods. "I'm with Conner."

Joshua gets up. "I think I'll go lay down in the U-Haul."

The four of them get up, leaving Manuel behind. He sits back down. "I'm just going to wait here for Parker." The double doors fly open, and Parker sticks her head out. "Come on back, Manuel. There's room for you."

He gets up and follows Parker back to Talia's room.

The other four walk out to the parking lot. Joshua heads over to the U-Haul. Conner turns to Alex as he unlocks the Subaru. "You guys can have the back. I'll lay down in the front seat."

Ali opens the back door, laying down the seats. She crawls in, and Alex follows, curling up next to her, as she looks out the back window at the sky. She settles into him, snuggling up, smiling. "You're so hot."

Conner answers from the front seat. "Shut up, Ali. I'm trying to sleep."

She giggles. "Fine, but I just want to say, I'm glad we're hospital parking lot buddies."

Alex chuckles, holding her tight. "Me, too."

Conner sighs. "Alright, alright. Now, goodnight everyone."

Morning comes, and Alex and Ali wake up slowly, watching the sunrise out the back window. She curls into him, as he wraps an arm around her. She whispers, "Hey, you."

He smiles back at her. "Hey back."

The two of them lay there quietly, unable to move, as if a

revelation has just come about, and they're seeing each other for the first time. She puts her hands down on the seat to steady herself. It's as if something shifted beneath her. He grins, pulling her close to whisper in her ear. "I love you, Ali."

She frowns. "You don't even know my whole name, so how can you know you love me? You don't know all my flaws, or how many times I yelled at my mom when I was growing up, or how awful I was as a teenager, or how I used to..."

He stops her by pinching her lips with his fingers. "I know the Ali I've been around all week; the girl who dropped everything and came running when her mom needed her, the girl who was faced with a difficult challenge and didn't turn tail and run, the girl who cares a lot about a grumpy old man even though she won't admit it, the girl creative enough to plan an awesome Valentine's Day Dinner." His voice gets quieter. "The girl who's not afraid of anything except admitting how she feels about me."

She stares out the back window, and a tear rolls down her cheek as she whispers. "It's not possible to fall in love in less than a week, Alex. It just isn't."

He frowns, crossing his arms over his chest. "Are you telling me you know my feelings better than I do? Is that what you are saying?"

She shakes her head. "Of course not. I'm saying you *think* you're in love with me, but you're not. Pretty soon, I'll be going back home, and you'll be staying here, writing your book, and everything will go back to normal. You'll see."

He smiles, shaking his head, despite the fact he feels like screaming. "So you think you can plan my life out for me, telling me who I can and can't love, and I'll just sit back and let you?"

She frowns at him. "You need a girl who will be happy to follow you around whenever you decide to pick up and move. I'm not that girl."

He looks at her imploringly. "Are you sure, Ali? Moving around can be lots of fun. You meet new people, try new things, see lots of sights. Besides, can't you work from home?"

She sighs, exasperated. "Yes, I can. I contract with online companies, but that's not the point."

His grin in the middle of their discussion infuriates her. "Then what is your point?"

She shrugs, feeling irritated. "Although I find you irresistible, that doesn't mean we are destined to be together." She studies him longer, answering in a louder voice, as if she's trying to convince herself. "It doesn't."

He gives her a squeeze. "Then what does it mean?"

She releases a sigh, irritated with herself that she finds his arms so comforting. "I'm still workin' on that."

He laughs out loud. "Just try to fight your feelings for me, Ali. You won't win."

"You two are sickening. I'm going to find some breakfast while I still have an appetite." Conner barks out from the front seat.

She stretches a long arm out toward the front seat, dropping a twenty. "Here. Bring me back two muffins and two coffees with creamer, please."

Conner nods, palming the twenty-dollar bill. "Thanks."

She cuddles up against Alex. "I'm going back to sleep. We'll be busy when we get home. It's the Valentine's Day Dance tonight. I'll be doing Parker's hair and finishing getting the café ready."

Alex starts talking like a girl. "Sooo, like what are you wearing to the dance tonight?"

She elbows him in the ribs. "Haha. You're so funny. I'll probably wear a dress."

He circles her wrist with his hand. "I'm getting you a wrist corsage."

She turns her face toward his. "Why would you do that?"

He gives her a peck on the lips. "I'm your date."

She smiles. "I like little pale pink roses. The lighter, the better."

He nods. "Noted."

He lets go of her wrist, wrapping an arm around her waist, splaying his hand across her back, growling in her ear. "Will you save a slow dance for me, Ali?"

She tries in vain to ignore his arm around her, sending little shock waves of awareness across her skin. "Maybe." She closes her eyes, determined to ignore him. "Now be quiet. I'm trying to rest."

Conner opens the front door and hops in. "You gotta get out and put the seat back. Parker and Manuel are coming."

Ali and Alex get around slowly, crawling out of the back of the Subaru. Ali moves the seats back up, and a sleepy Manuel and Parker come across the parking lot, carrying breakfast for everyone. "Here you go."

She takes the food, and Alex holds the two coffees. "Thanks." No sooner does Conner pull out of the parking lot, and Manuel and Parker are fast asleep.

Twenty minutes later, they arrive home, and she crawls out of the Subaru, taking the keys from Conner. "Thanks for driving us home, little brother."

Conner gets out, calling out over his shoulder as he heads inside. "Anytime."

forty-four

The much-anticipated night of the dance has finally arrived, and Ali can't wait. She's so excited to see all the kid's dresses and faces, and a little part of her can't wait to see Alex dressed up. She sits still in front of the mirror as Parker curls her wavy hair into tight curls, which she pulls up into a loose pony-tail with a few stray curls. Parker stands behind Ali, smiling. "I really like Alex, and I think he really likes you."

Ali's face is pensive, revealing nothing as she stares into the mirror, pondering. "Don't you think it's a little too soon to be serious?"

Parker laughs. "It's not like you're teenagers, Ali. Look at Mom and Joshua. They knew in like four days."

She looks at Parker in the mirror, and she can't believe she's asking for relationship advice from her little sister. "Do you think that's smart?"

Parker smiles back at her. "I'm not worried. You know Mom. She doesn't do anything without considering the risks. Besides, it's not as if she was marrying a stranger. She knew him when she was younger, and his sister was her best friend."

Ali nods. "I suppose that's true, but I barely know Alex."

Parker meets Ali's gaze in the mirror again. "That's true, but Mom and I know him. Mom has known him the longest. If she trusts his character, that's good enough for me."

Ali frowns. "Of course she likes Alex. He's a kiss-up."

Parker gives her a nudge from behind. "No, he's not."

Ali isn't done. "Yes, he is. He's always lingering to see if she needs any help. He agrees with pretty much everything she says." Parker pinches Ali's arm. "Ouch! What'd you do that for?"

"You're going to fault a guy for being helpful and kind, but you're not going to fault the one you were with for a year and a half for leaving you on the way to the altar?"

Ali sighs. "First of all, my relationships are not your business."

Parker snorts. "You just asked me for my opinion and now you don't want it?"

Ali goes on, ignoring her comment. "And second of all, it's different. A year and a half is a long time to just throw away."

Parker winks at Ali in the mirror. "It really isn't if it was just a waste of your time. From everything I've seen and heard, Jason wasn't worth the time or the heartache."

"Hey. I'll be the judge of that." Ali's tone is sharp, but Parker's not about to back down.

"Obviously." Parker frowns at Ali. "Just because we all like Alex doesn't mean he's not good for you."

Ali gives her sister a glare in the mirror. "If you like him so much, why don't you date him?"

Parker wrinkles her nose. "Hardly. I'm like eighteen and he's twenty-eight. And I think he's in *love* with my sister."

Ali shivers again at the thought. "That's what he said, but

I say, how can he know?"

Parker's hand freezes mid-air, curling iron in hand. "He said he loved you?"

Ali looks down. "Yeah."

"What did you say? Did you say it back?"

Ali shakes her head. "Of course not. I don't know if I do."

Parker eyeballs her. "That's just brutal, Ali. I can't believe you. He puts himself out there, and you say nothing?"

Ali feels defensive. "I didn't ask him to say it. Mom says you should always be honest. I didn't know what to say, so I didn't answer." She pauses. "It's not like I could say thank you."

Parker snorts. "I guess, but Ali, you're always telling me to let 'em down easy, and you just left him hanging. That's all I'm sayin'."

Ali snorts. "He's a writer. He'll be alright."

Parker bops her head with the curling iron. "Just 'cause he's a writer doesn't mean he's objective all the time. He still has feelings. Geez."

Ali's close to tears. "I don't know how I feel, Parker. It's scary. I thought Jason was the one and look how wrong I was about him."

Parker waits a few seconds before answering. "All I know is you're happy and smiling whenever you're with him. That should tell you something."

Ali fiddles with the nail polish bottles on the dresser. "Could we just not talk about this anymore? Let's have fun getting ready." She looks back at Parker with an ornery grin. "Is Manuel a good kisser?"

Parker blushes. "What kind of a question is that?"

Ali giggles. "You're right. You wouldn't like a guy who didn't know how to kiss."

Parker winks. "You're dang right. Some things can't be taught."

forty-five

The doorbell rings, and Parker flies to open it and her face falls. "Oh, hey, Alex."

Alex chuckles at the lack of enthusiasm in her greeting. "Gee, thanks, Parker. Nice to see you, too. Is your sister around?"

Parker turns and belts up the stairway. "Ali! Your date is here."

Ali floats down the stairs in the red dress she found earlier in the week at Bella's boutique. "Hey, Alex."

Alex walks to the foot of the stairs, sliding a corsage on her wrist. "Hey, Ali."

She lifts the corsage, sniffing the flowers. "I love them. They're beautiful."

He smiles down at her. "Like you."

"Alright, you two lovebirds, look over here. I need a picture for Mom," Parker announces.

Alex spins around, holding Ali's hand, and Parker snaps a picture. He tugs her to him, dipping her, and she squeals with delight while Parker snaps another photo. He plants a kiss on her lips before letting her out of the dip. "Shall we go, my lady?"

"Alright." They walk out the door together, passing Manuel on the sidewalk. Ali gives him a wink. "Looking very sharp, Manuel."

He puffs out his chest. "I know how to use a comb."

The door opens, and Parker steps out in her floor-length dress, all sparkles and poofy chiffon. "Hey, Manuel."

He takes a few seconds to answer. "Parker. You look like a princess."

She curtsies, touching her tiara. "Thanks. I even have a tiara." She giggles. "Do you want to walk to the café now?"

He whips something from behind his back. "Your corsage."

She giggles nervously. "You didn't have to."

He gets all serious. "I couldn't let Alex show me up."

She sticks out her hand, and he slides it on her wrist. "Thanks. I love it. It's perfect." She steps up closer. "Do you think I could get my goodnight kiss now?"

He leans in, and they share a kiss. He pulls back. "You ready to go?"

She nods her head. "As long as you think you can handle my mom and my sister being at the dance, yeah."

He grins and ducks his head. "I'm not worried. They love me."

She slips a hand inside his arm. "Let's go then."

The music blasts and the dance floor fills as the night flies by. Alex watches Ali dancing next to Parker, hamming it up. He knows she's the one for him, and he's not waiting a second longer. He goes to the DJ, asking for the mic. "Ali Louise Post, I've got something to say to you."

The music stops, and the dance crowd scatters, leaving Ali standing in the middle of the dance floor by herself. He looks at her, standing alone in the spotlight, as if she's waiting for him. He speaks into the mic. "Ali. Will you marry me?"

She doesn't answer. She's speechless. He steps away from the mic, and walks across the dance floor, going down on one knee before her. "Ali. Will you marry me?"

The crowd waits in hushed silence, and though they're surrounded, all Ali sees is Alex, her future, smiling up at her. "Yes. I'll marry you." He stands up, wraps his arms around her waist, lifts her off the ground, and spins a few times before releasing her to share a kiss.

"I love you, Ali. I've loved you since the moment I saw you dragging that sparkly red suitcase past me to shut the door in my face."

She laughs. "You really do like the chase, don't you?"

He chuckles, whispering low in her ear. "It only makes the catch that much sweeter. You're mine now, Ali Louise Post, and you won't soon forget it."

Her breath hitches at the possessiveness in his words, and she leans in for another long kiss, loving the cheer from the audience. She pulls back slowly, looking around at all the happy faces. "Maybe I am a small-town girl, after all."

Alex only has eyes for Ali as he answers. "I don't care what kind of girl you are, as long as you're mine."

She pecks him on the lips, gazing into his eyes that twinkle and shine. "I love you, Alex. I'm ready to be yours. I'll always be your Valentine."

epilogue

Alex and Ali married a few months later in April, at the café. He bought a house in town, leaving his old apartment to Talia and her baby girl, Valentine.

Joshua took on the role of adopted grandpa, watching Valentine during the day so Talia could

focus on her schoolwork. Maggie made the arrangement, telling Joshua it would be good practice for when their twins come along (nine months after their wedding day).

Manuel, Talia, and Parker graduated high school in May. Parker and Talia enrolled in classes at the local junior college while Manuel attends a tech college nearby. Joshua and Maggie continue to babysit Valentine while Talia's at college.

It's not long, and Valentine becomes a regular at the café, perfectly content to hang out in the playpen, keeping a careful eye on all of her grown-ups. Joshua leans over, picks her up, and holds her close. "How's my favorite Valentine? Give me some love."

She lays her pudgy little fingers on his cheeks, giving him a kiss on each side.

Joshua smiles as he winks at Valentine and her twinkling

eyes before looking over at his wife, Maggie, who catches his eye, smiling back at him with her pregnancy glow, as she blows him a kiss from the café sink, silently mouthing to him across the busy kitchen. "My cup is full."

~

Don't miss out on your next favorite book!

Join the Satin Romance mailing list
www.satinromance.com/mail.html

THANK YOU FOR READING

∼

Don't miss out on your next favorite book!

Join the Satin Romance mailing list
www.satinromance.com/mail.html

∼

Did you enjoy this book?

We invite you to leave a review at your favorite book site,
such as Goodreads, Amazon, Barnes & Noble, etc.

DID YOU KNOW THAT LEAVING A REVIEW...

- Helps other readers find books they may enjoy.
- Gives you a chance to let your voice be heard.
- Gives authors recognition for their hard work.
- Doesn't have to be long. A sentence or two about
  why you liked the book will do.

about the author

I'm a thankful wife of a wonderful and loving husband, and a blessed mom of three amazing children. I'm also a grateful nurse who has the privilege to work with some pretty great people every day.

I live in the Flint Hills of Kansas. I enjoy reading and writing in my spare time. I love meandering through bookstores and libraries. I love traveling, especially to the ocean. I love meeting new people and experiencing new places. I love baking in a quiet kitchen.

I enjoy watching romantic comedies and I'm a huge fan of "The Office."

I believe a good book is a great opportunity to welcome a new perspective.

 facebook.com/RachelAnneJonesAuthor

 twitter.com/Jones1974Ra

 instagram.com/diari1974

also by rachel anne jones

With Satin Romance

A Joy-Filled Christmas

Fill Your Cup Valentine

With Fire & Ice Young Adult Books

Novels

Marmalade Uncapped

Essence of Emma

Lovestruck: Kisses, Lies & Oatmeal Cream Pies

Ramblin' Nash: A Day in the Life of a Flower Shop Boy

All Or Nothing Series

Chasing Denver

Rough Terrain

A Firm Plateau

Radioactive Series

Love and Armageddon

House of Cinders

www.ingramcontent.com/pod-product-compliance
Lightning Source LLC
Chambersburg PA
CBHW050403260626
47156CB00003B/852